STAR
COLONIES

EDITED BY

Martin H. Greenberg
and John Helfers

DAW BOOKS, INC.

DONALD A. WOLLHEIM, FOUNDER

375 Hudson Street, New York, NY 10014

ELIZABETH R. WOLLHEIM
SHEILA E. GILBERT
PUBLISHERS

First Printing, June 2000

1 2 3 4 5 6 7 8 9

THE FAR FRONTIERS—

Humankind has always had the wanderlust, driven by curiosity to discover what lies downstream, over the mountain, across the ocean, beyond our own world. And though we have not yet managed to conquer the far reaches of space in reality, the original stories included in this volume allow us to make those journeys in the ever-expanding universe of our imaginations:

"The Boid Hunt"—Scientists, doctors, engineers, it didn't matter what they'd been before they'd colonized Coyote, now they were all farmers planting crops in order to survive. But by the end of a nine-month rainy season the pickings were lean. So when someone suggested a boid hunt, how could they say no?

"Coming of Age"—They'd had so many hopes when they'd come to this brave new world, and with hard work the colony had thrived. It wasn't until the first generation born on the planet came of age that they realized the world had changed them as much as they'd changed it. . . .

"No Place Like Home"—They were the advance team, searching for a world that could relieve the population burden back home. And it looked like they'd found it— until they were forced to decide what really constituted a life-form. . . .

STAR COLONIES

ACKNOWLEDGMENTS

CONTENTS

INTRODUCTION

by John Helfers

It has always been in mankind's nature to push beyond his known boundaries. From the origins of *Homo sapiens* in Africa to the days when the first Cro-Magnons crossed the land bridge in the Bering Strait to look upon the new continent they had found, humans have been driven by a desire to see what is on the other side of the hill, the mountain, the ocean, the planet. Whether it is for trade routes to the East or so-called manifest destiny in the western United States, under whatever name, humans will always be explorers.

Today, the vast majority of the Earth has been trodden upon, surveyed, satellite-photographed, and computer-mapped. From the desolate wastelands of the Arctic ice cap to the equally stark Sahara desert to the silent, once-mysterious depths of the ocean, there are few, if any, places mankind has not visited. Whether it is a modern-day explorer or an indigenous race of natives who have lived in their homeland for ten thousand years, humans have spread from their tiny roots in the cradle of civilization to become the dominant life-form on this planet, and also inhabit just about every place on Earth as well. There are no new vistas to see, no new lands to discover, not on Earth, not anymore. So where will the next generation of explorers look to discover the new horizons to push beyond?

The answer is right above our heads.

More than thirty years after Gene Roddenberry prophetically wrote the introduction for the *Star Trek* television series, space is still the final frontier. Back in the 1960s, the Apollo missions, culminating with Neil Armstrong uttering his famous words as he stepped out of the lunar landing craft on July 20th, 1969, led many people the world over to believe that we were poised on the brink of a great new era of exploration, one that would allow us to unlock the mysteries of the universe, and perhaps, of ourselves.

Sadly, it was not to be. After several more trips to the Moon, the National Aeronautics and Space Administration had to drastically cut back its space program as America became entangled in Vietnam. By the time the conflict was over, space exploration had fallen by the wayside as nations launched dozens of satellites for communication, spying, and research, but almost nothing dedicated to exploration. Even the space shuttle launches of the 1980s sparked little interest among a populace more concerned with matters here on Earth.

However, in 1997 NASA successfully landed a probe on the arid surface of Mars, collecting a wealth of previously unknown data about the surface of the red planet. Receiving major media attention, this mission rejuvenated NASA's standing, and renewed serious speculation about the possibility of exploring space and establishing a permanent colony on the Moon or elsewhere.

Before and after the Mars mission, several privately funded groups had started their own initiatives to reach the stars, claiming they could do it faster and less expensively than the government. The Artemis Project is a privately founded and funded concern dedicated specifically to starting a habitable, permanently-manned colony on the Moon. Many others are out there, eager to discover what challenges and perils await the settlers of the twenty-first century.

Throughout it all, from the launch of the first Sputnik satellite to the Mars landing and beyond, a group of people have followed mankind's tentative exploration of our galaxy, using NASA and the world's progress as springboards to flights of imagination into a world where mankind has not only explored the vast emptiness of space, but has colonized it as well, terraforming planets to suit human needs as well as finding new worlds to explore beyond our solar system. That group, of course, is science fiction writers.

If there is one thing science fiction has done, it has taken the dream of reaching the stars off the computers at NASA and put it in the minds of readers worldwide. From Isaac Asimov's and Ray Bradbury's space colony stories during the Golden Age of science fiction to Kim Stanley Robinson's groundbreaking Mars trilogy detailing the colonization and terraforming of the red planet, science fiction has always been right there alongside the advances mankind has made, from the Earth to the Moon and beyond. In its own way, science fiction has also spurred imagination and perhaps even progress into space further by providing a look at what a future among the stars might hold.

With this in mind, we asked the best and brightest of today's science fiction authors to give us their take on what a space colony might really be like. And they answered right back, showing us worlds and places we could hardly imagine. From Allen Steele's down and dirty settlers who get more than they bargained for on a local hunting trip to Pamela Sargent's meticulously detailed extrapolation of how Venus might be terraformed a millennia from now, the perils and rewards of living on other planets come alive in these thirteen stories about mankind's drive to colonize the stars. So turn the page and prepare to journey where no man has gone . . . yet. Come with us to the far-off corners of the galaxy, and discover the stories of the men and women who create the space colonies of tomorrow.

THE SHOULDERS OF GIANTS
by Robert J. Sawyer

Robert J. Sawyer's novels *The Terminal Experiment, Starplex, Frameshift,* and *Factoring Humanity* were all finalists for the Hugo Award, and *The Terminal Experiment* won the Nebula Award for Best Novel of the Year. His latest novel is *Calculating God.* He lives near Toronto; please visit his Web site at www.sfwriter.com.

It seemed like only yesterday when I'd died, but, of course, it was almost certainly centuries ago. I wish the computer would just *tell* me, dammitall, but it was doubtless waiting until its sensors said I was sufficiently stable and alert. The irony was that my pulse was surely racing out of concern, forestalling it speaking to me. If this was an emergency, it should inform me, and if it wasn't, it should let me relax.

Finally, the machine did speak in its crisp, feminine voice. "Hello, Toby. Welcome back to the world of the living."

"Where—" I'd thought I'd spoken the word, but no sound came out. I tried again. "Where are we?"

"Exactly where we should be: decelerating toward Soror."

I felt myself calming down. "How is Ling?"

"She's reviving, as well."

"The others?"

"All forty-eight cryogenics chambers are functioning properly," said the computer. "Everybody is apparently fine."

That was good to hear, but it wasn't surprising. We had four extra cryochambers; if one of the occupied ones had failed, Ling and I would have been awoken earlier to transfer the person within it into a spare. "What's the date?"

"16 June 3296."

I'd expected an answer like that, but it still took me back a bit. Twelve hundred years had elapsed since the blood had been siphoned out of my body and oxygenated antifreeze had been pumped in to replace it. We'd spent the first of those years accelerating, and presumably the last one decelerating, and the rest—

—the rest was spent coasting at our maximum velocity, 3,000 km/s, one percent of the speed of light. My father had been from Glasgow; my mother, from Los Angeles. They had both enjoyed the quip that the difference between an American and a European was that to an American, a hundred years was a long time, and to a European, a hundred miles is a long journey.

But both would agree that twelve hundred years and 11.9 light-years were equally staggering values. And now, here we were, decelerating in toward Tau Ceti, the closest sunlike star to Earth that wasn't part of a multiple-star system. Of course, because of that, this star had been frequently examined by Earth's Search for Extraterrestrial Intelligence. But nothing had ever been detected; nary a peep.

I was feeling better minute by minute. My own blood, stored in bottles, had been returned to my body and was now coursing through my arteries, my veins, reanimating me.

We were going to make it.

Tau Ceti happened to be oriented with its north

pole facing toward Sol; that meant that the technique developed late in the twentieth century to detect planetary systems based on subtle blue-shifts and red-shifts of a star tugged now closer, now farther away, was useless with it. Any wobble in Tau Ceti's movements would be perpendicular, as seen from Earth, producing no Doppler effect. But eventually Earth-orbiting telescopes had been developed that were sensitive enough to detect the wobble visually, and—

It had been front-page news around the world: the first solar system seen by telescopes. Not inferred from stellar wobbles or spectral shifts, but actually *seen*. At least four planets could be made out orbiting Tau Ceti, and one of them—

There had been formulas for decades, first popularized in the Rand Corporation's study *Habitable Planets for Man*. Every science-fiction writer and exobiologist worth his or her salt had used them to determine the *life zones*—the distances from target stars at which planets with Earthlike surface temperatures might exist, a Goldilocks band, neither too hot nor too cold.

And the second of the four planets that could be seen around Tau Ceti was smack-dab in the middle of that star's life zone. The planet was watched carefully for an entire year—one of its years, that is, a period of 193 Earth days. Two wonderful facts became apparent. First, the planet's orbit was damn near circular—meaning it would likely have stable temperatures all the time; the gravitational influence of the fourth planet, a Jovian giant orbiting at a distance of half a billion kilometers from Tau Ceti, probably was responsible for that.

And, second, the planet varied in brightness substantially over the course of its twenty-nine-hour-and-seventeen-minute day. The reason was easy to deduce:

most of one hemisphere was covered with land, which reflected back little of Tau Ceti's yellow light, while the other hemisphere, with a much higher albedo, was likely covered by a vast ocean, no doubt, given the planet's fortuitous orbital radius, of liquid water—an extraterrestrial Pacific.

Of course, at a distance of 11.9 light-years, it was quite possible that Tau Ceti had other planets, too small or too dark to be seen. And so referring to the Earthlike globe as Tau Ceti II would have been problematic; if an additional world or worlds were eventually found orbiting closer in, the system's planetary numbering would end up as confusing as the scheme used to designate Saturn's rings.

Clearly a name was called for, and Giancarlo DiMaio, the astronomer who had discovered the half-land, half-water world, gave it one: Soror, the Latin word for sister. And, indeed, Soror appeared, at least as far as could be told from Earth, to be a sister to humanity's home world.

Soon we would know for sure just how perfect a sister it was. And speaking of sisters, well—okay, Ling Woo wasn't my biological sister, but we'd worked together and trained together for four years before launch, and I'd come to think of her as a sister, despite the press constantly referring to us as the new Adam and Eve. Of course, we'd help to populate the new world, but not together; my wife, Helena, was one of the forty-eight others still frozen solid. Ling wasn't involved yet with any of the other colonists, but, well, she was gorgeous and brilliant, and of the two dozen men in cryosleep, twenty-one were unattached.

Ling and I were co-captains of the *Pioneer Spirit*. Her cryocoffin was like mine, and unlike all the others: it was designed for repeated use. She and I could be revived multiple times during the voyage, to deal with emergencies. The rest of the crew, in coffins that had cost only seven hundred thousand dollars apiece instead of the six million each of ours was worth, could only be revived once, when our ship reached its final destination.

"You're all set," said the computer. "You can get up now."

The thick glass cover over my coffin slid aside, and I used the padded handles to hoist myself out of its black porcelain frame. For most of the journey, the ship had been coasting in zero gravity, but now that it was decelerating, there was a gentle push downward. Still, it was nowhere near a full g, and I was grateful for that. It would be a day or two before I would be truly steady on my feet.

My module was shielded from the others by a partition, which I'd covered with photos of people I'd left behind: my parents, Helena's parents, my real sister, her two sons. My clothes had waited patiently for me for twelve hundred years; I rather suspected they were now hopelessly out of style. But I got dressed—I'd been naked in the cryochamber, of course—and at last I stepped out from behind the partition, just in time to see Ling emerging from behind the wall that shielded her cryocoffin.

" 'Morning," I said, trying to sound blasé.

Ling, wearing a blue-and-gray jumpsuit, smiled broadly. "Good morning."

We moved into the center of the room, and hugged, friends delighted to have shared an adventure together. Then we immediately headed out toward the bridge, half-walking, half-floating, in the reduced gravity.

"How'd you sleep?" asked Ling.

It wasn't a frivolous question. Prior to our mission,

the longest anyone had spent in cryofreeze was five years, on a voyage to Saturn; the *Pioneer Spirit* was Earth's first starship.

"Fine," I said. "You?"

"Okay," replied Ling. But then she stopped moving, and briefly touched my forearm. "Did you—did you dream?"

Brain activity slowed to a virtual halt in cryofreeze, but several members of the crew of *Cronus*—the Saturn mission—had claimed to have had brief dreams, lasting perhaps two or three subjective minutes, spread over five years. Over the span that the *Pioneer Spirit* had been traveling, there would have been time for many hours of dreaming.

I shook my head. "No. What about you?"

Ling nodded. "Yes. I dreamed about the Strait of Gibraltar. Ever been there?"

"No."

"It's Spain's southernmost boundary, of course. You can see across the Strait from Europe to northern Africa, and there were Neandertal settlements on the Spanish side." Ling's Ph.D. was in anthropology. "But they never made it across the Strait. They could clearly see that there was more land—another continent!— only thirteen kilometers away. A strong swimmer can make it, and with any sort of raft or boat, it was eminently doable. But Neandertals never journeyed to the other side; as far as we can tell, they never even tried."

"And you dreamed—"

"I dreamed I was part of a Neandertal community there, a teenage girl, I guess. And I was trying to convince the others that we should go across the Strait, go see the new land. But I couldn't; they weren't interested. There was plenty of food and shelter where we were. Finally, I headed out on my own, trying to swim it. The water was cold and the waves were high, and half the time I couldn't get any air to breathe, but I swam and I swam, and then . . ."

"Yes?"

She shrugged a little. "And then I woke up."

I smiled at her. "Well, this time we're going to make it. We're going to make it for sure."

We came to the bridge door, which opened automatically to admit us, although it squeaked something fierce while doing so; its lubricants must have dried up over the last twelve centuries. The room was rectangular with a double row of angled consoles facing a large screen, which currently was off.

"Distance to Soror?" I asked into the air.

The computer's voice replied. "1.2 million kilometers."

I nodded. About three times the distance between Earth and its moon. "Screen on, view ahead."

"Overrides are in place," said the computer.

Ling smiled at me. "You're jumping the gun, partner."

I was embarrassed. The *Pioneer Spirit* was decelerating toward Soror; the ship's fusion exhaust was facing in the direction of travel. The optical scanners would be burned out by the glare if their shutters were opened. "Computer, turn off the fusion motors."

"Powering down," said the artificial voice.

"Visual as soon as you're able," I said.

The gravity bled away as the ship's engines stopped firing. Ling held on to one of the handles attached to the top of the console nearest her; I was still a little groggy from the suspended animation, and just floated freely in the room. After about two minutes, the screen came on. Tau Ceti was in the exact center, a baseball-sized yellow disk. And the four planets were clearly visible, ranging from pea-sized to as big as grape.

"Magnify on Soror," I said.

One of the peas became a billiard ball, although Tau Ceti grew hardly at all.

"More," said Ling.

The planet grew to softball size. It was showing as a wide crescent, perhaps a third of the disk illuminated from this angle. And—thankfully, fantastically—Soror was everything we'd dreamed it would be: a giant polished marble, with swirls of white cloud, and a vast, blue ocean, and—

Part of a continent was visible, emerging out of the darkness. And it was green, apparently covered with vegetation.

We hugged again, squeezing each other tightly. No one had been sure when we'd left Earth; Soror could have been barren. The *Pioneer Spirit* was ready regardless: in its cargo holds was everything we needed to survive even on an airless world. But we'd hoped and prayed that Soror would be, well—just like this: a true sister, another Earth, another home.

"It's beautiful, isn't it?" said Ling.

I felt my eyes tearing. It *was* beautiful, breathtaking, stunning. The vast ocean, the cottony clouds, the verdant land, and—

"Oh, my God," I said softly. "Oh, my God."

"What?" said Ling.

"Don't you see?" I asked. "Look!"

Ling narrowed her eyes and moved closer to the screen. "What?"

"On the dark side," I said.

She looked again. "Oh . . ." she said. There were faint lights sprinkled across the darkness; hard to see, but definitely there. "Could it be volcanism?" asked Ling. Maybe Soror wasn't so perfect after all.

"Computer," I said, "spectral analysis of the light sources on the planet's dark side."

"Predominantly incandescent lighting, color temperature 5600 Kelvin."

I exhaled and looked at Ling. They weren't volcanoes. They were cities.

Soror, the world we'd spent twelve centuries traveling to, the world we'd intended to colonize, the world that had been dead silent when examined by radio telescopes, was already inhabited.

The *Pioneer Spirit* was a colonization ship; it wasn't intended as a diplomatic vessel. When it had left Earth, it had seemed important to get at least some humans off the mother world. Two small-scale nuclear wars—Nuke I and Nuke II, as the media had dubbed them—had already been fought, one in southern Asia, the other in South America. It appeared to be only a matter of time before Nuke III, and that one might be the big one.

SETI had detected nothing from Tau Ceti, at least not by 2051. But Earth itself had only been broadcasting for a century and a half at that point; Tau Ceti might have had a thriving civilization then that hadn't yet started using radio. But now it was twelve hundred years later. Who knew how advanced the Tau Cetians might be?

I looked at Ling, then back at the screen. "What should we do?"

Ling tilted her head to one side. "I'm not sure. On the one hand, I'd love to meet them, whoever they are. But . . ."

"But they might not want to meet us," I said. "They might think we're invaders, and—"

"And we've got forty-eight other colonists to think about," said Ling. "For all we know, we're the last surviving humans."

I frowned. "Well, that's easy enough to determine. Computer, swing the radio telescope toward Sol system. See if you can pick up anything that might be artificial."

"Just a sec," said the female voice. A few moments later, a cacophony filled the room: static and snatches of voices and bits of music and sequences of tones, overlapping and jumbled, fading in and out. I heard what sounded like English—although strangely inflected—and maybe Arabic and Mandarin and . . .

"We're not the last survivors," I said, smiling. "There's still life on Earth—or, at least, there was 11.9 years ago, when those signals started out."

Ling exhaled. "I'm glad we didn't blow ourselves up," she said. "Now, I guess we should find out what we're dealing with at Tau Ceti. Computer, swing the dish to face Soror, and again scan for artificial signals."

"Doing so." There was silence for most of a minute, then a blast of static, and a few bars of music, and clicks and bleeps, and voices, speaking in Mandarin and English and—

"No," said Ling. "I said face the dish the *other* way. I want to hear what's coming from Soror."

The computer actually sounded miffed. "The dish *is* facing toward Soror," it said.

I looked at Ling, realization dawning. At the time we'd left Earth, we'd been so worried that humanity was about to snuff itself out, we hadn't really stopped to consider what would happen if that didn't occur.

But with twelve hundred years, faster spaceships would doubtless have been developed. While the colonists aboard the *Pioneer Spirit* had slept, some dreaming at an indolent pace, other ships had zipped past them, arriving at Tau Ceti decades, if not centuries, earlier—long enough ago that they'd already built human cities on Soror.

"Damn it," I said. "God damn it." I shook my head, staring at the screen. The tortoise was supposed to win, not the hare.

"What do we do now?" asked Ling.

I sighed. "I suppose we should contact them."

"We—ah, we might be from the wrong side."

I grinned. "Well, we can't *both* be from the wrong side. Besides, you heard the radio: Mandarin *and* English. Anyway, I can't imagine that anyone cares about a war more than a thousand years in the past, and—"

"Excuse me," said the ship's computer. "Incoming audio message."

I looked at Ling. She frowned, surprised. "Put it on," I said.

"*Pioneer Spirit*, welcome! This is Jod Bokket, manager of the Derluntin space station, in orbit around Soror. Is there anyone awake on board?" It was a man's voice, with an accent unlike anything I'd ever heard before.

Ling looked at me, to see if I was going to object, then she spoke up. "Computer, send a reply." The computer bleeped to signal that the channel was open. "This is Dr. Ling Woo, co-captain of the *Pioneer Spirit*. Two of us have revived; there are forty-eight more still in cryofreeze."

"Well, look," said Bokket's voice, "it'll be days at the rate you're going before you get here. How about if we send a ship to bring you two to Derluntin? We can have someone there to pick you up in about an hour."

"They really like to rub it in, don't they?" I grumbled.

"What was that?" said Bokket. "We couldn't quite make it out."

Ling and I consulted with facial expressions, then agreed. "Sure," said Ling. "We'll be waiting."

"Not for long," said Bokket, and the speaker went dead.

Bokket himself came to collect us. His spherical ship was tiny compared with ours, but it seemed to have about the same amount of habitable interior space; would the ignominies ever cease? Docking adapters had changed a lot in a thousand years, and he wasn't able to get an airtight seal, so we had to transfer over to his ship in space suits. Once aboard, I was pleased to see we were still floating freely; it would have been *too* much if they'd had artificial gravity.

Bokket seemed a nice fellow—about my age, early thirties. Of course, maybe people looked youthful forever now; who knew how old he might actually be? I couldn't really identify his ethnicity either; he seemed to be rather a blend of traits. But he certainly was taken with Ling—his eyes popped out when she took off her helmet, revealing her heart-shaped face and long black hair.

"Hello," he said, smiling broadly.

Ling smiled back. "Hello. I'm Ling Woo, and this is Toby MacGregor, my co-captain."

"Greetings," I said, sticking out my hand.

Bokket looked at it, clearly not knowing precisely what to do. He extended his hand in a mirroring of my gesture, but didn't touch me. I closed the gap and clasped his hand. He seemed surprised, but pleased.

"We'll take you back to the station first," he said. "Forgive us, but, well—you can't go down to the planet's surface yet; you'll have to be quarantined. We've eliminated a lot of diseases, of course, since your time, and so we don't vaccinate for them anymore. I'm willing to take the risk, but . . ."

I nodded. "That's fine."

He tipped his head slightly, as if he were preoccupied for a moment, then: "I've told the ship to take us back to Derluntin station. It's in a polar orbit, about 200 kilometers above Soror; you'll get some beautiful views of the planet, anyway." He was grinning from ear to ear. "It's wonderful to meet you people," he said. "Like a page out of history."

"If you knew about us," I asked, after we'd settled in for the journey to the station, "why didn't you pick us up earlier?"

Bokket cleared his throat. "We didn't know about you."

"But you called us by name: *Pioneer Spirit*."

"Well, it *is* painted in letters three meters high across your hull. Our asteroid-watch system detected you. A lot of information from your time has been lost—I guess there was a lot of political upheaval then, no?—but we knew Earth had experimented with sleeper ships in the twenty-first century."

We were getting close to the space station; it was a giant ring, spinning to simulate gravity. It might have taken us over a thousand years to do it, but humanity was finally building space stations the way God had always intended them to be.

And floating next to the space station was a beautiful spaceship, with a spindle-shaped silver hull and two sets of mutually perpendicular emerald-green delta wings. "It's gorgeous," I said.

Bokket nodded.

"How does it land, though? Tail-down?"

"It doesn't land; it's a starship."

"Yes, but—"

"We use shuttles to go between it and the ground."

"But if it can't land," asked Ling, "why is it streamlined? Just for aesthetics?"

Bokket laughed, but it was a polite laugh. "It's streamlined because it needs to be. There's substantial length-contraction when flying at just below the speed of light; that means that the interstellar medium seems much denser. Although there's only one baryon per cubic centimeter, they form what seems to be an appreciable atmosphere if you're going fast enough."

"And your ships are *that* fast?" asked Ling.

Bokket smiled. "Yes. They're that fast."

Ling shook her head. "We were crazy," she said. "Crazy to undertake our journey." She looked briefly at Bokket, but couldn't meet his eyes. She turned her gaze down toward the floor. "You must think we're incredibly foolish."

Bokket's eyes widened. He seemed at a loss for what to say. He looked at me, spreading his arms, as if appealing to me for support. But I just exhaled, letting air—and disappointment—vent from my body.

"You're wrong," said Bokket, at last. "You couldn't be more wrong. We *honor* you." He paused, waiting for Ling to look up again. She did, her eyebrows lifted questioningly. "If we have come farther than you," said Bokket, "or have gone faster than you, it's because we had your work to build on. Humans are here now because it's *easy* for us to be here, because you and others blazed the trails." He looked at me, then at Ling. "If we see farther," he said, "it's because we stand on the shoulders of giants."

Later that day, Ling, Bokket, and I were walking along the gently curving floor of Derluntin station. We were confined to a limited part of one section; they'd let us down to the planet's surface in another ten days, Bokket had said.

"There's nothing for us here," said Ling, hands in her pockets. "We're freaks, anachronisms. Like somebody from the T'ang Dynasty showing up in our world."

"Soror is wealthy," said Bokket. "We can certainly support you and your passengers."

"They are *not* passengers," I snapped. "They are colonists. They are explorers."

Bokket nodded. "I'm sorry. You're right, of course. But look—we really are delighted that you're here. I've been keeping the media away; the quarantine lets me do that. But they will go absolutely dingo when you come down to the planet. It's like having Neil Armstrong or Tamiko Hiroshige show up at your door."

"Tamiko who?" asked Ling.

"Sorry. After your time. She was the first person to disembark at Alpha Centauri."

"The first," I repeated; I guess I wasn't doing a good job of hiding my bitterness. "That's the honor—that's the achievement. Being the first. Nobody remembers the name of the second person on the moon."

"Edwin Eugene Aldrin, Jr.," said Bokket. "Known as 'Buzz.' "

"Fine, okay," I said. "*You* remember, but most people don't."

"I didn't remember it; I accessed it." He tapped his temple. "Direct link to the planetary web; everybody has one."

Ling exhaled; the gulf was vast. "Regardless," she said, "we are not pioneers; we're just also-rans. We may have set out before you did, but you got here before us."

"Well, my ancestors did," said Bokket. "I'm sixth generation Sororian."

"*Sixth* generation?" I said. "How long has the colony been here?"

"We're not a colony anymore; we're an independent world. But the ship that got here first left Earth in 2107. Of course, my ancestors didn't immigrate until much later."

"Twenty-one-oh-seven," I repeated. That was only fifty-six years after the launch of the *Pioneer Spirit*. I'd been thirty-one when our ship had started its journey; if I'd stayed behind, I might very well have lived to see the real pioneers depart. What had we been thinking, leaving Earth? Had we been running, escaping, getting out, fleeing before the bombs fell? Were we pioneers, or cowards?

No. No, those were crazy thoughts. We'd left for the same reason that *Homo sapiens sapiens* had crossed the Strait of Gibraltar. It was what we did as a species. It was why we'd triumphed, and the Neandertals had failed. We *needed* to see what was on the other side, what was over the next hill, what was orbiting other stars. It was what had given us dominion over the home planet; it was what was going to make us kings of infinite space.

I turned to Ling. "We can't stay here," I said.

She seemed to mull this over for a bit, then nodded. She looked at Bokket. "We don't want parades," she said. "We don't want statues." She lifted her eyebrows, as if acknowledging the magnitude of what she was asking for. "We want a new ship, a faster ship." She looked at me, and I bobbed my head in agreement. She pointed out the window. "A *streamlined* ship."

"What would you do with it?" asked Bokket. "Where would you go?"

She glanced at me, then looked back at Bokket. "Andromeda."

"Andromeda? You mean the Andromeda *galaxy?* But that's—" a fractional pause, no doubt while his web link provided the data "—2.2 *million* light-years away."

"Exactly."

"But . . . but it would take over two million years to get there."

"Only from Earth's—excuse me, from Soror's—point of view," said Ling. "We could do it in less subjective time than we've already been traveling, and, of course, we'd spend all that time in cryogenic freeze."

"None of our ships have cryogenic chambers," Bokket said. "There's no need for them."

"We could transfer the chambers from the *Pioneer Spirit.*"

Bokket shook his head. "It would be a one-way trip; you'd never come back."

"That's not true," I said. "Unlike most galaxies, Andromeda is actually moving toward the Milky Way, not away from it. Eventually, the two galaxies will merge, bringing us home."

"That's billions of years in the future."

"Thinking small hasn't done us any good so far," said Ling.

Bokket frowned. "I said before that we can afford to support you and your shipmates here on Soror, and that's true. But starships are expensive. We can't just give you one."

"It's got to be cheaper than supporting all of us."

"No, it's not."

"You said you honored us. You said you stand on our shoulders. If that's true, then repay the favor. Give us an opportunity to stand on *your* shoulders. Let us have a new ship."

Bokket sighed; it was clear he felt we really didn't understand how difficult Ling's request would be to fulfill. "I'll do what I can," he said.

Ling and I spent that evening talking, while blue-and-green Soror spun majestically beneath us. It was our job to jointly make the right decision, not just for ourselves but for the four dozen other members of the *Pioneer Spirit*'s complement that had entrusted their fate to us. Would they have wanted to be revived here?

No. No, of course not. They'd left Earth to found a colony; there was no reason to think they would have changed their minds, whatever they might be dreaming. Nobody had an emotional attachment to the idea of Tau Ceti; it just had seemed a logical target star.

"We could ask for passage back to Earth," I said.

"You don't want that," said Ling. "And neither, I'm sure, would any of the others."

"No, you're right," I said. "They'd want us to go on."

Ling nodded. "I think so."

"Andromeda?" I said, smiling. "Where did that come from?"

She shrugged. "First thing that popped into my head."

"Andromeda," I repeated, tasting the word some more. I remembered how thrilled I was, at sixteen, out in the California desert, to see that little oval smudge below Cassiopeia from the first time. Another galaxy, another island universe—and half again as big as our own. "Why not?" I fell silent, but, after a while, I said, "Bokket seems to like you."

Ling smiled. "I like him."

"Go for it," I said.

"What?" She sounded surprised.

"Go for it, if you like him. I may have to be alone until Helena is revived at our final destination, but you don't have to be. Even if they do give us a new ship, it'll surely be a few weeks before they can transfer the cryochambers."

Ling rolled her eyes. *"Men,"* she said, but I knew the idea appealed to her.

Bokket was right: the Sororian media seemed quite enamored with Ling and me, and not just because of our exotic appearance—my white skin and blue eyes; her dark skin and epicanthic folds; our two strange accents, both so different from the way people of the thirty-third century spoke. They also seemed to be fascinated by, well, by the pioneer spirit.

When the quarantine was over, we did go down to the planet. The temperature was perhaps a little cooler than I'd have liked, and the air a bit moister—but humans adapt, of course. The architecture in Soror's capital city of Pax was surprisingly ornate, with lots of domed roofs and intricate carvings. The term "capital city" was an anachronism, though; government was completely decentralized, with all major decisions done by plebiscite—including the decision about whether or not to give us another ship.

Bokket, Ling, and I were in the central square of Pax, along with Kari Deetal, Soror's president, waiting for the results of the vote to be announced. Media representatives from all over the Tau Ceti system were present, as well as one from Earth, whose stories were always read 11.9 years after he filed them. Also on hand were perhaps a thousand spectators.

"My friends," said Deetal, to the crowd, spreading her arms, "you have all voted, and now let us share in the results." She tipped her head slightly, and a moment later people in the crowd started clapping and cheering.

Ling and I turned to Bokket, who was beaming. "What is it?" said Ling. "What decision did they make?"

Bokket looked surprised. "Oh, sorry. I forgot you don't have web implants. You're going to get your ship."

Ling closed her eyes and breathed a sigh of relief. My heart was pounding.

President Deetal gestured toward us. "Dr. Mac-Gregor, Dr. Woo—would you say a few words?"

We glanced at each other, then stood up. "Thank you," I said looking out at everyone.

Ling nodded in agreement. "Thank you very much."

A reporter called out a question. "What are you going to call your new ship?"

Ling frowned; I pursued my lips. And then I said, "What else? The *Pioneer Spirit II*."

The crowd erupted again.

*   *   *

Finally, the fateful day came. Our official boarding of our new starship—the one that would be covered by all the media—wouldn't happen for another four hours, but Ling and I were nonetheless heading toward the airlock that joined the ship to the station's outer rim. She wanted to look things over once more, and I wanted to spend a little time just sitting next to Helena's cryochamber, communing with her.

And, as we walked, Bokket came running along the curving floor toward us.

"Ling," he said, catching his breath. "Toby."

I nodded a greeting. Ling looked slightly uncomfortable; she and Bokket had grown close during the last few weeks, but they'd also had their time alone last night to say their good-byes. I don't think she'd expected to see him again before we left.

"I'm sorry to bother you two," he said. "I know you're both busy, but . . ." He seemed quite nervous.

"Yes?" I said.

He looked at me, then at Ling. "Do you have room for another passenger?"

Ling smiled. "We don't have passengers. We're colonists."

"Sorry," said Bokket, smiling back at her. "Do you have room for another colonist?"

"Well, there *are* four spare cryochambers, but . . ." She looked at me.

"Why not?" I said, shrugging.

"It's going to be hard work, you know," said Ling, turning back to Bokket. "Wherever we end up, it's going to be rough."

Bokket nodded. "I know. And I want to be part of it."

Ling knew she didn't have to be coy around me. "That would be wonderful," she said. "But—but why?"

Bokket reached out tentatively, and found Ling's hand. He squeezed it gently, and she squeezed back. "You're one reason," he said.

"Got a thing for older women, eh?" said Ling. I smiled at that.

Bokket laughed. "I guess."

"You said I was one reason," said Ling.

He nodded. "The other reason is—well, it's this: I don't want to stand on the shoulders of giants." He paused, then lifted his own shoulders a little, as if acknowledging that he was giving voice to the sort of thought rarely spoken aloud. "I want to *be* a giant."

They continued to hold hands as we walked down the space station's long corridor, heading toward the sleek and graceful ship that would take us to our new home.

EDEN STAR

by Jack Williamson

Jack Williamson was born in 1908 and has been writing science fiction for nearly three quarters of a century, with the novels *Darker Than You Think, The Humanoids, Star Bridge,* and *Lifeburst,* as well as many others as a result. He has also written nonfiction on such topics as the teaching of science fiction and a study of H.G. Wells. A winner of the Nebula Grand Master Award and the Hugo Award, he lives in New Mexico. His most recent works are the novel *Black Sun* and the second volume of his collected stories, *Wolves of Darkness*.

"**M**ister Big, it's worse than murder." Dirk had once been taught to call our father sir, a habit he had broken long ago. He paused to look our father in the eye. "Do you want to kill a world?"

We were still back on old Earth, sitting over coffee in the kitchen of the old adobe ranch house in New Mexico. Colin McArr had come there elated with the discovery of the Lone Star and his dream of a human colony on its single planet. Our father scowled and asked Dirk what geocide meant.

Two years younger than I, he is a feisty little guy with a shock of stiff coppery hair he seldom bothers to comb. He hates to take orders and loves to compete. I gave up the battles with our father long ago, but it's still a game to him.

"A world's a live being." He spoke very gravely, as

if instructing a slow student. "Call it a biocosm. A great community of separate organisms that aren't all that separate. They keep one another alive by symbiosis. Here on Earth the plants make free oxygen for us. We give it back in carbon dioxide."

"So what?" our father muttered.

"So your grand scheme is total geocide." Dirk grinned with the pleasure of his argument, and turned serious again. "All life on earth is one single being, if you get the point. I doubt that two biocosms can exist together. One would surely feed like a cancer on the other. I don't want a planet's death on my own conscience."

He turned to McArr. "Doctor Wise, you?"

McArr is a raw-boned giant with a tangle of fiery yellow beard. I had never quite liked or trusted him, perhaps because our father has always trusted him too well. They had been roommates at Caltech, and our father had showered him with millions for his labs and expeditions and research satellites.

"A silly quibble," he sniffed at Dirk through the beard. "Charles Darwin gave us the answer. To stay alive, we all compete. The fittest survive. We may die there if we happen to meet something more fit than we are. If we're fitter, we'll survive. A law of nature, and no nonsense about it."

Dirk shrugged and turned back to our father.

"The nonsense is your grand scheme itself. A crazy lottery."

McArr had bubbled all morning about the solitary star. It really shone alone. Some cosmological accident had flung it into the void, twenty million light-years from any galaxy.

"I don't doubt Molly or her star." Dirk gave him a cynical squint. "It's the planet that bothers me. Even she hasn't seen it because it's too far off for her telescopes. How do you know it's even there?"

"She says it is."

Dr. Molly McArr was his daughter, a slim, green-eyed brunette with a far better brain than his. A competent astrophysicist and a pioneer xenobiologist, she had identified life in her brine specimens from Europa before she ever found the star. I had once dreamed of dating her, but she seemed to love her cosmic riddles and alien microbes more than mere men.

"She spent the summer on the spectroscope." McArr raised his voice to answer Dirk. "She says the Doppler wobble shows just one planet, sized right and in the right orbit. An Earthlike world, and great good luck for us!"

"But still," Dirk frowned doubtfully, "it's a long way to go."

"Not by quantum wave, flying at the speed of light." Short of patience, McArr rapped the table with his empty cup. "True, we'll be leaving twenty million years of objective time on Earth behind us, but relativity will stop time for us aboard the ship. The isolated star ought to be a safe destination, with no nearby masses to break the quantum wave."

"Maybe." Dirk shook his head. "I've heard about the launches. I hear the pilot craft don't come back."

"How could they?" McArr blinked at him like a judicial owl. "Real time, our time, runs on while they're in flight. It can't run back to tell us where they got to, but quantum theory is well proven. The technology exists." He turned back to our father. "We can get there, Jim. All we need is funds to launch the ship."

"Even if you had it," Dirk raised his voice again,

"your scheme is a call for quantum suicide. Who would volunteer?"

Our father had been a refugee from misfortune, staggered by the hostile takeover of the great corporation he had spent his life to build, again by his defeat in a hard race for the Senate, finally by my mother's sudden death. After her funeral he retired to the desert ranch and spent his aimless days with *The Wall Street Journal* or riding the range on his old roan mare. I had thought his own life was over, but he spent half that night listening to McArr. Next morning he came down to breakfast with his grizzled beard shaved off and a new light in his eyes.

"We've going to call it the Eden Star." His voice had a ring I hadn't heard for years. "The planet will be Eden Two. A new chance, Vince! The second chance for me. A great break for the future of our kind."

He found funds to build the quantum ship and rounded up his volunteers, an even hundred of them, all desperate enough to take the desperate risk. A few political exiles, a few perhaps in flight from scandal or the law or some secret sorrow, more simply disappointed with life on a troubled Earth and hoping to find something better for themselves and their children.

Dirk had trained for a Mars exploration flight, but lost out in the final cut. Somewhat to my surprise, he agreed to study quantum navigation and come along as our pilot. Perhaps he was bored with life on Earth. I think he was half in love with Molly McArr.

I remember our last night on Earth. After all the final handshakes and tearful kisses at the farewell dinner, Dirk and I sat together in a taxi on our way out

to the old military missile range where the quantum
ship stood waiting, a tall silver pillar gleaming in the
light of a waning moon.

He was cheerfully recalling the gifts he had left for
friends he would never see again: books and paintings,
a horse ranch in Wyoming, a fast jet. With less to
leave, I thought sadly of our dead mother and how
she used to spoil Dirk, happily calling him her great
little man.

Molly hadn't been at the party, and I asked him why.

"She's already aboard, rechecking her destination
data." He turned to study me soberly before he went
on. "Vince, I know you wonder why I'm going. Let's
say just for the hell of it. But I've thought about you."

He paused again. The flash of a headlight caught a
grave expression, and his voice had fallen when he
spoke.

"If you'll forgive me for saying this, and if you really
want to get away from anything, you'll stay right here
on Earth. You've lived under the Iron Man's iron
thumb far too long."

"Could be," I had to say. "I've thought enough
about it, but he wants me to come as the colony's
official historian."

His short laugh was almost mockery. "Looking at
the odds against us, I hope you live to see some
history."

We have seen history. A brassy desert sun stood at
the zenith of a dusty desert sky when we took off,
dusty desert mountains on the brown horizon all
around us. In a relative instant of ship time, Earth
had flickered out. We found ourselves lost in black
and starless space, the ship in orbit around Eden Two.

Dirk kept us there a month in orbit, searching the planet for any hint of intelligent life.

Scanning the two major continents from high orbits and low, we saw no roads, no dams, no walls, no cities, no evidence of intelligent engineering. Monitoring the spectrum, we heard no radio signal. Cheers echoed through the ship when Dirk's voice rang from the speakers with the word that we were down from orbit, safe on the west coast of the equatorial continent.

McArr and I came off the ship together. A sun as bright and kind as our old one smiled out of cloudless blue. Odd, flat-topped trees lined the bank of a river that wound near. He shouted "Eureka!" and we turned together with arms spread wide to embrace the boom of distant surf and the clean fresh scent of a brisk west wind. The turf was bright green velvet, spangled with snow-white blooms that spread rainbow wings to flutter away from our feet.

"Flying pollen." He gestured at them. "We must expect surprises here."

Herds of little yellow-brown quadrupeds had scattered from our landing. Now they were grazing back toward us. Comic little creatures, high in the rear, heads on the ground, they make golden towers when they stand erect to watch us.

"Game animals." McArr grinned and shook his head at me. "And no predators! Have we blundered into an actual Eden?"

Late that afternoon we came off the ship again. McArr brought a torsion balance that he set up on a little tripod to measure the planet's gravity. I was still lost in the excitement of the landing, trying to absorb all the impressions and emotions of it, groping for words to record the moment for our history.

"Eden Two!" I called to him. "And no snakes in sight!"

Busy with his gear, he said nothing, but I soon began to wonder if we had really reached a second virgin Earth. The sea breeze had died. The motionless air took on a faint foul taint. The flying blooms had died and fallen. A splendid crimson sunset dimmed quickly into night. McArr turned off his instrument lights, and blackness fell upon me.

A total darkness that plunged me into panic. He had been close beside me, the ship not twenty yards away, but they were gone. Looking up, I found no moon, no stars, no ray of light. Of course I had known the planet had no moon or stars, but that shock of strangeness caught me unprepared.

Eden Two had a sudden scent of Satan. Shaking, weak in the knees, I couldn't breathe. Feeling a coward and a fool, I was overwhelmed with a sudden sick longing for the remembered moments of my infancy when I lay in the dark waiting for my mother to come and tuck me in.

"Ready?" McArr's casual voice saved my sanity. "Let's get back aboard."

His lantern found the ship. He gathered up his gear and I followed him up the ramp and into the comforts of light and human fellowship, feeling a little ashamed of that jolt of terror and enormously grateful for the safety of my tiny cabin. It was home, and it gave me a fresh awareness of what we were, doubtless now the only human beings in the universe, the whole human future in our hands. Whatever the hazards we had to survive!

I was half asleep when the ship phone rang.

"Vince!" Dirk's urgent voice. "Better get up here."

He didn't explain. I rushed up to the control room

in the nose cone. Molly and McArr were already with him there, peering out into the dark. She turned to shake her head at me, a finger to her lips. Dirk twisted a knob on the instrument panel, and I heard a sound I can't describe, strange as the scream of the tropic bird that startled me once when my mother took me to visit an aviary in that last sad summer of her life.

"The outside mikes," Dirk murmured. "We've woken something up."

Something in that shriek sent a shiver through me. I stood frozen, staring with Molly and McArr out into the blackness, listening until it paused and came again from nowhere we could see, hoarse and strange and meaningless, yet piercing me with a sense of something trapped in the agony of death.

To help us see, Dirk blacked out the inside lights. Kneeling against the windows, staring out into that suffocating dark, we found the things at last, but only in flickering glimpses. A horde of them swarmed over the windows, flickering so faintly I never really made them out.

I blinked and strained and rubbed my eyes. A long black spider face that licked the glass with a three-fingered tongue? A slick black tentacle that struck like a snake at my face? Black-taloned claws that slashed at the glass? Or were they images out of my own imagination?

The windows were heavy quartz glass, but I shrank back in spite of myself. The microphones were picking up a bedlam of shrieks and howls and grunts, squeaks and squeals and chirps, bangs and clicks and pops.

"They're tapping!" McArr whispered. "Trying to talk."

Listening, he had Dirk turn up the speakers till the din was deafening, finally had him turn on the searchlight. It caught a few of the creatures, if only for a moment. Huge and ungainly, with slick black bodies and tangled hairy legs. They brought back memories of a pet tarantula Dirk had used to terrify me when we were kids, till our mother made him get rid of it.

They scattered out of the light as if it blinded them, tumbling to the ground, diving into the shadows before I could find heads or limbs or shapes. In a moment, all I saw was the howling dark.

"The light's killing them."

Dirk turned it off.

"Keep it on," our father told him. "If it keeps them off the ship."

I dreamed that night that they had gotten aboard and filled the ship with blinding blackness. I heard their scraping claws, their muffled chirps and squeaks. They were everywhere, snatching the kids out of their bunks and eating them alive. I heard little Linda Marquez screaming for help, but I couldn't find her in the dark.

I woke to the silence of the sleeping ship and found the golden sun rising into another serene blue sky. The high-tailed herbivores were grazing peacefully around us. The creatures had left no sign I could see, but my father gathered us in the main cabin for what he called a council of war.

"War or not," Dirk spoke first, "we're at a dicey point."

"Dicey?" That yelp came from a gaunt woman with a baby girl asleep in her arms. "I'd say desperate. The monsters woke little Lillian. She screamed all night. We've got to get out."

Somebody asked if we could look for another planet.

"Impossible." Molly McArr frowned through black-rimmed glasses. "The star has no other planets. We have no interstellar launch facility. No telescopes big enough to find another destination star."

What about the other continent?

"Would it be better?" Dirk shrugged. "Our midnight visitors did no actual harm. As little as we know, we could blunder into something worse."

That afternoon my father sent me out with McCarr and Molly to survey our surroundings and search for the screamers.

"Whatever they are." His uneasy shrug was almost a shudder. "We know they're more than any collective nightmare. They left queer footmarks in the mud around the ship. I want to know what they are, where they went, what they mean for us."

"Nothing good," McArr muttered. "Or they'd have stayed to tell us."

"Find them," he said. "Any trace you can."

We tried. McArr drove the light vehicle. Molly sat in the front seat with him. In the rear seat, I used binoculars to sweep the sunlit landscape, the flat-topped trees along the river, the small brown quadrupeds gazing the green velvet plain. The flying blooms scattered away from our wheels, and their scent rose about us in a cloud of exotic sweetness.

"An actual Eden!" Molly turned to smile at me, with a quizzical quirk of her lips. "And a new library of life for us to read. New science for us to write. A wonder world, at least by daylight."

She murmured something to her father. I laid the glasses aside to admire her and wish she liked me as well as she did those winged blooms. She marveled at them, filmed them, caught one in a plastic jar, broke a little tube of something gas to stabilize it, and mounted it carefully on a pin.

We followed the riverbank down to the beach and circled back far around the ship. Some of the little brown quadrupeds stood up to watch us pass and dropped their heads again as we drove east toward the hills, perhaps twenty miles away.

The herds thinned as the land sloped upward. Thickets of thorny yellow growth replaced the velvet turf. The flat-topped trees were gone, and the river's rocky bed grew deeper until we drove into the dark-walled canyon it had cut. That narrowed as we pushed farther, jolting over rocks and picking a way between boulders scattered where flood and rockfalls had left them.

Noon passed. I felt uneasy that night might catch us away from the ship, but McArr drove us on and farther on. The canyon narrowed. Its walls shut out the sun. The way ahead looked impossible. Molly wanted to turn back, but he ignored her. We were creeping around a sharp curve when the front wheels dropped.

The fall threw me against the front seat and dazed me for a moment. Molly and McArr were out of the vehicle when I could sit up. I found them staring at a wide slab of rock swinging into the cliff ahead.

"We've found them!" McArr shouted. "Troglodytes!"

I was scrambling out of the car, rubbing my bruises. Molly came back to see if I was hurt, and we stood with him, watching a hidden door lift to reveal a dark tunnel mouth.

"Intelligence," Molly murmured. "A problem for Dirk."

The door stopped with a dull thud a dozen feet overhead. I shaded my eyes to make out a wide gateway into darkness, paved and walled and arched with smoothly cut stone blocks. Cold air came out of it, and a strange bitter mustiness. I stepped back to breathe clean air. McArr examined the hinged stone slab that had dropped under the car.

"They're stonemasons," he muttered. "And engineers."

Fumbling in the toolbox, he found a flashlight and started into the tunnel. Anxiously, Molly called him back.

"Haven't we gone far enough?" I asked him. "Till we can get back and report?"

"Report what?" He scowled impatiently. "A hole in the ground? A trapdoor to conceal it? That's not enough."

But he helped me push at the car while Molly backed it back to level ground. It showed no damage. She found a spot where she could turn, but McArr wasn't ready to go.

"Give me time for a peek inside." He looked at his watch. "An hour ought to do. If I'm not out by then, get back to the ship with the story."

"Father!" Molly caught his arm. "You shouldn't—"

He shook off her hand and stalked into the tunnel. Waiting in its dank breath, we watched the feeble flicker of his light on bare stone walls. It dimmed and vanished. The echo of his footsteps faded away.

Listening, we said little, but I found Molly's hand clutching mine. I watched the time. The hour was gone, and most of another, before we heard his boots on the stone. Stumbling out of the dark, he shaded his eyes to search for us.

"Tell Dirk." He was breathing fast. "We've found

his alien biocosm. And found a million questions to answer before we know we can survive here. I'm going back for a longer look."

We had brought a lunch. Molly spread it out on the back seat of the car and begged him to tell us what he had seen.

"Seen?" He snorted at her. "In the dark? I heard their voices ahead, but I think they ran from my light." Scowling into the dark, he shook his head. "The tunnels branch; the complex must be enormous. They are old; I saw deep wheel ruts worn in the stone. We've got to know them, if they're willing to be known."

In no mood for food, he dug into the tool box for spare flashlight batteries and found none.

"No matter." He shrugged. "They don't want light."

Molly begged him to wait, to return to the ship with us for another council of war.

"Who wants war?" He was sharply sardonic. "We must make a move for peace, if they can understand peace. Get back to the ship while you can. I'll try to be out tomorrow, I hope with some better hint of what they are and how we can try to deal with them. Look for me at noon."

He walked back into the tunnel.

That night we heard them again, closer when Dirk blacked out the ship's lights. Shrieks of jungle birds, screams of tortured animals, howls and wails and bellows that never came from anything on Earth.

At dawn next day we set out to be waiting when McArr got out of the tunnel. By midmorning, following our tracks into the hills, we reached the spot where the hidden door had opened.

Or was it the spot? Our wheels had left clear prints

on dry sandbars but no traces on bare rock. The door
had opened out of a sharp turn, but the canyon was
never straight. Perhaps a quarter mile of it wound
between the last wheel prints and a rockfall too steep
to climb. We left the car and walked the canyon, finding no tunnel mouth, no sign of any doorway.

Tired of walking, we waited in the car. McArr did
not appear. Noon went by. We walked and searched
and kept on waiting until the shadows had begun to
darken. Molly agreed at last that we must get back to
the ship.

That night we heard another bedlam in the sky.
Next day we came back to search again and wait
again. Molly cried when she thought her father was
dead. She blamed herself for letting him go down the
tunnel alone, though I knew she could never have
stopped him. When the fall of night forced us to leave
again without him, she cursed the unseen troglodytes
with a vocabulary that amazed me.

Every day for three more weeks, we came back and
found nothing. Tired and disheartened, Molly talked
forlornly of her life back on Earth. An only child, she
had lived with her father after a bitter divorce.

"He and I were close," she said. "I know he loves
me, but he never really showed it. What he always did
was always to challenge me to be better than he was.
I guess I was precocious, but you know how brilliant
he is—if he's still alive—with an ego of his own. He
never let me feel quite his equal." Emotion twisted
her face. "He made me feel inferior."

I told her how my own father had always ruled my
life. Those confessions brought us closer together. Trying to lift her feelings, I talked of our future on the
planet.

"If we survive!" I heard no cheer in her voice. "Dirk seems excited about making our place in this new biocosm and learning its laws of life. But those howling demons! They—they've taken my father. They're more than I can take."

She was suddenly sobbing. I put my arm around her. She melted against me. We kissed, but after a moment she drew abruptly away.

"Sorry, Vince." Her bitter little laugh was almost another sob. "I forgot my father."

After those long weeks of disappointment, we had to halt the search. Dirk and my father put Molly on a task group assigned to learn if Terran plants could grow here. They had me begin a census of our group, reporting work history and useful skills.

One morning four months later, I was out with her on a test farm, where the young corn had grown as high as our knees. Suddenly she screamed and ran from me. She had seen McArr stumbling toward us across the field. A human scarecrow, he was ragged and bearded and drawn thin, a strip of filthy cloth wrapped like as bandage over his eyes. He pushed it up, squinted to find Molly, and staggered to meet her.

He was near collapse, starved and sunburned and dehydrated. We loaded him on a tractor cart and carried him on to the ship. The medics took possession of him, and we saw no more of him till that evening. Shaved and clean by then, clad in a yellow jumpsuit, he looked pale and haggard but able enough to attack his dinner.

Dirk asked what he had learned.

"What could a blind man learn?" He looked impatiently up from a bowl of new potatoes out of Molly's gardens. "The flashlight died. The trogs do sometimes emit light, maybe when they mate, but only in firefly flashes too faint to show me anything. All I know is what I felt and touched."

"Were you a prisoner?"

"Not exactly." He stabbed his fork into another potato. "But they did try to keep me. They were always huddling around me, speaking to me. If their squeaks and grunts really are a language. They fed me queer-tasting stuff I never saw. It sometimes made me sick, but I think they worshiped me."

He shaded his eyes to survey the table and reached for a red tomato.

"I kept trying to escape." He made a dismal shrug. "Helpless. Lost in a world I never understood. I think they kept leading me deeper when I tried to get out, till finally they took me down to where I did see a light."

He looked up, his hollow eyes staring off at nothing.

"An actual light, but still very feeble, too faint to show me much. From the echoes, I think the chamber was large and probably round. A mob of the creatures lay huddled on the floor under a pale white globe that hung from the roof.

"They were singing, chanting, howling, their voices a weird cacophony that I have no word for, in the same sequence of yowls and hoots was repeated over and over. They were all looking up at that light. I couldn't see them well, but their eyes all reflected it. I think they fear light and hide from it. I think they were praying. I think they worship the sun."

He reached for another chicken wing.

"I've been famished, dreaming of food. Afraid I'd never eat again." He grinned gratefully at Molly and turned back to Dirk. "I think you can forget your apprehensions about a new biocosm. I've been your guinea pig, living with them all that time and eating what they gave me. And you see me still alive."

"I think we've found the reason." Dirk nodded at Molly. "And a new view of biocosms. I think they're not all that separate. Molly says the molecules of life start forming in the cosmic clouds before the stars are gone. She thinks evolution everywhere has to follow the same universal path. That would make the whole cosmos kin, all one great organism."

"Perhaps." McArr blinked uncertainly. "Perhaps."

I asked him what we could expect from the troglodytes.

"I never got to know them." Wild for an instant, his eyes darted around the room as if searching for monsters among us. "They didn't want to let me go. I'm afraid they'll follow."

Molly wanted him to sleep, but at sunset he came with us to the control cone. Dirk sat by the hooded instrument board. Molly and I stood by McArr, watching blackness fall. We were all of us silent, listening uneasily to the microphones, but I liked the warm quick pressures of her hand in mine.

Until long past midnight, all we heard was the rustle of the wind. Molly got a chair for McArr. I heard him snoring. He woke hungry again, and she found him a ration pack.

"Perhaps I was wrong." He asked Dirk to turn up the lights. "Perhaps there's no danger."

The speakers were silent for another hour, before we heard the first shriek. Ignoring the searchlight, the creatures came swarming around the ship, flapping thin black bat wings against the windows, peering inside with strange black eyes, fighting the glass with skeletal hairy limbs. Their bawling grew deafening, till

Dirk turned the speakers down. Molly asked McArr what they were after.

"If you want a guess—" He shrugged unhappily. "They worship light. I believe they worshiped me because they thought I came from the sun. I believe they think we came to carry them there."

Dirk turned on the searchlight, but still they kept on coming. They plastered the windows till the light crimped and twisted their wings and drove them down. Dirk turned up the speakers to hear their squalling. I tried to imagine what they might be trying to say, but all I heard was agony.

Day broke, but still they came by scores and hundreds and thousands. Flying down from the hills, they ripped a thin dark streak across the pink veil of dawn. The rising sun hit them cruelly, but still they came on, raining out of the sky. Even on the ground, they kept on crawling toward us, tumbling into the dead black tangle around us, reeking and bloating under the sun.

Next day we moved the ship.

THE MUFFIN MIGRATION

by Alan Dean Foster

Alan Dean Foster was born in New York City and raised in Los Angeles. He has a bachelor's degree in political science and a Master of Fine Arts in Cinema from UCLA. He has traveled extensively around the world, from Australia to Papua, New Guinea. He has also written fiction in just about every genre, and is known for his excellent movie novelizations. Currently, he lives in Prescott, Arizona, with his wife, assorted dogs, cats, fish, javelina, and other animals, where he is working on several new novels and media projects.

It was a beautiful day on Hedris. But then, Bowman reflected as he stood on the little covered porch he and LeCleur had fashioned from packing scrap, every day for the past four months had been beautiful. Not overwhelming like the spectacular mornings on Barabas, or stunningly evocative like the sunsets on New Riviera: just tranquil, temperate, and bursting with the crisp fresh tang of unpolluted air, green growing grasses, and a recognition of the presence of unfettered, unfenced life-force.

In addition to the all-pervasive, piquant musk of millions of muffins, of course.

The muffins, as the two advance agents had come to call them, were by incalculable orders of magnitude the dominant life-form on Hedris. They swarmed in inconceivable numbers over its endless grassy plains, burrowed deep into its unbelievably rich topsoil, turned streams and rivers brown with their bathing, frolicking bodies. Fortunately for Bowman and LeCleur, the largest of them stood no more than six inches high, not counting the few thicker, lighter-hued bristles that protruded upward and beyond the otherwise concise covering of soft brown fur. A muffin had two eyes, two legs, a short furry blob of a tail, and an oval mouth filled with several eruptions of toothlike bone designed to make short work of the diverse assortment of foot-high grass in which they lived. They communicated, fought, and cooed to one another via appealing sequences of chirruping, high-pitched peeping sounds.

It was a good thing, Bowman reflected as he inhaled deeply of the fresh air that swept over the benign plains of Hedris, that the local grasses were as fecund as the muffins, or the planet would have been stripped bare of anything edible millions of years ago. Even though a patient observer could actually watch the grass grow, it remained a constant source of amazement to him and his partner that the local vegetation managed to keep well ahead of the perpetually foraging muffins.

The uncountable little balls of brown-and-beige fur were not the only browsers, of course. On a world as fertile as Hedris, there were always niches to fill. But for every *kodout, pangalta,* and slow-moving, thousand-toothed *jerabid,* there were a thousand muffins. No, he corrected himself. Ten thousand, maybe more. Between the higher grass and the deeper burrows it was impossible to get an accurate account, even with the aid of mini-satellite recordings.

With such qualified stats were his and LeCleur's reports filled. They had another five months in which to refine and perfect their figures, hone their observations, and condense their opinions. The House of Novy Churapcha, the industrial-commercial concern that had set them up on Hedris, was anxious to formulate a bid and stake its claim in front of the Commonwealth concession courts before any of the other great trading Houses or public companies got wind of the new discovery. By keeping their outpost on Hedris tiny and isolated, and without contact for almost a year, the managers hoped to avoid the unwanted attention of curious competitors.

So far the strategy seemed to have worked. In the seven months since the fabrication crew, working around the clock, had erected the outpost, not even a stray communication had come the way of the two agents. That was fine with Bowman. He didn't mind the isolation. He and LeCleur were trained to deal with it. And they were very well compensated for maintaining their lack of offworld contact.

A few clouds were gathering. There might be an afternoon rain shower, he decided. If it materialized, it would be gentle, of course, like everything else on Hedris. No dangerous lightning, and just enough distant thunder to be atmospheric. Then the sun would come out, attended by the inevitable rainbow.

The sweet smell of muffin on the grill reached him from inside and he turned away from the brightening panorama. It was LeCleur's week to do the cooking, and his partner had long since mastered different ways of preparing the eminently edible indigene. Not only were the multitudinous muffins harmless, cute beyond words, and easy to catch, their seared flesh was tender and highly palatable, with a sugary, almost honeyed flavor to the whitish flesh that was nothing at all like chicken. Tastewise, it far surpassed anything in their inventory of prepackaged concentrates and dehydrates. There wasn't a lot of meat on a muffin, but then, neither was there a shortage of the hopping, preoccupied, two-legged creatures.

The slim, diminutive humanoid natives virtually lived on them, and lived well. Only their metabolism kept them thin, Bowman reflected as he closed the front door of the station behind him. Overawed by the much larger humans, the native Akoe were occasional visitors to the outpost. They were invariably polite, courteous, and quietly eager to learn about their extraordinary visitors. Their language was a simple one and with the aid of electronic teaching devices, both experienced agents had soon mastered enough of it to carry on a rudimentary conversation. The Akoe were always welcome at the outpost, though sometimes their quiet staring got on Bowman's nerves. An amused LeCleur never missed an opportunity to chide him about it.

"How's it look outside?" LeCleur was almost as tall as Bowman, but not nearly as broad or muscular. "Let me guess: clear and warm, with a chance of a sprinkle later in the day."

"What are you, psychic?" Grinning, Bowman sat down opposite his friend and partner. The platter of grilled muffin, neatly sliced, sizzled in a warmer in the center, ringed by reconstituted bread, butter, jams, scrambled rehydrated eggs from three different kinds of fowl, and two tall self-chilling pitchers containing juice. Coffee and tea arrived in the form of the self-propelled carafes that followed the men whenever they verbally expressed their individual thirst.

"Thought we might run a predator census between rivers Six EW and Eight NS today." Having finished his meal, LeCleur was adding sweetener to his mug of hot high-grown tea.

Bowman was amenable to the suggestion. "Maybe we'll see another *volute*." They'd only encountered one of the pig-sized, loop-tailed carnivores so far, and that from a distance. He was smearing rehydrated blackberry jam on his toast when the perimeter alarm went off. Neither man was alarmed.

"I'll get it." LeCleur rose from his seat. "My turn."

While Bowman finished the last of his breakfast, LeCleur activated the free-ranging headsup. A cylindrical image appeared in the middle of the room, a perfect floating replica in miniature of a 360° view outside the outpost. A spoken command from LeCleur caused the image to enlarge and focus on the source of the alarm. This was followed by an order to shut down the soft but insistent whine.

The agent chuckled into the ensuing silence as he recognized the slim, standing figure that had set off the alert. Its image looked, as always, slightly bewildered. "It's only old Malakotee."

Wiping his mouth, Bowman rose. "Let him in and we'll see what he wants." It was always interesting and instructive to observe the elderly native's reaction to the many miracles the outpost contained. Also fun. He and LeCleur had few enough diversions.

Precisely enunciated directives caused the circumferential viewer to be replaced by a floating command board. In seconds LeCleur had shut down the station's external defenses, rotated the bridge to cross the excavated ravine that encircled the outpost, and opened the front door. By the time Bowman was finishing up the dishes, the Akoe elder had arrived at the front door.

Old Malakotee was a leader among his people, wizened and much respected. The Akoe were led not by one chief, but by a group of chosen seniors. Decisions were made by group vote. All very democratic, LeCleur mused as he greeted the alien in its own language. Malakotee responded in kind, but declined to enter, though he could not keep his eyes from roving. Nor did he accept the offer of one of the chairs that sat invitingly on the porch. His much slighter, smaller body and backside tended to find themselves engulfed by the massive human furniture. Also, he never knew what to do with his tail. It switched back and forth as he chattered, the tuft of kinky black hair at the tip swatting curious flying arthropods away.

Dark, intelligent eyes peered out from beneath smooth brows. The alien's face was hairless, but the rest of his body was covered with a fine charcoal-gray fuzz. When he opened his mouth, an orifice that was proportionately much wider than that of a comparably sized human, LeCleur could see how the pointed incisors alternated with flattened grinding teeth. In place of a nose was a small trunk with three flexible tips that the Akoe could employ as a third, if very short, hand.

A cloak comprising the skins of many native animals, especially the ubiquitous muffin, was draped elegantly over his slim form. It was decorated with bits of carved bone, hand-made beads of exceptional quality (the two humans had already traded for examples), and shiny bits of cut and worked shell. The Akoe were very dexterous and of reasonable artistic skill. Necklaces hung from Old Malakotee's throat, and bracelets jangled on his wrists. He leaned on a ceremonial *kotele* staff, the wood elaborately garnished with feathers, beads, and paint.

"Thanking you for offer to come into your hut," the native explained to LeCleur, having to crane his neck to meet the much taller human's eyes, "but I not stay long today. Come to tell you my people, they are moving now."

The agent was openly surprised. Recovering from their initial shock and stupefaction at the humans' arrival, the Akoe had been a fixture on the shores of river One NS ever since. Calling for his partner to join them, LeCleur queried their visitor.

"The Akoe are moving? But where, and why?"

Raising his primitively florid staff, the elder pointed. "Go north and west soon. Long trek." Bowman appeared on the porch, wiping his hands against his pants as Malakotee finished, "Find safety in deep caves."

"Safety?" Bowman made a face. "What's this about 'safety'? Safety from what?"

The elder turned solemn eyes to the even bigger human. "From migration, of course. Is time of year. When migration over, Akoe come back to river."

The two men exchanged a glance. "What migration?" LeCleur asked their pensive visitor. "What's migrating?" Uncertainly, he scanned the vast, barely undulating plain beyond the outpost's perimeter.

"The muffins. Is the time of year. Soon now, they migrate."

A modest herd of less than a hundred thousand of the small brown browsers was clustered in the grass in front of the outpost, grazing peacefully. Their familiar soft peep-peeping filled the morning air. LeCleur watched as several, each no bigger than his closed fist, hopped as close as they dared to the edge of the perpendicular-sided ravine that surrounded the station to graze on the *ninicumb* flowers that were growing there.

"We'll see you when you come back, then."

"No, no!" Old Malakotee was surprisingly insistent. "I come warn you." He gestured emphatically. "You come with Akoe. You big skypeople good folk. Come with us. We keep you safe during migration."

Bowman smiled condescendingly at the native, whose appearance never failed to put him in mind of an anorexic munchkin. "That's very kind of you and your people, Malakotee, but Gerard and I are quite comfortable here. We have protections you can't see and wouldn't understand if I tried to explain them to you."

The miniature snout in the center of the Akoe's face twitched uneasily. "Malakotee know you sky-people got many wondrous things. You show Malakotee plenty. But you no understand. This is *ixtex,*" he explained, using the native word for the bipedal muffins, "migration!"

"So you've told us. I promise you, we'll be all right. Would you like some tea?" The chemical brew that was Terran tea had been shown to produce interesting, wholly pleasurable reactions within the Akoe body.

Ordinarily, Old Malakotee, like any Akoe, would have jumped at the offer. But not this morning. Starting off the porch, he gestured purposefully with his staff. Beads jangled and bounced against the light-colored, streaky wood.

"I tell you. You come with Akoe, we take care of you. You stay here," he rendered the Akoe gesture for despair, "no good." Reaching the ground, he promptly launched into a slow-spinning, head-bending, tail-flicking tribal chant-dance. When he was through, he saluted one final time with his ornamented staff before turning his back on them and striding deliberately away from the outpost.

As LeCleur called forth the headsup and rotated

the bridge shut behind the retreating native, Bowman contemplated what they had just seen. "Interesting performance. Wonder if it had any special significance?"

LeCleur, who was more of a xenologist than his partner, banished the command panel display with a word and nodded. "That was the 'Dance for the Dead.' He was giving us a polite send-off."

"Oh." Bowman squinted at the sky. Just another lovely day, as always. "I'll get the skimmer ready for the census."

The Akoe had been gone for just over a week when LeCleur was bitten. Bowman looked up from his work as his partner entered. The bite was not deep, but the bright blood streak running down the other man's leg was clearly visible beneath the hem of his field shorts, staining his calf. Plopping himself down in another chair, LeCleur put the first-aid kit on the table and flicked it open. As he applied antiseptic spray and then coagulator, Bowman watched with casual interest.

"Step on something?"

A disgruntled, slightly embarrassed LeCleur finished treating the wound with a dose of color-coded epidermase. "Like hell. A damn muffin bit me."

His partner grunted. "Like I said; step on something?"

"I did not step on it. I was hunting for burrowing arthropods in the grass in the east quad when I felt something sharp. I looked back, and there was this little furry shitball gnawing on my calf. I had to swat it off. It bounced once, scrambled back onto its feet, and shot off into the grass." He closed the first-aid kit. "Freakish."

"An accident, yeah." Bowman couldn't keep himself from grinning. "It must have mistaken your leg for the mother of all *casquak* seeds."

"It wasn't the incident that was freaky." LeCleur was not smiling. "It was the muffin. It had sharp teeth."

Bowman's grin faded. "That's impossible. We've examined, not to mention eaten, hundreds of muffins since we've been here. Not one of them had sharp teeth. Their chewing mechanism is strictly molaric dentition, for grinding up and processing vegetation."

His partner shook his head slowly. "I saw them, Jamie. Sharp and pointed. Saw them and felt them. And there was something funny about its eyes, too."

"That's a description that'll look nice and scientific in the record. Funny how?"

Clearly distressed, LeCleur pursed his lips. "I don't know. I didn't get a good look. They just struck me as funny." He tapped his leg above the now hermetized bite. "This didn't."

"Well, we know they're not poisonous." Bowman turned back to his work. "So it was a freak muffin. A break in the muffin routine. An eclectic muffin. I'm sure it was an isolated incident and won't happen again."

"It sure won't." LeCleur rose and extended his mended leg. "Because next time, you do the arthropod survey."

It was a week later when Bowman, holding his coffee, walked out onto the porch, sat down in one of the chairs, and had the mug halfway to his lips when he paused. Lowering the container, he stared for a long moment before activating the com button attached to the collar of his shirt.

"Gerard, I think you'd better come here. I'm on the porch."

A drowsy mumble responded. The other agent was sleeping in. Bowman continued to nag him until he finally appeared, rubbing at his eyes and grumbling. His vision and mind cleared quickly enough as soon as he was able to share his partner's view.

On the far edge of the ravine, muffins were gathering. Not in the familiar, tidily spaced herd cluster in which they spent the night for protection from roving carnivores, nor in the irregular pattern they employed for browsing, but in dense knots of wall-to-wall brown fur. More muffins were arriving every minute, filling in the gaps. And from the hundreds going on thousands rose an unexpectedly steady, repetitive peep-peeping that was somehow intimidating in its idiosyncratic sonority.

"What the hell is going on?" LeCleur finally murmured.

Bowman remembered to take a drink of his coffee before pulling the scope from its pocket on the side of the chair. What he saw through the lens was anything but reassuring. He passed it to his partner. "Take a look for yourself."

LeCleur raised the instrument. The view it displayed resolved into groups of two to three muffins, bunched so tightly together it seemed impossible they could breathe, much less peep. They had swollen slightly, their compact bodies puffed up about an additional ten percent, brown hair bristling. Their eyes—LeCleur had seen harbingers of that wild, collective red glare in the countenance of the one that had bit him a week ago. When they opened their mouths to peep, the change that had taken place within was immediately apparent. Instead of a succession of smooth, white eruptions of bone, the diminutive jaws were now filled with a mixture of grinding projections and triangular, assertively sharp-edged canines.

He lowered the scope. "Christ—they're metamorphosing. And moving. I wonder how much?"

Bowman already had the command headsup in place. A few verbal directives were sufficient to materialize an image. Atop the single-story station, remote instrumentation was responding efficiently.

The surface around the outpost was swarming with rustling, stirring movement. By midday, they no longer needed the instruments to show them what was happening. The two men stood on the porch, observing manually.

All around them, as far as they could see and beyond, the grass was coming down, mowed flat by a suddenly ravenous, insatiable horde. Within that seething ocean of brown fur, red eyes, and snapping teeth, nothing survived. Grass, other plants, anything living was overwhelmed, to disappear down a sea of brown gullets. From the depths of the feeding frenzy arose a relentless, ostinato peeping that drowned out everything from the wind to the soft hum of the outpost's hydrogen generator.

Bowman and LeCleur watched, recorded, and made notes, usually without saying a word. By evening the entire boundless mass of muffins, like a moving carpet, had begun advancing as one being in a southeasterly direction. The Akoe, Bowman recalled, had gone north. The two agents needed no explanation of the phenomenon they were observing.

The migration was under way.

"I suppose we could have offered to let the Akoe stay here," he commented to his partner.

LeCleur was tired from work and looking forward

to a good night's sleep. It had been a busy day. "Don't believe it would've mattered. I think they would've gone anyway. Besides, such an offer would have constituted unsupported interference with native ritual. Expressly forbidden by the xenological protocols."

Bowman nodded. "You check the systems?"

His friend smiled. "Everything's working normally. Wake-up alarm the same time tomorrow?"

Bowman shrugged. "That works for me." He glanced out at the heaving, rippling sea of brown. "They'll still be here. How long you estimate it will take them to move on through?"

LeCleur considered. "Depends how widespread the migration is." Raising a hand, he pointed. "Check that out."

So dense had the swarm become that a number of the muffins at its edge were being jostled off into the ravine. The protective excavation was thirty feet deep, with walls that had been heat-treated to unclimbable slickness. A spider would have had trouble ascending those artificial perpendicularities. The agents retired, grateful for the outpost soundproofing that shut out all but the faintest trace of mass peeping.

The station's pleasant, synthesized female voice woke Bowman slightly before his partner.

"What. . . ?" he mumbled. "What's going on?"

"Perimeter violation," the outpost replied, in the same tone of voice it used to announce when a tridee recording was winding up, or when mechanical food pre-prep had been completed. "You are advised to observe and react."

"Observe and react, hell," Bowman bawled as he struggled into a sitting position. Save for the dim light provided by widely-spaced night illuminators, it was dark in his room. "What time is it, anyway?"

"Four AM, corrected Hedris time." The outpost voice was not abashed by this pronouncement.

Muttering under his breath, Bowman shoved himself into shorts and a shirt. LeCleur was waiting for him in the hall.

"I don't know. I just got out of bed myself," he mumbled in response to his partner's querulous gaze.

As they made their way toward outpost central, Bowman queried the voice. "What kind of perimeter violation? Elaborate."

"Why don't you just look outside?" soft artificial tones responded. "I've put on the lights."

Both men headed for the main entrance. As soon as the door opened, Bowman had to shield his eyes. LeCleur adapted faster. What he exclaimed was not scientific, but it was descriptive.

Bathed in the bright automated beams positioned atop the roof of the outpost was a Dantean vision of glaring red eyes, gnashing teeth, and spattering blood; a boiling brown stew of muffins whole, bleeding, dismembering, and scrambling with their two tiny legs for a foothold among their seething brethren. Presumably the rest of the darkened plain concealed a similar vision straight from Hell. Presumably, because the astounded agents could not see it. Their view was blocked by the thousands upon thousands of dead, dying, and frenetic muffins that had filled the outpost-encircling ravine to the brim with their bodies. At the same time, the reason for the transformation in the aliens' dentition was immediately apparent.

Having consumed everything green that grew on the plains, they had turned to eating flesh. And each other.

Bulging eyes flared, tiny feet kicked, razor-sharp teeth flashed and tore. The curdling miasma of gore, eviscerated organs, and engorged muffin musk verged on overpowering. Rising above it all was the odor of cooked meat. Holding his hand over mouth and nose, LeCleur saw the reason why the outpost had awakened them.

Lining the interior wall of the artificial ravine was a double fence of waved air. Frenzied with instinct, the muffins were throwing themselves heedlessly onto the lethal barrier, moving always in a southeasterly direction. The instant it contacted the electrically waved air, a scrambling muffin body was immediately electrocuted. As was the one following behind it, and the next, and the next. In their dozens, in their hundreds, their wee corpses were piling up at such a rate that those advancing from behind would soon be able to cross unhindered into the compound. Those that didn't pause to feast on the bodies of their own dead, that is.

"I think we'd better get inside and lock down until this is over," LeCleur murmured quietly as he stood surveying the surging sea of southward-flowing carnage.

An angry Bowman was already heading for the master console. Though it held an unmistakable gruesome fascination, the migration would mean extra work for him and his partner. The perimeter fence would have to be repaired, and even with mechanical help it would take weeks to clear out and dispose of the tens of thousands of muffin corpses that filled the ravine, turning it into a moat full of meat. They would have to do all that while keeping up with their regular work schedule. He was more than a little pissed.

Oh, well, he calmed himself. Everything had gone so smoothly, Hedris had been so accommodating, from the first day they had occupied the outpost, that it would be churlish of him to gripe about one small, unforeseen

difficulty. They would deal with it in the morning. Which
wasn't that far off, he noted irritably. As soon as the
greater part of the migration had passed them by, or
settled down to a more manageable frenzy, he and
LeCleur could retire for an extended rest and leave
the cleaning up to the automatics. Surely, despite the
muffins' numbers, such furious activity could not be
sustained for more than a day or two.

His lack of concern stemmed from detailed knowledge of the station's construction. It had been designed, and built, to handle and ride out anything from
three-hundred-mile-an-hour winds, to temperatures
down to a hundred-and-fifty below and the same
above. The prefab duralloy walls and metallic glass
ports were impervious to windblown grit, flying acid,
ordinary laser cutters, micrometeorites up to a diameter of one inch, and solid stone avalanches. The interior was sealed against smoke, toxic gases, volcanic
emissions, and flash floods of water, liquid methane,
and anything else a planet could puke up.

Moving to a port, he watched as the first wave of
migrating muffins to crest the wave fence raced toward
the now impervious sealed structure. Their small feet,
adapted for running and darting about on the flat
plains, did not allow them to climb very well, but before long sufficient dead and dying bodies had piled
high enough against the north side of the outpost to
reach the port. Raging, berserk little faces gazed hun-
grily in at him. Metamorphosed teeth gnawed and bit
at the port, their frantic scratching sounds penetrating
only faintly. They were unable even to scratch the
high-tech transparency. He watched as dozens of muffins smothered one another in their haste to sustain
their southeasterly progress, stared as tiny teeth

snapped and broke off in futile attempts to penetrate the glass and get at the food within.

Once again, LeCleur made breakfast, taking more time than usual. The sun was rising, casting its familiar benign light over a panorama of devastation and death the two team members could not have imagined at the height of the worst day during the past four halcyon, pastoral months. As for the migration itself, it gave no indication of abating, or of even slowing down.

"I don't care how many millions of muffins there are inhabiting this part of the world." Seated on the opposite side of the table, LeCleur betrayed an uncharacteristic nervousness no doubt abetted by his lack of sleep. "It has to slow down soon."

Bowman nodded absently. He ate mechanically, without his usual delight in the other man's cooking. "It's pitiful, watching the little critters mass asphyxiate themselves like this, and then be reduced to feeding on each other's corpses." He remembered cuddling and taking the measurements of baby muffins while others looked on, curious but only mildly agitated, peeping querulously. Now that peeping had risen to a tyrannical, pestilential drone not even the outpost's soundproofing could mute entirely.

"It's not pitiful to me." Eyes swollen from lack of sleep, LeCleur scratched his right leg where he had been assaulted. "You didn't get bit."

Holding his coffee, Bowman glanced to his right, in the direction of the nearest port. Instruments and the time told them the sun was up. They could not observe it directly because every port was now completely blocked by a mass of accumulated muffin cadavers.

Still, both men were capable of surprise when the voice of the outpost announced that evening that it was switching over to canned air. Neither man had to ask why, though Bowman did so, just to confirm.

The station was now buried beneath a growing mountain of dead muffins. Their accumulated tiny bodies had blocked every one of the shielded air intakes.

Still, neither agent was worried. They had enough bottled air for weeks, ample food, and could recycle their waste water. In an emergency, the station was almost as self-sufficient a closed system as a starship, though quite immobile. Their only real regret was the absence of information, since the swarming bodies now obstructed all the outpost's external sensors.

Three days later a frustrated LeCleur suggested cracking one of the doors to see if the migration had finally run its course. Bowman was less taken with the idea.

"What if it's not?" he argued.

"Then we use the emergency door close. That'll shut it by itself. How else are we going to tell if the migration's finally moved on and passed us by?" He gestured broadly. "Until we can get up top with some of the cleaning gear and clear off the bodies, we're sitting blind in here."

"I know." Bowman found himself succumbing to his partner's enticing logic. Not that his own objections were vociferous. He knew they would have to try and look outside sooner or later. He just wasn't enthusiastic about the idea. "I don't like the thought of letting any of the little monsters get inside."

"Who would?" LeCleur's expression was grim. "We'll draw a couple of rifles from stores and be ready when the door opens, even though the only thing that might spill in are dead bodies. Remember, the live muffins are all up top, migrating southeastward. They're traveling atop the ones who've been suffocated.''

Bowman nodded. LeCleur was right, of course. They had nothing to fear from the hundreds of compressed muffins that now formed a wall enclosing the outpost. And if anything living presented itself at the open door, the automatic hinges would slam it tight at a word from either man, without them having to go near it.

With a nod, Bowman rose from the table. After months of freely roaming the plains and rivers beyond the outpost, he was sick and tired of being cooped up in the darkened station. "Right. We'll take it slow and careful, but we have to see what's going on out there."

"Migration's probably been over and done with for days, and we've been wasting our time squatting here whining about it."

The rifles fired needle-packed shells specifically designed to stop dangerous small animals in their tracks. The spray pattern that resulted subsequent to ignition meant that those wielding the weapons did not have to focus precisely on a target. Aiming the muzzles of the guns in the approximate direction would be sufficient to ensure the demise of any creature in the general vicinity of the shot. It was not an elegant weapon, but it was effective. Though they had been carried on field trips away from the outpost by both Bowman and LeCleur as protection against endemic carnivores both known and unknown, neither man had yet been compelled to fire one of the versatile weapons in anger. As they positioned themselves fifteen feet in from the front door, Bowman hoped they would be able to maintain that record of non-use.

Responding to a curt nod from his partner signifying that he was in position and ready, LeCleur gave the command to open the door exactly two inches. Rifles raised, they waited to see what would materialize in response.

Seals releasing, the door swung inward slightly. Spilling into the room came a stench of rotting, decaying flesh that the outpost's atmospheric scrubbers promptly whirred to life to deal with. A line of solid brown showed itself between door and reinforced jamb. Half a dozen or so crushed muffin corpses tumbled into the room. Several exhibited signs of having been partially consumed.

After a glance at his partner, LeCleur uttered a second command. Neither man had lowered the muzzle of his weapon. The door resumed opening. More tiny, smashed bodies spilled from the dike of tiny carcasses, forming a small, sad mound at its base. The stink grew worse, but not unbearably so. From floor to lintel, the doorway was blocked with dead muffins.

Lowering his rifle, Bowman moved forward, bending to examine several of the bodies that had tumbled into the room. Some had clearly been dead longer than others. Not one so much as twitched a leg.

"Poor little bastards. I wonder how often this migration takes place?"

"Often enough for population control." LeCleur was standing alongside his partner, the unused rifle now dangling from one hand. "We always wondered why the muffins didn't overrun the whole planet. Now we know. They regulate their own numbers. Probably store up sufficient fat and energy from cannibalizing themselves during migration for enough to survive until the grasses can regenerate themselves.

"We need to record the full cycle: duration of migration, variation by continent and specific locale, influencing variables such as weather, availability of water, and so on. This is important stuff." He grinned. "Can you imagine trying to run a grain farm here under these conditions? I know that's one of the operations the company had in mind for this place."

Bowman nodded thoughtfully. "It can be done. This is just the primary outpost. Armed with the right information, I don't see why properly prepared colonists can't handle something even as far ranging as this migration."

LeCleur agreed. That was when the wall of cadavers exploded in their faces. Or rather, its center did.

Still sensing the presence of live food beyond the door, the muffins had dug a tunnel through their own dead to get at it. As they came pouring into the room, Bowman and LeCleur commenced firing frantically. Hundreds of tiny needles bloomed from dozens of shells as the rapid-fire rifles took their toll on the rampaging intruders. Dozens, hundreds of red-eyed, on-rushing muffins perished in the storm of needles, their diminutive bodies shredded beyond recognition. A frantic LeCleur screamed the command to close the door, and the outpost did its best to comply. Unfortunately, a combination of deceased muffins and live muffins had filled the gap. Many died between the heavy-duty hingers, crushed to death, as the door swung closed. But—it did not, could not, shut all the way.

A river of ravenous brown poured into the room, swarming over chairs and tables, knocking over equipment, snapping and biting at everything and anything within reach. Above the fermenting chaos rose a single horrific, repetitive, incessant sound.

"PEEP PEEP PEEP PEEP . . . !"

"The storeroom!" Firing as fast as he could pull the trigger, heedless of the damage to the installation stray needle-shells might be doing, Bowman retreated as fast as he could. He glanced down repeatedly. Trip here, now, and he would go down beneath a wave of teeth and tiny, stamping feet. LeCleur was right behind him.

Stumbling into the storeroom, they shut the door manually, neither man wanting to take the time to issue the necessary command to the omnipresent outpost pickups. Besides, they didn't know if the station voice would respond anymore. In their swarming, the muffins had already shorted out a brace of unshielded, sensitive equipment. The agents backed away from the door as dozens of tiny thudding sounds reached them from the other side. The storeroom was the most solidly built internal component of the station, but its door was not made of duralloy like the exterior walls. Would it hold up against the remorseless, concerted assault? And if so, for how long?

Then the lights went out.

"They've cut or shorted internal connectors," Bowman commented unnecessarily. Being forced to listen to the rapid-fire pounding on the other side of the door and not being able to do anything about it was nerve-racking enough. Having to endure it in the dark was ten times worse.

There was food in the storeroom in the form of concentrates, and bottled water to drink. They would live, LeCleur reflected—at least until the air was cut off, or the climate control shut down.

Bowman was contemplating similar possibilities. "How many shells you have left, Gerard?"

The other man checked the illuminated readout on the side of the rifle that provided the only light in the sealed storeroom. "Five." When preparing to open the front door, neither man had, reasonably enough at the time, considered it necessary to pocket extra ammunition. "You?"

His partner's reply was glum. "Three. We're not going to shoot our way out of here."

Trying to find some additional light in the darkness, LeCleur commented as calmly as he could manage, "The door seems to be holding."

"Small teeth." Bowman was surprised to note that his voice was trembling slightly.

"Too many teeth," LeCleur responded. Feeling around in the darkness, he found a solid container and sat down, cradling the rifle across his legs. He discovered that he was really thirsty, and tried not to think about it. They would feel around for the food and water containers later, after the thudding against the door had stopped. Assuming it would.

"Maybe they'll get bored and go away," he ventured hopefully.

Bowman tried to find some confidence in the darkness. "Maybe instinct will overpower hunger and they'll resume the migration. All we have to do is wait them out."

"Yeah." LeCleur grunted softly. "That's all." After several moments of silence broken only by the steady thump-thumping against the door, he added, "Opening up was a dumb idea."

"No, it wasn't," Bowman contended. "We just didn't execute smartly. After the first minute, we assumed everything was all right and relaxed."

LeCleur shifted his position on his container. "It won't be repeated, but it doesn't matter. I don't care what the situation: I'll never be able to relax on this world again."

"I hope we'll both have the opportunity not to." Bowman's fingers fidgeted against the trigger of the rifle.

Eventually they found the water, and the food. The latter tasted awful without machine pre-prep, but the powder was filling, and nourishing. Unwilling to go to sleep and unable to stay awake, their exhausted bodies finally forced them into unconsciousness.

LeCleur sat up sharply in the darkness, the hard length of the rifle threatening to slip off his chest until he grabbed it to keep it from falling. He listened intently for a long, long moment before whispering loudly.

"Jamie. Jamie, wake up!"

"Huh? Wuzzat . . . ?" In the dim light provided by the illuminated rifle gauges, the other man bestirred himself.

"Listen." Licking his lips, LeCleur slid off the pile of containers on which he had been sleeping. His field shorts squeaked sharply against the smooth polyastic.

Bowman said nothing. It was silent in the store-room. More significantly, it was equally silent on the other side of the door. The two men huddled together, their faces barely discernible in the feeble glow of the gauge-lights.

"What do we do now?" LeCleur kept glancing at the darkened door.

Bowman considered the situation as purposefully as his sore back and unsatisfied belly would permit. "We can't stay cooped up in here forever." He hesitated. "Anyway, I'd rather go down fighting than suffocate when the air goes out or is cut off."

LeCleur nodded reluctantly. "Who's first?"

"I'll do it." Bowman took a deep breath, the soft wheeze of inbound air sounding abnormally loud in the darkness. "Cover me as best you can."

His partner nodded and raised the rifle. Positioning himself at the most efficacious angle to the door, he waited silently. In the darkness, he could hear his own heart pounding.

Holding his own weapon tightly in his left hand, Bowman undid the seals. They clicked like the final ticks of his own internal clock counting down the remainder of his life. Light and fresher air entered the room as the door swung inward. Exhaling softly, Bowman opened it further. No minuscule brown demons flew at his face, no nipping tiny teeth assailed his ankles. Taking a deep breath, he wrenched sharply on the door and leaped back, raising the muzzle of his weapon as the badly dented barrier pivoted inward. Light from the interior of the station made him blink repeatedly.

It was silent inside the outpost. A ridge of dead muffins two feet high was piled up against the door. None of the little horrors moved. Together, the two men emerged from the storeroom.

Light poured down from the overheads. They still had power. The interior of the outpost was heaped high with tiny cadavers. There were dead muffins everywhere: on the dining table, in opened storage cabinets, under benches, beneath exposed supplies, and all over the kitchen area. They were crammed impossibly tight together in corners, in the living quarters, on shelves. Their flattened, furry, motionless bodies had clogged the food prep area and the toilets, filled the showers and every empty container and tube.

Bright daylight poured through the still open front door. Scavengers, or wind, or marauding muffins had reduced the avalanche of dead muffins on the porch to the same height of two feet that had accumulated against the storeroom portal. The wasted agents could go outside, if they wished. After weeks of unending peep-peeping, the ensuing silence was loud enough to hurt Bowman's ears.

"It's over." LeCleur was brushing dead muffins off the kitchen table. "How about some tea and coffee? If I can get any of the appliances to work, that is."

Setting his rifle aside, Bowman slumped into a chair and dropped his head onto his crossed forearms. "I don't give a damn what it is or if it's ice cold. Right now my throat will take anything."

Nodding, LeCleur waded through dunes comprised of dead muffins and began a struggle to coax the beverage maker to life. Every so often, he would pause to shove or throw dead muffins out of his way, not caring where they landed. The awful smell was no better, but by now their stressed bodies had come to tolerate it without comment.

A large, mobile shape came gliding through the gaping front door.

Forgetting the beverage maker, LeCleur threw himself toward where he had left his rifle standing against a counter. Bowman reached for his own weapon, caught one leg against the chair on which he was sitting, and crashed to the floor with the chair tangled up in his legs.

Gripping his staff, Old Malakotee paused to stare at them both. "You alive. I surprised." His alien gaze swept the room, taking in the thousands of deceased muffins, the destruction of property, and the stench. "Very surprised. But glad."

"So are we." Untangling himself from the chair, a chagrined Bowman rose to greet their visitor. "Both of those things. What are you doing back here?"

"I know!" A wide smile broke out on the jubilant LeCleur's face: the first smile of any kind he had shown for days. "It's over. The migration's over, and the Akoe have come back!"

Old Malakotee regarded the exultant human somberly. "The migration is not over, skyman Le'leur. It still continue." He turned to regard the uncertain Bowman. "But we like you people. I tell my tribe: we must try to help." He gestured outside. Leaning to look, both men could see a small knot of Akoe males standing and waiting in the stinking sunshine. They looked competent, but uneasy. Their postures were alert, their gazes wary.

"You come with us now." The elder gestured energetically. "Not much time. Akoe help you."

"It's okay." Bowman gestured to take in their surroundings. "We'll clear all this out. We have machines to help us. You'll see. In a week or two everything here will be cleaned up and back to normal. Then you can visit us again, and try our food and drink as you did before, and we can talk."

The agent was feeling expansive. They had suffered through everything the muffin migration could throw at them, and had survived. Next time, maybe next year, the larger, better equipped team that would arrive to relieve them would be properly informed of the danger and appropriately equipped to deal with it. What he and LeCleur had experienced was just one more consequence of being the primary survey and sampling team on a new world. It came with the job.

"Not visit!" Old Malakotee was emphatic. "You come with us now! Akoe protect you, show you how to survive migration. Go to deep caves and hide."

LeCleur joined in. "We don't have to hide, Malakotee. Not anymore. Even if the migration's not over, it's obviously passed this place by."

"Juvenile migration passed." Stepping back, Old

Malakotee eyed them flatly. Outside, the younger Akoe were already clamoring to leave. "Now adults come."

Bowman blinked, uncertain he had heard correctly. "Adults?" He looked back at LeCleur, whose expression reflected the same bewilderment his partner was feeling. "But—the muffins." He kicked at the half-dozen quiescent bodies scattered around his feet. "These aren't the adults?"

"They juveniles." Malakotee stared at him unblinkingly. His demeanor was assurance enough this was not a joke.

"Then if every muffin we've been seeing these past seven months has been a juvenile or an infant . . ." LeCleur was licking his lips nervously. "Where are the adults?"

The native tapped the floor with the butt of his staff. "In ground. Hibernating." Bowman struggled to get the meaning of the alien words right. "Growing. Once a year, come out."

The agent swallowed. "They come out—and then what?"

Old Malakotee's alien gaze met that of the human. "Migrate." Raising a multifingered hand, he pointed. To the southeast. "That way."

"No wonder." LeCleur was murmuring softly. "No wonder the juvenile muffins flee in such a frenzy. We've already seen that the species is cannibalistic. If the juveniles eat one another, then the adults . . ." His voice trailed off.

"I take it," Bowman inquired of the native, surprised at how calm his voice had become, "that the adults are a little bigger than the juveniles?"

Old Malakotee made the Akoe gesture signifying concurrence. "*Much* bigger. Also hungrier. Been in ground long, long time. Very hungry when come out." He started toward the doorway. "Must go quickly now. You come—or stay."

Weak from fatigue, Bowman turned to consider the interior of the outpost; the ruined instrumentation, the devastated equipment, the masses of dead muffins. Juvenile muffins, he reminded himself. He contemplated the havoc they had wrought. What would the adults be like? Bigger, Old Malakotee had told them. Bigger, and hungrier. But not, he told himself, necessarily cuter.

Outside, the little band of intrepid Akoe was already moving off, heading at a steady lope for the muffin-bridged ravine, their tails switching rhythmically behind them. Standing at the door, Bowman and LeCleur watched them go. What would the temperature in the deep caves to the north be like? How long could they survive on Akoe food? Could they even keep up with the well-conditioned, fast-moving aliens, who were in their element running for days on end over the grassy plains? The two men exchanged a glance. At least they had a choice. Didn't they? Well, didn't they?

Beneath their feet, something moved. The ground quivered, ever so slightly.

THE BOID HUNT

by Allen Steele

Allen Steele's most recent works include *Oceanspace* and a collection of short fiction entitled *Sex and Violence in Zero G.* He made an impact on the science fiction field with his first novel *Orbital Decay,* published in 1987. He has won the Hugo Award twice for his short fiction, most recently in 1998 for the novella, "Where Angels Fear to Tread," which also won the Locus Award for Best Novella. He currently lives in Massachusetts with his wife, a local disc jockey.

As so many things often do, the boid hunt began with an argument, and gradually escalated into something far more serious. When it was all over, two men lay dead and a third had been forever changed. I was there, and this was how it happened.

It was the spring of CY 1, or AD 2156 by Gregorian reckoning. Although we had been on Coyote for less than one of its years, by then the colony was a little more than three Earth-years old. We had endured the first long winter on the fourth moon of 47 Ursae Majoris A, the superjovian gas giant we had come to call Bear; the snows which had blanketed the grassy plains of New Florida had melted and the ice had receded from its labyrinthine creeks and streams, and now we were suffering through the rainy season. Gray clouds covered the azure skies above the island, sometimes shrouding Bear from sight for days on end, while cold rain fell constantly upon Liberty and threatened to wash away the crops we had just planted in the fields surrounding town. The incessant downpour was enough to drive men to drink and talk crazy, and that was how the whole sorry affair got started.

Late one evening several of us were gathered in Lew's Cantina, the small blackwood shack which Lew Geary had built at the end of town. According to Colony Law, there weren't supposed to be any bars, only cafés which served liquor as part of their regular menu, but Lew got around this by offering chicken sandwiches and creek crab stew. Chicken was too scarce for anyone to eat more than once a week, though, and no one ever voluntarily dined on creek crab in any form unless they were truly ravenous. The menu was simply a front to keep the Prefects at arm's length, but even so we often found some blueshirts hunkered up at the bar, quietly putting away a pint or two after making their rounds. Indeed, Captain Lee himself was known to drop by, albeit on rare occasion; he'd order a bowl of that foul stew, if only for appearances' sake, then ask Lew for a pint of sourgrass ale. Thus the Cantina was left unmolested; so long as its patrons behaved themselves, its presence was tolerated.

And so it was a rainy night in late spring, and about a dozen or so men and women were crowded together in the one-room shack, either seated at tables or leaning against the plank bar behind which Lew held court. The air was humid and just warm enough to make everything moist and sticky. The rain pattered upon the cloverweed-thatched sheet-metal roof and drooled down the eaves outside the door, where it formed a shallow puddle which everyone had to step across on their way in or out. No one was dry, either inside or out; even after you hung up your poncho and slouch hat on the hooks near the door, your boots were caked with reddish-brown mud and your hair and beard were ready to be wrung out, and if you weren't at the Cantina to do some serious drinking, then you should have stayed home.

Almost everyone there that night was a farmer. I don't think anyone in Liberty ever intended to be a farmer; when we left Earth, we had been scientists and engineers, doctors and life-control specialists, astrogators and biologists. Yet the colony's survival depended upon agriculture, so we put down our computers and books and picked up hoes and shovels, and through trial and error managed to learn enough about Coyote's ecosystem—or at least New Florida's—to grow sufficient food to keep the colony alive during that first winter. Yet with almost a hundred mouths to feed, the autumn harvest had been severely stretched during the nine-month freeze, and everyone eventually learned what it was like to tighten their belts. Spring brought warmer days and nights, but when we weren't struggling to divert the waters of the flooded creeks away from our fields, we were constantly fighting a war of attrition against the native insects and small animals which threatened to devour the crops. Farming was never an easy task, and it was even more difficult when you were still learning about the world you had settled. Coyote might be Earthlike, but it wasn't Earth.

I was on my second or third pint when Gill Reese started talking about food.

"I remember . . ." He stopped, gazing into the depths of his ceramic beer stein as if fondly recalling the face of a long-lost love. "I remember steak," he finished. "Kansas City prime rib, an inch thick." Raising a hand, he held his thumb and forefinger an inch and a half apart. "Medium-well, with a little juice on top, grilled with sliced mushrooms and onions, with potatoes au gratin on the side."

"When the potatoes come up, we'll have plenty of that." Jim Levin sat on the wooden stool next to Reese, a mug parked in front of him. "Tomatoes, too, if we can keep the swoops and pinch-beetles off 'em." He turned to Bernie Cayle, the biochemist sitting on the other side of him. "How are you coming with the new pesticide, by the way? Find anything yet?"

Bernie gave a forlorn shrug. "I'm getting close, but I . . ."

"I wasn't talking about potatoes. Jesus!" Reese slammed a calloused hand down on the bartop, hard enough to make everyone's mugs shudder. "I was talking about steak . . . *meat,* for the luvva Christ!"

I didn't like Reese very much, even when he was sober. Reese had been a lieutenant-colonel in the URA Combined Service, one of the half-dozen soldiers stranded aboard the *Alabama* when Captain Lee and his coconspirators had stolen the starship from Earth orbit. Reese and his men had unsuccessfully attempted to retake the ship just before launch; they had been confined to the main airlock until the ship was two days into its boost phase and released only after Lee surrounded them with several armed men and marched them straight to the hibernation deck. When he was revived from cold sleep nearly eighty-six years later—seventy-seven years shiptime—Captain Lee had forced Colonel Reese and the others to accept the fact, since they were now forty-four light-years from Earth, their sworn loyalty to the United Republic of America had become a moot point. Since it was either that or be jettisoned, Reese had reluctantly allowed himself to be stripped of his rank, yet he remained a Service officer at heart.

But that wasn't why I disliked Reese. He was one of those hard-eyed men whom the Academy of the Republic had taken in as idealistic, patriotic youngsters and gradually beaten into mean-spirited, self-centered bastards. R.E. Lee had been an Academy graduate as well, a first-year skinhead when Reese was an upperclassman, but somehow Lee had managed to reject the inhumanity which Reese had come to embrace. Many of the colonists considered them to be two of the same kind, but I knew there was a difference: Captain Lee searched for solutions, while Reese looked for problems.

Bernie shied away, pretending to study the water dripping from a crack in the ceiling into a pan Lew had placed on the bar. Lew himself stood at a distance behind the counter, washing the mugs his wife Carrie had made in the community kiln. "No sense in wanting what you can't have, Colonel," he observed quietly. A few people in Liberty still addressed Reese by his former rank, if only for sake of politeness. "And as I recall, a K.C. prime rib was tough to come by even then."

Lew had a point, but Reese wasn't about to be mollified. "You're missing the point. I'm talking about real food, man. Something you can sink your teeth into." He gestured toward the pot of stew simmering in the fireplace on the far side the cantina. "And I don't mean creek crab . . . man, sometimes I think if I ever have another bowl of that stuff, I'm going to hurl."

"So don't have any." Lew turned away to place the clean mugs on the shelf above the ale kegs. "I'm not going to clean up your mess."

There were scattered chuckles from down the bar, and I smiled into my beer. I couldn't blame Lew for being insulted; the crab stew he served was his wife's recipe. "Give it a rest, Gill," I said. "The nearest steak is forty-four light-years away. Like he said, no sense whining about something you can't have."

Wrong choice of words. Reese slowly turned to glare at me. "I wasn't whining, Johnson," he slurred, his voice low and threatening. "I was giving my opinion. You got a problem with that?"

I didn't have a problem with his opinion, such as it was, only with the bully who had expressed it. But Gill Reese was a combat-trained soldier who outweighed me by at least fifteen kilos, while I was an astrophysicist—an unemployed astrophysicist, I hastily add—who hadn't thrown a serious punch at anyone since childhood. Out of the corner of my eye, I could see Cayle and Levin carefully edging away. Reese was drunk and spoiling for a fight, and I had made the mistake of giving him a target of opportunity.

"No problem here, Colonel," I replied, shamed by my own cowardice. "I just . . . think you're complaining about something we can't do much about, that's all."

Reese glowered at me but didn't say anything for a moment. Like it or not, I had cold facts on my side. Although we had brought livestock with us from Earth—chickens, turkeys, goats, sheep, pigs, even llama, along with dogs and cats—cattle had been deliberately left behind by the mission planners; they required too much feed and grazing land to be worth the effort. Moreover, most of the animals we had were still frozen embryos. So far, only a handful of chickens, pigs, and dogs had been successfully decanted; the rest remained in orbit aboard the *Alabama,* where they would be safe until Captain Lee determined that we had tamed New Florida. His decision had been correct; we had lost most of the pigs to ring disease during the first summer on Coyote, and predators like swoops and creek cats had killed most of the chickens until we trained the dogs to guard their pens at night.

Yet Reese wasn't about to let it go. "You're wrong there, Dr. Johnson," he said, still challenging me with his humorless brown eyes. "There is something we can do about it . . . we can go hunting."

I blinked, and he smiled as he relished my startled expression. "And what do you suggest we hunt, Gill?" I asked, already suspecting the answer.

Savoring the moment, Reese picked up his mug, slugged down the last of his ale. "Boid," he said. "We hunt boid."

An uncertain silence fell across the Cantina as every eye turned toward him. And in that moment, as fortuitous circumstance would have it, the front door creaked open and who should happen to walk in but Carlos Montero.

Had I known what was going to happen next, I would have grabbed Carlos by the back of the neck, turned him around, and hurled him back out into the rainy night. Either that or, if I had the courage, picked up my beer stein and bashed it over Reese's head, and gladly paid my dues when he recovered consciousness. Since I'm neither precogniscient nor particularly brave, though, I thought of doing neither.

Carlos Montero was tall for his sixteen Earth-years, loose-limbed and muscular, yet still possessing the gawky immaturity of youth. Downlike blond whiskers on his chin and upper lip, an uncertain swagger in his step, he was a nice, good-looking kid trying hard to be a man. So far, he was doing a good job; although Carlos had only been thirteen when his family joined the thirty political detainees who had fled the Republic aboard the *Alabama,* during the colony's first year he had not only survived the untimely deaths of his father and mother but had also become the man of his family, taking care of his younger sister while putting in time in the community farms. Since no one on the Council had thought of setting a minimum drinking age, Lew had recently started letting him into the Cantina. Like many of us, he tended to think of young Mr. Montero as something of a surrogate son.

In the stillness of the moment, everyone watched as he stamped his boots on the floor and removed his drenched cap. Carlos couldn't help but notice the attention he was getting. "Am I missing something?" he asked as he pulled off his rain-slicked poncho and cap and hung them next to the door. "Is there a problem or what?"

"No problem." Lew had already taken a stein off the shelf and was holding it beneath the keg. Eventually, once the colony got large enough that everyone stopped knowing everyone else, we got around to reinventing money; as it stood then, though, your currency was the sweat of your brow. You received as good as you gave, and that was pretty much the end of it. "We were just . . ."

"Lew," I said quietly.

Lew saw the look on my face and shut up. Too late, he remembered how Jorge and Amelia Montero died. Now was a good time to drop the subject.

"We were talking about hunting for game." Reese half-turned to face Carlos, one hand on the handle of his stein, the other tucked into his old uniform belt.

"I was just saying that we don't get enough meat in our diet, and it's time we start living off the land."

"Seems to me we're doing that already, Gill." Jim pushed his stein across the bar and shook his head when Lew silently asked whether he wanted a refill. "Once the rain ends, we'll have a ten- or eleven-month growing season, and at the last town meeting Captain Lee told us we'd be bringing down the rest of the embryos once we've figured out how to take care of the swoops."

"I'm just saying that we've got an island full of game which we've barely touched." Reese glanced over his shoulder at Lew to point to his mug and raise a finger. "They're all coming out of hibernation now, but so far all we've done is trap creek crab . . . and I don't know about you, but I'm getting a little tired of pulling bones out of my teeth."

Scattered chuckles from around the shack, and more than a few nods this time. Lew remained quiet as he finished filling Carlos' stein. As he placed it on the bar, the colonel stepped aside to make room for him. "Here y'go, Mr. Montero," he said, pulling the mug a little closer. "Elbow up here and have one on the Service."

The Service. I almost winced when I heard that. After all, the Combined Service had rounded up left-wing intellectuals like Jorge Montero when they didn't go along with the draconian measures of its Federal Renewal Program. Yet Carlos was either blissfully ignorant of what his parents had suffered through, or he had simply chosen to ignore it as a thing of the past, for I'd noticed how he recently taken to treating Gill Reese with more than a small measure of respect. His father and mother would have sickened . . . but then, his folks had been on Coyote for less than three days before they had been killed.

"Thanks, sir." Carlos squeezed in between me and Reese. There wasn't a vacant stool, so he had to lean against the counter. He ignored me as he picked up the stein and took a tentative sip; noticing Reese's watchful eye, he drank more deeply, and Gill gave him an ever-so-slight nod of approval. "So what are you thinking about hunting? Creek cat?"

Oh, no, I thought. *Don't go there . . .*

Reese shrugged. "Well, that's a possibility, I guess. Might be good for fur, but they look a little too stringy for meat." He paused, then looked Carlos straight in the eye. "I was thinking more about boid."

No one said anything, although everyone in the room seemed to be watching Carlos. I can't say I wasn't curious myself, for it was a boid that had killed his parents.

Carlos stared at the colonel for a moment, then dropped his gaze. "What makes you think they're worth hunting?" he asked quietly. "Seems to me like they're nothing but feathers and claws."

"So's a chicken, if you look at it the wrong way," Reese said in the exact same tone. "But there's a lot of meat beneath those feathers and there's got to be some muscle behind those claws. I've taken a close look at the ones we've taken down . . ."

"Like the one that killed his parents?" Without realizing what I was doing, I found myself speaking up. Carlos stiffened, and I immediately regretted what I had said.

But Reese didn't. "The very same one which killed his folks, yes, now that you ask, Dr. Johnson." Although he was speaking to me, it was clear that he was also talking to Carlos. "Since you don't remember, I was the one of the guys who located its nest and shot it along with its mate . . . and their whole brood, for that matter. Take my word for it, they're not bullet-proof."

"So long as you've got enough bullets," I muttered.

"Bullets and courage, yes." Now he was addressing the rest of the Cantina, twisting every word I uttered in his favor. "We've set up perimeter guns around town, sure, and that's kept them away, but what do you hear late at night when you're lying awake in bed? Why do we send no fewer than three people . . . three armed people . . . into the brush at any time?"

"Because they're the dominant species, that's why." Lew reluctantly pushed Reese's stein across the bar. He had refilled his mug, but it seemed to me that he done so only to avoid trouble; any other person that carried on a rant in his place usually got cut off.

"That's where you're wrong." Gill ignored the beer stein as he gave Lew a patronizing smile. "We're here to stay, and the sooner we get that across to those . . . overgrown ostriches, the better off everyone's going to be."

Then he picked up the stein and turned to Carlos. "And I think you've got some payback time coming to you," he added quietly, hefting his stein. "Are you in?"

"Carlos . . ." I began.

"Let him make up his own mind, Doc," Reese said. "He's a man now."

Carlos hesitated, and in that moment I glimpsed a flicker of fear in his solemn blue eyes. He was being challenged, not only by someone whose respect he wished to earn, but also in front of everyone in the Cantina. If he said no, he'd never be able to walk into this place again . . . or at least not as a man, but as a boy. Reese stared at him, silently awaiting his reply.

"I'm in," Carlos said at last. He met Reese's forthright gaze, and raised his own mug. "Hell, yeah, I'm in."

Murmurs around the room. A couple of men clapped their hands in approval. Reese grinned and tapped his stein against Carlos', then he turned to look at the others. "Anyone else who wants to join us, you're welcome to tag along. The more the merrier." He glanced over his shoulder at me. "So, Doc . . . are you coming or not?"

To this day, I still don't know for certain why he did that. I didn't like Reese, and he didn't like me; there was no reason why he would want me in his hunting party. Perhaps he was just drunk, or perhaps he believed I'd wimp out and thus humiliate myself. Nonetheless, he now had me cornered as well.

"Yeah, I'm with you," I muttered, and had the satisfaction of seeing a glimmer of surprise in Reese's face. I told myself that it was only to keep an eye on Carlos, but the fact of the matter was that I had my own pride to uphold. "When do we go?"

"Tomorrow morning." Ignoring me once more, he turned to the others. "If you're coming, we'll meet at the grange hall. We'll be heading south down Sand Creek, so bring overnight gear . . . bedrolls, lamps, and two days' rations. We'll check out guns and kay- aks before we leave. Any questions?"

"What happens if you find a boid?" Lew asked.

"Are you coming?" Reese inquired, and chuckled as Lew slowly shook his head. "Then keep the fire- place warm and whip up some barbecue sauce. We're bringing home supper."

* * *

An hour or so later, I left the Cantina and began making my way home. I'd tapped the keg more than a few times, and my boots sloshed through the mud as I staggered down the middle of Main Street, passing the darkened windows and bolted doors of wood-slate houses. At the far end of town I could make out the white drumlike shapes of the *Alabama*'s cargo cylinders, still resting where they had been dropped from orbit three Earth years ago, since then cannibalized and turned into water tanks and grain elevators.

I neglected to take my flashlight from the pocket of my slicker, but I didn't really need it to see where I was going. The rain had stopped, at least for a few hours, and the clouds had temporarily parted. Looming above the horizon was the vast hemisphere of Ursa Majoris 47b, the pale blue gas giant around which Coyote revolved, its ring plane jutting straight up into space. Although Coyote was now undergoing the daily planetary eclipse which gave us a regular day-night cycle, on clear nights enough sunlight was reflected from Great Father to give the semblance of a full-moon night on Earth.

I stopped in the street to take in the view. Also, I badly needed to take a leak, and the nearest communal outhouse was a couple of hundred meters away. There weren't any Prefects in sight, though, and with this much mud in the street a small puddle of urine would go unnoticed, so I unbuttoned my fly.

The night sky was brilliant with alien constellations and new worlds. Bear's ringed brother Wolf was rising to the east, and directly above me I could make out three of Coyote's companion moons, Dog, Hawk, and Eagle. If I waited a little while longer, I might see the *Alabama* fly over. I was searching for the orbiting starship when my meditation was shattered by a scream.

Think of a madman in a sanitarium. Think of a victim of the Spanish Inquisition being tortured in a prison dungeon. Think of an insane rooster crowing after midnight. Think of what you'd sound like if someone shoved a needle beneath one of your fingernails.

That's the mating cry of a boid.

When the advance team from the *Alabama* heard that high-pitched nocturnal scream rippling across the marshes three years ago, they wisely abandoned their campsite and spent the rest of their first night on Coyote aboard the *Plymouth*. It wasn't until almost a week later, when two colonists ventured into the marshes near the landing site, that they discovered exactly what made that hellish sound.

Neither of them survived the experience. I don't think I have to tell you who they were.

I froze, waiting for it to come again, praying that it wouldn't be any closer. Down the dark street behind me, I heard someone hastily opening a window to clap their storm shutters closed. The motion detectors had always been able to detect the boids when they approached Liberty, and the boids had eventually learned to respect the perimeter guns. Nonetheless, no one took chances.

The boid screamed again. It sounded a little less near this time, a little farther away from town. Yet now the night wasn't quite so peaceful, the stars not quite so benign.

Six men met in front of the grange early the following morning . . . or rather, five men and a boy wanting to become a man.

I had half expected Jim Levin and Bernie Cayle to

show up; despite his earlier skepticism, Jim had been one of the first to sign up, and wherever Jim went, his best friend wasn't far behind. When I arrived, they were already helping Carlos Montero haul the creek cat-skin kayaks from the storage shed out to the boat ramp behind the grange; through the shed door, I could see Gill Reese signing out six semi-auto rifles from the community armory. Yet it came as a surprise when Lew Geary came walking into the yard, back-pack slung over his shoulder, bedroll beneath his arm. Carrie was with him, but she didn't seem very happy about his last-minute change of mind; she scowled in Reese's direction when Lew sheepishly explained that, if he was going to cook something in his Cantina, he preferred to kill and dress it himself. I don't know if that was the full truth, or whether Lew simply wanted to take an adventure, but since the kayaks were two-seaters and there weren't any other volunteers, we welcomed him to the party. Carrie gave Lew a fare-well hug and kiss, then turned and silently stalked away.

We spent another half hour carefully loading our gear into the beached kayaks. By then a small crowd had gathered around the ramp. Jim's and Bernie's wives showed up to see their husbands off, and Carlos put his sister Marie in Sissy Levin's care while he was gone. I didn't have a wife or family, so I stood off to one side, chatting with friends as I waited for the oth-ers to make their good-byes. Captain Lee made his appearance just as we were about to depart; appar-ently he had been among the last to hear about this impromptu expedition, and he wasn't very pleased. He and Reese stepped into the grange and had a brief argument among themselves; we didn't hear most of it, yet just as I was beginning to think—and secretly hope—that R.E. would order the sortie to be canceled, the two men emerged from the meeting hall. Reese, with a smug grin on his face, walked to his kayak, picked up his two-bladed paddle, and proclaimed to one and all that we were ready to go. The Captain said nothing; arms folded across his chest, he silently observed the rest of us pick up our own paddles and shove the kayaks into the creek.

The weather was on our side that morning; the rain clouds had parted, allowing the warm sun to beat down upon the narrow, serpentine banks of Sand Creek. We had removed our jackets and peeled back the sleeves of our shirts before casting off, but the day soon became hot and before long we were taking off our shirts as well. When I looked back from the stern of the boat I shared with Lew, the rooftops and farm fields of Liberty had disappeared far behind us, and even the radio tower was nowhere to be seen. Less than two klicks downstream from town, it was impossible to tell that there was a human colony on Coyote.

Sand Creek weaved its way through dense marshlands thick with grass, brush, and trees. My shoulders and arms ached as the blades of my paddle dipped right and left, right and left, into the tepid brown water, until my lungs became accustomed to working hard in the thin atmosphere and I settled into a regular rhythm. A pair of curious swoops found us and circled our boats for a while, their harsh screeches echoing off the river banks, until they gradually lost interest and drifted away on their broad leathery wings, and again the flat landscape was quiet and peaceful.

All except for the sound of Gill Reese's voice. He insisted on keeping ahead of the rest of us, telling Carlos to paddle a little harder whenever Jim and Bernie threatened to catch up with them, as if we were in some sort of race. Lew and I brought up the rear, calmly moving along, in no particular hurry to get anywhere soon, yet even from twenty meters away I could hear Reese, even after the rest of us had fallen silent, telling stories about basic training at the Academy (". . . second in my class . . ."), about rowing a canoe down the entire length of the Suwanee River (". . . from the Okefenokee Swamp clear down the Gulf of Mexico . . ."), rock-climbing in the Utah badlands (". . . and there I was, clinging to the side of Pistol Peak . . ."), his first shuttle launch (". . . and so I grabbed the stick and . . ."), and after a while it was just one, long, endless liturgy. The life and times of Colonel Gilbert Reese, a true man among men.

"Hemingway would have loved this guy," Lew muttered over his shoulder at one point.

"Hemingway, hell," I replied. "Let's try Aesop."

All the while, Carlos remained quiet. At first he interjected a question or comment now and then—"So what happened then?" "Really?" "And did he . . . ?"—until eventually he became silent altogether, still giving Reese his audience, yet letting his gaze drift to the savannah which stretched out around us. I couldn't tell whether he was actually listening or simply pretending, but his reticence made me uneasy in a way I couldn't quite fathom.

Shortly after midday we reached a fork where Sand Creek branched off into a tributary. By now Great Father was blazing hot and we had been paddling for over four hours, so we lashed our boats together and dropped anchor just a few meters from the point. While we lunched on the sandwiches Carrie had sent with us, Jim dug out an orbital map of New Florida and stretched it across the gunnels. Studying it, we saw that the tributary split off to the southeast for about twenty kilometers before meandering westward again to rejoin Sand Creek just south of the long, skinny sandbar formed by the two streams. Past the confluence, the creek gradually became wider until it ended in a waterfall which cascaded down the high bluffs overlooking East River, one of the two major rivers which bordered New Florida and eventually flowed into Big River, the vast equatorial channel which completely encircled Coyote.

No one had yet charted this tributary; in fact, it didn't even have a name on the map. Perhaps that was what prompted Reese to urge that we should take it instead of continuing down Sand Creek, even though it would take us farther away from Liberty. Since we hadn't yet spotted any signs of boids, he argued that it made sense for us to explore the tributary, but I think he had another motive. Maybe he was only curious, or perhaps it simply appealed to his vanity to name a stream after himself.

"Let's try it out," Carlos said after awhile. "If we don't find anything, we can always paddle back to where we started, right?"

This was the first time he had said much of anything. After listening to Reese talk about himself for four straight hours, you would have thought that he would be aching for decent conversation. Instead he had sat quietly in the bow of their kayak, hunched over his paddle as he stared at the grasslands surrounding us. The sun must be getting to him, I thought. Either that, or he was regretting his decision to go on this trip. I knew I certainly was.

"No, no." Reese shook his head as he talked around a mouthful of crab salad sandwich. "If we go down that way, I don't want to come back until we've reached the end." He brushed the crumbs off his hands, then jabbed a finger at the map. "If we need to, we can pull off down there and make camp for the night, but I want to see where this takes us."

He gave us a challenging look, and once again I wondered how he had become the *de facto* leader of this expedition. Probably because he was so accustomed to command, he automatically assumed it whenever possible. He couldn't be in charge of the colony so long as Captain Lee was still around, and since he hadn't been elected to the Council, this was his way of asserting himself. Bernie mumbled something about trying to get back home before sunset, but Jim nodded as if surrendering himself to the inevitable. Neither Lew nor I said anything. For better or worse, this was Reese's trip and Carlos' rite of manhood. The rest of us were just along for the ride.

The tributary wasn't like Sand Creek. After the first kilometer, its banks became so narrow that we had to paddle single-file, so shallow that we could easily touch bottom with our oars. Dense walls of spider bush crowded in upon us from all sides, their roots extending into the stream like veins, their branches arching over our heads like a tangled canopy, casting angular shadows across the water. We had entered a swamp darker and more forbidding than the sun-drenched grasslands we had left behind, and it wasn't long before I was certain that we had taken a wrong turn.

Yet Reese insisted that we continue, even after Bernie and Lew begged him to reconsider. He had stopped bragging about his exploits, a small favor for which I was thankful; now his eyes prowled the stream banks, and I noticed that he had shifted his rifle between his knees where he could reach it more quickly. I soon found myself doing the same.

We were about three klicks down the tributary when we came upon a small clearing on the left side of the stream, a place where the spider bush parted almost like a doorway. As he and Carlos rowed closer to the clearing, Reese suddenly raised a hand, then silently pointed to the stream bank. Lew and I looked at each other, then we slowly paddled up alongside the two other kayaks, carefully sliding next to Jim and Bernie.

Sourgrass grew in the clearing, yet it lay low along the ground, as if something large had recently passed through here, pushing down the grass on its way to the water. Reese used his paddle to point to the very edge of the stream bank, and in the waning light of the midafternoon sun I saw what he had spotted: a distinctive three-clawed impression in the mud.

"This is it," Reese whispered. "Here's where we'll find 'em."

Once we beached the kayaks and gathered our rifles, we set out on foot through the opening in the spider bushes, following the trail of trampled grass left by the boid. It led us out of the brush and into a broad, open meadow surrounded by groves of blackwood and fauxbirch. On either side of the narrow trail the sourgrass grew shoulder-high, so dense that we could barely see a meter through it. The meadow was humid in the midafternoon sun, hot as a furnace and as still as a painting.

We marched two abreast down the trail, clutching our guns next to our chests, trying our best to remain quiet. It wasn't easy; the grass crunched softly beneath our boots with each step that we took, and Bernie's canteen sloshed and clanked on his belt until Reese irritably motioned for him to take it off and leave it behind. Reese and Jim were in the lead, with Carlos and Bernie trailing them; as before, Lew and I were in the rear, not an enviable position since boids were sometimes known to attack from behind. I found myself frequently glancing over my shoulder, trying to watch every corner of the meadow at once.

Soon the entrance to the path, and the tributary hidden behind the wall of spider bush, could no longer be easily discerned, and even the path itself seemed to be disappearing behind us. A warm breeze wafted through the meadow, drifting through the grass in a way that suggested movement. Sweat flowed down my forehead, stinging the corners of my eyes, tasting sour on my lips. But we were almost halfway through the meadow; if we could only reach the far end, I prayed, perhaps Reese would give up and we could return to the safety of the kayaks.

I glanced at Lew. Without having to ask, I knew that he had the same thought. It was then that it occurred to me that everything was too damn quiet. No swoops, no swampers, no creek cats . . . nothing moved except the wind in the grass.

And us.

Reese stopped. He raised a hand, bringing the column to a halt, then he crouched on his hips, studying something he had found on the trail. Jim glanced around, then bent over to look at the same thing. Although I couldn't see what it was, I intuitively knew what they had found: a pile of boid scat, the ropy brown turds we sometimes found just outside town. The wind shifted a little just then, and I picked up a heavy fecal scent. The droppings were fresh.

There was something else, something I couldn't

quite put my finger on. Again, I looked all around, searching for any movement within the meadow. Everything lay still. The breeze died, and now nothing stirred the high curtains of grass, yet there was a chill prickling at the nape of my neck. The atavistic sensation of being watched, studied . . .

Reese stood up, raised his hand again, beckoned for us to continue forward. As he and Jim started walking again, Carlos glanced over his shoulder at me. There was a boyish grin on his face, but I saw fear deep within his eyes, and that was moment the boid chose to attack.

The boid had been lurking only a few meters away, keeping breathlessly still, perfectly camouflaged within the tall grass. Perhaps it had been stalking us ever since we entered its territory. The moment that it saw that our guard was relaxed, if only for a second, it took advantage of us and moved in for the kill.

Jim Levin was dead before he knew it. He heard a swift motion to his right side, whipped around just as Bernie yelled, and then the creature was upon him. Its massive orange beak darted forward on its long neck, snapped and twisted in one swift movement, and I caught a glimpse of a large lump flying off into the tall grass. I didn't even realize that it was Jim's head until long after it hit the ground.

After that, the next few seconds became minutes, as if everything was rushing at light-speed and time itself had dilated. In those moments, this is what I saw:

The boid in the middle of the path: a enormous, flightless avian, like a pale-yellow ostrich crossed with a small dinosaur, standing upright on long backward-jointed legs, still holding Jim's decapitated corpse in its slender, winglike arms and its oversized, parrotlike mouth. Two and half meters and a hundred kilos of instant death.

Reese, somehow having managing to dash past the boid, in a perfect position to fire, yet standing stock-still, staring agape at the creature, his gun limp in his hands.

Bernie, on his knees and scrabbling for his gun where he had dropped it, screaming in inchoate terror as the boid dropped his friend's body and turned its enormous round eyes toward him.

Carlos, standing his ground in the middle of the path, bringing up his rife, settling its stock against his shoulder, squeezing off a round that went wild.

The boid, startled by the flash-bang of the shot, stopping in mid-charge, its bloodstained beak open as if in dumbfounded surprise.

Bernie was still screaming, and I was just beginning to raise my own gun, when Carlos fired again. Two shots, three, four . . . at least two of them missed, but I saw bits of orange bone splinter from the boid's beak and small feathers spray from its body.

The boid staggered backward, making that awful screech I had heard only last night.

Just behind me, Lew fired, the muzzle of his gun so close to my right ear that I was deafened. I couldn't tell whether he missed or hit, but it was enough to make the boid change its mind.

Abandoning Jim's body, it turned and began loping back down the path.

Heading straight for Gill Reese.

Reese saw the boid coming. He was at least ten meters away, and by now he had his gun half-raised to his shoulder. The boid was at full-charge, but it was wounded and in panic. He had all the time in the world to empty his rifle into the creature, at point-blank range.

But he didn't.

He remained frozen in place, his mouth open, even as the boid descended upon him.

And at those last few moments of slow time, while Lew and I were firing as fast as we could squeeze our triggers, I saw Carlos lower his rifle.

"Shoot!" I yelled. "Carlos, shoot. . . !"

The boid lowered its head, snagged Reese within its beak. I heard Reese scream once, a terrible howl abruptly cut short a half-second later as the creature, dragging his body with it, plunged back into the tall grass.

As quickly as the boid had appeared, it had vanished.

We made it back to Liberty a few hours after sundown. The rain clouds had moved in again, so it was in a cold, dark drizzle that we rowed the last few klicks up Sand Creek. The most welcome sight of my life were the lights of town as we rounded the last bend, but even then we didn't ease up from the paddles. We could already hear the boids making their nocturnal cries behind us, as if they were reasserting their domain and challenging us to a rematch.

Our first task was unloading Jim Levin's blanket-wrapped corpse from the bow of Bernie's kayak, and then going to his home to tell Sissy what had happened. Perhaps it's just as well that I leave what happened next unsaid; it wasn't pleasant. Yet Jim was lucky to have a grave, for although we managed to drag his remains back to the kayaks, we never located Gill Reese's body, and so no tombstone was ever erected in his honor.

The fact of the matter is that we never searched for Reese. The boid had taken its victim away into the grass, and we weren't about to go looking for him. But the more pragmatic truth is that none of us felt much remorse over his death. He had bullied us into this trip, then turned coward when he had to walk the walk. Coyote is a hard world; we had named it after a trickster demigod, and you can't lie to the gods and expect to live.

I think this was the lesson Carlos learned.

Just as Gill Reese intended, he became a man that day. He grew up straight and tall, and he never let us down after that. Yet although I eventually became one of his closest friends, doing many hard jobs together and sharing drinks afterward in Lew's Cantina, never once did I ever dare ask him why he chose to lower his gun at that critical moment on Levin Creek.

I never asked, and he never told me.

THE DRYAD'S WEDDING
by Robert Charles Wilson

Robert Charles Wilson is known and acclaimed for his emotionally touching, finely tuned science fiction. His novels include *Gypsies, The Divide, The Harvest,* and *Mysterium.* He lives in Toronto, Canada.

Chaia Martine was nineteen years old. In seven days she would marry the man she had been married to once before, in another life. And she suspected that something was terribly wrong with her.

Not the familiar something. She was actually thirty-five years old, not nineteen. She felt nineteen because nineteen years ago her skull had been fractured by a falling tree in a fierce summer storm. She had lain in the flooded Copper River for almost an hour before her rescuers reached her, and had lost so much dura mater and brain tissue that her memories could not be saved. The Humantown clinic had salvaged her body, but not her mind. She had had to wear diapers and learn to walk and talk all over again, as nanobacters built her a new cerebral hemisphere from fetal stem cells out of the colony's medical reserves. She had almost died and had been born a second time—awkwardly, painfully. Yes, certainly, *that* was wrong with her. (And problem enough for one person, Chaia thought.)

But that didn't explain why she sometimes heard

the voice of the forest calling her name. And it didn't explain, above all else, the way the spiders had assembled themselves into the shape of a man.

The spider incident happened in a glade uphill from the Copper River. The Copper was a gentle river now, herds of epidonts grazing peacefully at the grasses and faux-lilies that grew along the banks. Chaia loved the look of it, at least at the end of a placid Isian summer. (She was inevitably nervous, frightened on some fundamental physiological level, whenever mountain rains made the river run fast and white.) This glade was one of Chaia's private places, a place she came to be alone, away from the crowds and confusing expectations of Humantown, away from the hovering mystery of her once-and-future husband Gray McInnes. Standing, she could watch the river unfold like a perfect blue ribbon into the western prairies.

For the most part she was enclosed here, wrapped in green shade. Chaia was not now and never had been afraid of the Isian forest. Guardian remensors, small as sandflies, flew a twenty-meter perimeter around her wherever she went. They would warn her if any dangerous animal—a triraptor or a digger— came too close; they would sting and bite the creature if it attempted to stalk her.

There were Isian insects in the glade, a great many of them, but Chaia wasn't troubled by insects. Her skin exuded pheromones that repelled the most dangerous species. If one should somehow chance to bite, her enhanced immune system would quickly neutralize the poison. In fact, she had grown familiar with the insect population of the glade, some species of which she had studied in her bios and taxonomy classes. She often spent a lazy afternoon here doing nothing more than watching the bugs: the black noonbugs, like tiny pompous cartoon men, rolling balls of sticky fungal spores; or the diogenes flies, with their pollen sacs like miniature Victorian lanterns.

The spiders were less obvious but no less plentiful. They were called "spiders" because they resembled a namesake Terrestrial insect Chaia had never seen (or could not remember seeing, though she had once, in her lost life, lived on Earth). They looked like button-sized, rust-red marbles equipped with a radial mass of legs. The spiders were harvesters, cutting leaves and taking the fragments back to their ground nests, which rose like ankle-high pyramids from the forest floor.

She was not ordinarily aware of the spiders—they passed through the fallen leaves and green reeds as lightly as idle thoughts—but today they were numerous and active, as if vying for her attention. Chaia sat on a fallen log and watched, fascinated, as they marched among the damp thread-mosses, gathering in pale clumps and clinging together.

This was unusual behavior, and Chaia supposed it must reflect some event of great significance in the spider universe, a mass mating or the founding of a new colony. She lifted her feet so that she wold not inadvertently disturb the complex protocols of the creatures.

A breeze from the west rattled the long brella leaves above her head. Chaia was due back at Human-town for the evening meal (and a wedding rehearsal at the Universalist chapel), but that was still two hours away. Her afternoon was her own, and she meant to spend it doing absolutely nothing useful or productive. She watched the spiders gather in the glade, watched them idly at first but then with increasing attention, until it became obvious that what was happening here was not, perhaps, wholly natural.

Still, the feverish activity of the insects fascinated her. Spiders poured into the glade from several directions and several nests at once, parade lines of them. They avoided Chaia systematically but gathered before her in lacy sheets, stacked one atop another until the combined mass of their pale bodies took on a smoked-glass color and they rose in a seething mound to half her own height.

Carefully—disquieted but not yet terrified—Chaia stood and took a step backward. The spider-mass moved in response, shifting its borders until it became (and now Chaia's fear began to intensify) a nearly human shape. The spiders had made a man. Well, not a man, exactly, but a human form, neither male nor female, really just the suggestion of a torso, arms, a head. The head was the most detailed part of the spider-sculpture. Its eyes were a shadowed roundness, its nose a pale protruberance.

Chaia was about to flee the glade when the spider-thing opened its uncertain mouth and spoke.

The voice was very faint, as if the massed insects had enclosed a volume of air in a kind of leaky lung, expelling moist breezes through vocal cords made of insect parts or dried reeds. Or perhaps only Chaia heard the voice; she thought this was possible. But the spider-thing spoke, and the awful thing about this was, Chaia recognized its voice.

She hadn't heard it for a long time. But she had heard it often when she was younger, in the woods, in her dreams. She called it the voice of the forest because it had no real name, and she never spoke of it because she knew, somehow, she mustn't.

"Chaia," the spider-thing whispered.

It knew her name. It had always known her name. It had called her name from wind-tossed trees, from the rippling flow of the Copper River. She sensed an uneasiness in the voice, an anxiety, an unfulfilled need.

"Chaia," the spider-thing said. (The voice of the forest said.)

That was all. That was enough.

Then the man-shaped mass began to lose its form, to collapse into a collection of mere insects, thousands of them flowing like water at her feet, and she thought she heard the voice say, "No, not like this, not this." Chaia tried to answer it, to say *something,* because surely a sound of her own would disperse the hallucination (it *must* be a hallucination) and jolt the forest back to reality. But her throat was as dry and breathless as a sealed room. Her courage collapsed; she turned and ran downhill until she found the trail to Humantown, a cloud of guardian remensors following her like agitated gnats; ran all the way back with the forest singing in her ears, certain that something was wrong with her, that some part of her was deeply and permanently broken . . . and how could she bring herself to marry Gray McInnes, how could she even have contemplated it, when she was probably not even sane?

Humantown had been established half a century ago, deep in the arboreal hinterland of the Great Western Continent. It was the first truly successful human settlement on Isis. But it was not, strictly speaking, the first.

There had been human beings on Isis more than a century earlier. That had been when the great Trusts ruled the Earth, when the outer solar system had been a checkerboard of independent republics (Mars, the

asteroids, the Uranian moons, and the Kuiper kib-
butzim), when a single interstellar launch had consumed a significant fraction of the system's gross
economic product. People had come to Isis because
Isis was one of the few biologically active worlds
within practical reach, and because it seemed so invitingly Earthlike in its size, mass, climate, and atmosphere.

The problem: Isis was toxic.

It was, in fact, deadly. Its biosphere had evolved far
before the Earth's, and without the periodic massive
diebacks that punctuated Terrestrial evolution. The
Isian ecology was deeply complex, driven by predation
and parasitism. The Isian equivalents of viruses, bacteria, and prions made short work of any unprotected
Terrestrial organic matter. From an Isian point of
view, human beings were nothing more than an ambu-
latory buffet of choice long-chain proteins waiting pas-
sively to be devoured.

The first settlers—scientists living in the sterile cores
of multilayered biohazard facilities—had underestimated the virility of the Isian bios. They had died. All
of them, including thousands in the Isian orbital station, when their defenses were breached. Lovely as
she was, Isis was also a murderess.

Humanity had not returned to the planet for a hundred years, by which time the oligarchy of the Trusts
had collapsed and a gentler regime controlled the
Earth.

And still, no unprotected human being could survive
more than a few minutes in the Isian bios. But protection had grown more subtle, less intrusive. Chaia, for
instance, possessed immune system prostheses clustered in genned sacs around her abdominal aorta;

countless genetic fixes had hardened her cellular barriers against Isian invasion as well. With periodic upgrades, she could live here indefinitely.

She felt as if she had lived here all her life. She was not a true Isian, like the babies born in Humantown, because she had lived another life on Earth; but that life was lost to her. All she remembered was Isis. She knew the forests and uplands around Humantown intimately because they were her cradle and her home. She knew the wildlife. She knew the town itself, almost too well. And she knew the people.

She knew there was no one she could talk to about the spiders.

Humantown had grown up above an S-curse in the Copper River, a ploughed terrace dotted with simple Turing-fabricated structures. It was fenced to keep dangerous wild animals away, but the fence recognized Chaia and opened to admit her (chiming "Welcome, Chaia Martine!" from a hidden sonodot). Chaia suppressed her anxiety as she walked down dusty Main Street. She passed the hardware shelter, where Gray McInnes wrote Turing protocols for the assembly robots; she was obscurely relieved not to see him there. She passed the health center where she had spent her first five years under the care of her trauma-mother Lizabeth Chopra and a half-dozen surrogate fathers in the form of therapists and doctors. She passed the Universalist Chapel, where all the religious people except Orthodox Jews and Reform Mormons gathered once a week to worship . . . then she turned back, rang the rectory bell, and told Clergyman Gooding to cancel tonight's rehearsal. She wasn't feeling well, she said. No, nothing serious. A headache. She just needed to lie down.

Then she walked up Main Street, past Reyes Avenue where her own small private shelter stood, and down a back lane through a stand of cultivated brella trees where children played with brightly-colored mentor robots, and then—surprising herself—through the fence and out into the wildwood once more.

Dusk was slow on Isis. Sunsets lingered. The forest grew shadows as Chaia walked. She would be missed at the evening meal at the town kitchen, but perhaps Rector Gooding would make excuses for her.

That would not prevent Gray McInnes (wonderful, patient, enduring Gray) from seeking her out. And she wouldn't be at home, but she didn't think Gray would be terribly surprised at that. Chaia often went walking late in the woods and had even spent some nights there. After all, she had her remensors to protect her; the Humantown computers could pinpoint her location if some need arose. Would Gray follow her into the woods? No, she thought, not likely. He understood her periodic need to be alone. He understood all her quirks. If Gray had a fault, it was this relentless understanding. It suggested he still thought of her as a kind of invalid, as if she were the original Chaia Martine he had married back on Earth, only suffering from a long-term amnesia.

But she was not that Chaia Martine. She was only the sum of what she had been on Isis. Plus a few random delusions.

She followed an old path up the foothills above the human settlement and the river. She had no destination in mind, at least not consciously; but she walked for more than an hour, and when she awoke to herself she saw lights in the distance. Glaring portable flarelights, much brighter than the setting sun. This was a remote research site, an abandoned digger complex where the planetary ecologist Werner Eastman had excavated a nest of ancient tunnels.

She came out of the woods into a blizzard of light and sound.

Most of the heavy work here had been done by construction and mining robots. The huge yellow machines still roamed the site, sectioning the earth with a delicacy that belied their great size and noise. They sorted what they found, excreting chipped flint and knapping stones into neat mesh trays.

Werner and his two apprentices should have been finished for the night, but they seemed absorbed in their work, huddling in a polyplex shelter over some choice discovery. Chaia simply stood at the edge of the excavation, peering down the steeply terraced border into a layer of resected tunnels like limestone wormtracks. A cooling breeze tangled her long hair.

Werner must have noticed her at some point. She looked up from her thoughts and he was there, gazing at her with a gentle concern. "Hello, Chaia. Come to watch?"

"Not really. Just . . . walking."

"Late for that, isn't it? You'll be missing dinner."

"I felt restless."

She liked Werner Eastman. He was an old Isis hand, dedicated to his work. A tall man, graying at the temples after at least two juvenation cycles. He was older than Humantown itself, though still young by Terrestrial standards. He had been one of her surrogate fathers.

They had drifted apart in recent years. Werner disapproved of her marriage to Gray McInnes. He felt that Gray was taking advantage of her, exploiting the fact of his prior marriage to that other Chaia Martine,

the one who had died in the Copper River. Gray
wanted everything to slide back in time to the way it
had been before, Werner insisted. And that was maybe
true, Chaia thought. But she couldn't forget or ignore
Gray's many kindnesses. And Gray, after all, had been
the only courtier in her brief new life. The only one
not repelled or at least dismayed by her strangeness,
her awkward in-betweenness.

But Werner meant no harm. Her concern had always touched her, even when she considered it mis-
placed. She said, "You're working late, too."

"Yes. Well, we found something quite interesting in
the lower excavations. Care to have a look?"

She agreed, but only to be polite. What could be
interesting, except to a specialist, about these old digger tunnels? She had seen diggers often enough—live
ones, clutching crude spears in their manipulating
arms. They were occasionally dangerous, but nothing
about them inspired her curiosity. They were not truly
sentient, though they manufactured simple levers and
blades. In fact they were emotionally affectless, bland
as turtles. She couldn't imagine befriending a digger,
even the way she might befriend an ordinary animal.
They had no true speech. They lived in tunnels lined
with hardened excreta, and their diet consisted of rotting carrion and a few roots and vegetables. If food
was scarce, they would devour their own young.

Werner took her to the shelter where the day's dis-
coveries were laid out on a table. Here were the usual
simple flint tools, the kind Werner had been catalog-
uing since Chaia was young. But a few other items,
too. The ones he had called "interesting." Bits of cor-
roded metal. (Diggers weren't metalworkers.) This
one, for instance, clotted with clay, looked like the

kind of firefly lamp every colonist carried in his pouch. Here, a sort of buckle. Chipped fragments of glass.

"Humans made these," Chaia said, an odd uneasiness haunting her.

"Yes. But they're old. They date from the first Isian settlement, almost two hundred years ago."

"What are they doing in these old digger tunnels?"

"That's the interesting question, isn't it? But we also found this."

Werner reached into a specimen box and withdrew something already washed free of its embedding mud and clay, something smooth and white.

A jawbone.

A human jawbone.

"My God," Chaia breathed.

Werner began to explain what the jawbone represented . . . something about the first research colonists who had occupied the modern site of Humantown, and how one of them must have ventured into the digger colony when it was still active, or had been carried there, or . . .

But Chaia didn't really hear him.

The jawbone—dead, motionless on the table—spoke to her.

Werner went on talking. Werner couldn't hear.

But Chaia heard it quite plainly.

"Chaia," the jawbone said.

And Chaia fainted.

There is a phenomenon in the universe called, loosely, "sentience." It occurs in quasi-homeostatic systems of a certain complexity. Human beings are an example of such a system. Certain of their machines are also sentient. Elsewhere in the known universe, sentience is elusive.

Chaia, dreaming, remembered this much from her bios textbooks.

She dreamed of herself, of her brain regrown from fetal stem cells. Sentience requires communication. Nerve cells talk to nerve cells. They talk electrically; they talk chemically. Her fresh, new neurons had exfoliated into a mind.

"Mind," the textbooks said, was what happened in the gaps between the neurons. Signals were exchanged or inhibited. But the space between neurons is essentially empty. "Mind" was a hollowness where patterns bloomed and died.

Like flowers growing between the stars.

What were the places that mind could live? In a human nervous system. In the countless virtual gates of a quantum computer. And—and—

But the dream-thought drifted away, a pattern that had blossomed and withered before she could grasp it.

She woke to find Gray McInnes at her bedside, frowning.

She said, idiotically, "Am I sick?"

(Because of course she was sick; that was why she heard voices. . . .)

But Gray shook his head reassuringly. "Overtired, or so the therapist tells me. I guess you've been under a lot of stress. The wedding plans and all. What were you doing out in the wildwood?"

His expression was open and guileless, but she heard an accusation. "Just walking. Thinking."

He smiled. "The nervous bride?"

"Maybe some of that."

She turned her head. She was home, in her own shelter. They hadn't put her in the clinic, which was a good sign. Through the bedroom window she could see a patch of sky, clouds racing out of the west. When those clouds broke against the flanks of the Copper Mountains there would surely be rain. Summer was over.

Gray brushed a strand of hair away from her eyes. His hand was gentle. He smelled warm and solid. He was a big man, robust, stocky in the way that distinguished Earth-born colonists from their Martian or Kuiper-born colleagues. Chaia always felt tiny next to him.

He said, "The doctor gave you something. You'll probably want to sleep some more."

Chaia wondered whether it was Gray she loved or just his constant presence—the reassurance of him, like a favorite chair or a familiar blanket. She dreaded hurting him.

But how could she go through with the wedding, when she was probably not even sane? How much longer could she pass among people and pretend to be normal? They would notice, soon enough; Gray would notice first, was perhaps even now in that first awful stage of discovery, the warmth of him hiding a kernel of repugnance. . . .

"Close your eyes," he said, smoothing her forehead.

Cloud shadows stole across the room.

He stayed with her that night.

Humantown's particle-pair communications link with Earth had lately downloaded a series of fresh entertainments, and Gray picked one to watch while Chaia dimmed the ambient light. The videostory was called *The American's Daughter* and was set in the wild years of the twentieth century, when there were hundreds of quasi-independent Terrestrial nation-states and not even the moon had been settled. Gray, a history buff, pointed out some factual errors the producers had missed or ignored—the robotic servant that carried messages between the President's daughter and the penniless alchemy student was almost certainly an anachronism, for instance.

The story was placed in North America, with most of the conventional settings of an *histoire americain:* huge concrete buildings, pavement streets crowded with beggars and bankers, a cathedral, a "factory," a carnival. The story ended with a reunion, supposedly in New York City, but Chaia thought the buildings looked like the old city of Brussels, gently morphed to more closely resemble a twentieth-century city.

Gray turned to her curiously when she remarked on it. "What do you know about Brussels?"

"Well, I—" She was suddenly puzzled. "I guess I must have seen pictures."

Brussels.

A place on Earth.

But it had seemed so familiar. She just . . . well, *recognized* it.

Remembered it.

When had she seen Brussels? Can you remember a place you've never been? Or was this another neurological tic, like seeing spiders turn into people, like hearing jawbones talk?

Chaia's mood darkened. Gray stayed with her, and she was grateful for his company. But when they went to bed she turned her back to him, nestled against his big body in a way that meant she was ready to sleep. Only sleep. Or try to sleep.

Soon he was snoring. Chaia, restless, opened her eyes and watched the pebble-sized moon dart across the sky beyond the window. She thought of "lunacy," an old English word that had figured in *The Ameri-*

can's Daughter. After "Luna," the Earth's moon, linked in ancient mythology to madness, strangeness, the uncertainties of great distances and time.

Isis was a stepping stone to the stars.

Star travel was not a simple business even today. Interstellar launches were more efficient than the original Higgs translations of two hundred years ago, but they still consumed enormous resources—in the energy and materials necessary to produce the exotic-matter Higgs lenses; and in sheer real estate, each launch requiring the conversion to its nascent energy of an entire small asteroid or Kuiper body. And all of that would take you no farther than the nearest thousand stars.

But from Isis, a living world at the periphery of the human diaspora, a thousand new stars became (at least theoretically) accessible. Isis didn't have the industrial base to support even a single outward-bound Higgs launch, not yet, but the time would come. Already self-reproducing Turing factories had colonized the icy fringes of the Isian system, building planetary interferometers to scout likely stars. Already, remensors and industrial robots had begun digging into selected cometary bodies, hollowing them out for the Higgs launches that would happen, if all went well, in fifty or a hundred years. Chaia herself might well live another hundred or two hundred years; she might see some of these great public works come to fruition.

In the meantime the daily work of Humantown went on: tending robots, harvesting food and medicinals from the wilderness, writing and revising Turing protocols, making sense of the strange Isian bios. And the simple work of living. Making love, making babies; growing up, even dying.

Getting married.

In the morning she went to the Universalist chapel with Gray for a brief rehearsal: essentially a walk up the aisle, a feigned exchange of yubiwa (finger rings made of gold mined from the mountains by robots), the pronunciation of the banns. Weddings were a Terrestrial custom; relations among Martians and Kuiper folk were more fluid, less formal. Not that a Universalist ceremony was exactly formal. Universalism was not even really a religion in the old sense. Its only dogma was a prescribed humility in the face of the mysteries of the natural world, the unfathomables of ultimate beginning and ultimate end. Its icon was a black circle: the abyss, the primordial singularity; the infinitely receding spacetime of a black hole.

Chaia walked listlessly through the rehearsal. She noticed, but could not bring herself to care, when Gray exchanged glances with Rector Gooding, their expressions reflecting—what? Disappointment? Doubt? Had she been too restrained, too distant? Maybe it would be better if Gray came to doubt her sincerity. Then maybe he could set aside the quest that had consumed him for almost twenty years: to recreate and remarry the woman he had married once on Earth, the other Chaia Martine, her old shadow-self.

After the rehearsal she led fatigue and left Gray at the chapel. She would go home and rest, she said. A lie. Instead she went to see Werner Eastman, determined to confront the mystery of her madness before she married Gray McInnes and perhaps widowed him again, a fate he hardly deserved.

"How much do you know about the first Isian colonists?" Werner asked, sipping coffee from a shiny blue mug.

He wasn't at the tunnel excavation today. He was in his laboratory in the medical-biological complex, a large space strewn with Isian bones and fossils, insects killed and mounted on card stock, loose terminal scrolls with cladistic charts sketched onto them. There was another human skull section on the table in front of him. Chaia carefully avoided looking at it, lest it call her name.

"Not much," she said. "Just what you learn in school. They weren't hardened against the bios. They died."

"More or less correct. Did you know one of the original research stations was located just west of here? The ruins were cleared for farmland thirty years ago—the old hands wanted to preserve it as a historical site, but we were outvoted. We saved what we could from the antique data-storage systems, however, anything that hadn't been hopelessly corrupted by weather and time."

"Do you know who *that* is?" Chaia asked, meaning the skull fragment that lingered in her peripheral vision like a warning sign.

"I think so," Werner said. He sounded pleased with himself at this bit of detective work—he had obviously been ransacking the archives. "I think what we have here are the remains of a young Terrestrial woman named Zoe Fisher."

Chaia didn't recognize the name, though perhaps she had heard it once long ago—it seemed familiar in that faraway fashion.

"Zoe Fisher," Werner continued, "was out in the wildwood testing new isolation and immune-enhancement technologies when the research station lost its perimeters and went hot. She missed the evacuation. She was abandoned on Isis, captured by the local diggers and carried into their warren, where she died and was presumably devoured.''

The diggers didn't like fresh meat. They preferred their victuals predigested by decay enzymes. Ghastly, Chaia thought. She imagined, far too vividly, that early explorer, Zoe Fisher, lost in the woods with no hope of rescue, the toxic bios slowly but certainly eroding her defenses.

(Had it been raining back then? It was raining today: gently, on Humantown, and fiercely, far up the foothills of the Copper Mountains. The first explorers had never even felt the touch of Isian rain on their skin. Without their barriers of steel and latex and smartgels they had been horribly vulnerable; a single drop of rain contained enough Isian disease vectors to kill one of them literally within minutes.)

She thought of Zoe Fisher, lost in the rain, dragged unwilling into the deep and foul complexities of the digger tunnels. The picture was almost too vivid in her mind, too painfully close.

''An awful way to die,'' Chaia said.

''She was delirious at the end. In a way, almost happy.''

Delirious, Chaia thought. Like me. ''How do you know that?''

''She was in sporadic radio contact with another colonist. Some fragments of her dialogue were stored to local cyberspace and recovered when we archived the ruins. Zoe Fisher thought the bios of the planet had somehow entered her mind—that is, she believed she was talking to Isis itself. And not just Isis. All the living worlds of the galaxy, linked by some kind of shadowy quantum connection on the cellular level.''

Chaia was startled.

The bios, she thought. The voice of the forest. Had

the voice of the forest spoken to Zoe Fisher, down there in the darkness of the digger middens?

She said carefully, "Could there be any truth to that?"

Werner smiled. "I doubt it. We have some evidence that DNA-based life spread through the galaxy in a slow panspermia—at least that's the prevailing theory. But as far as we know, the only objects that can communicate at greater than relativistic speed are highly-engineered particle-pair links. Certainly not microscopic unicells."

She had dreamed, had she not, of the way a mind grows out of the chemically-charged spaces between neurons? Well, how *else* might a mind grow? In the bios of a planet? In the stew of virtual particles seething in the vacuum between the stars?

"But it's possible," she whispered, "isn't it?"

"Well, no, probably not. Zoe Fisher wasn't a biologist or a physicist, and she wasn't exactly presenting a scientific thesis. But she *was* an orphan, and she talked about Earth as an "orphan planet," cut off somewhere from the galactic bios. Essentially, she was talking about herself. She imagined she'd found the family she'd never had, even if it was a family of inconceivably vast intelligences."

But that's glib, Chaia thought. *That's not the whole story. It can't be.*

Nor was any of this the reason she had come to see Werner Eastman. He sat patiently, sharing the room with her, waiting for her to speak. The silence grew weighty until at last she confessed: "I'm worried about Gray. What I might be doing to him."

Werner's expression softened. He became a kind of father again, and she felt unbearably young and unbearably lonely next to him. "Chaia," he said. "Maybe you should be worried about yourself."

"No . . . it's Gray." She pictured Gray the way she had seen him last night, curled in bed, vulnerable for all his husky size. "He lost me once. . . ."

"Chaia, that's not true. I know Gray sees it that way. The Chaia Martine you used to be . . . the woman who almost died in the river . . . Gray loved her deeply. He's never abandoned the hope that some part of her would resurface in you. But that's simply not going to happen. You're what that Chaia Martine might have been, if she had been born and raised on Isis. That's all, and it ought to be enough. If he loved you on that basis, I would bless the marriage. But what moves Gray is a combination of loss and guilt. He misses his wife, and he blames himself because he couldn't save her from the river. He thinks he should have been out there with her in that awful storm, tying down beacon pylons. Well, he can't go back and rescue her. So he's doing the next best thing. He's marrying the woman he will always think of, on some level, as Chaia's ghost."

"No one has ever been nicer to me than Gray."

"And he'll go on being nice to you, year after year, and concealing his disappointment, year after year. And you deserve better than that."

Maybe. But Werner had failed to grasp the subtlety, the nuance of her relationship with Gray. *I am not a diagram,* she thought. *I'm not one of your cladistic charts.*

"I think my memory's coming back," she said, surprising herself.

"Pardon me?"

"My memory of Earth. Of being that other Chaia Martine."

Gray shook his head sadly. "It can't happen, Chaia.

It's even less plausible than the idea of talking planets."

"I saw Brussels in a videostory last night. And I recognized it. Not, you know, from a photograph or a book. I *knew* I'd been there. I had walked those streets."

"Brussels? On Earth?"

It sounded ridiculous—another delusion—but she blushed and nodded.

"Chaia, that couldn't be a genuine memory."

"Why not?"

"I was one of your therapists, remember? You ought to read your own file more closely. Chaia Martine was born and lived in Brisbane. She was educated in the Emigre Academy in Near Earth Orbit from the age of ten, then traveled to the Kuper Belt for pre-Isian training. She couldn't have seen Brussels because she was never there."

An Isian day is slightly longer than the Terrestrial day. The circadian rhythms of the colonists had been adjusted to suit. Still, something in the ancient human biology took notice of the discrepancy. Afternoons were long; nights could be endless.

Chaia went to bed alone, far later than she had planned. Her head was throbbing. A thousand half-formed ideas flickered through her mind. She fell asleep almost inadvertently, between one fevered notion and the next.

A rattle of thunder woke her deep in the belly of the night.

Storms came hard out of the west this time of year, rolling over the basinlands toward the spine of the continent. Wind whispered around the facets of her personal shelter.

You ought to read your own file more closely, Werner had said. But she never had, had she? She had explicitly avoided learning very much about the Chaia Martine who had once inhabited this body, the Terrestrial woman who had married Gray McInnes once long ago . . . not because she was incurious but because that woman was dead, and it was better, her therapists had insisted, not to disturb her ghost, not to confuse the issue of her own fragile identity.

But perhaps some ghosts needed disturbing.

Sleepless, Chaia took her personal scroll into her lap and addressed the Humantown archives.

She had been trained in archival management and it was simple enough for her to scroll into the medical and personnel records and root out Chaia Martine's detailed *curriculum vitae.* Chaia Martine—*that* Chaia Martine—had been groomed from birth for Isis duty. Biologically, she was the daughter of a Catalonian peasant couple who bartered a half-dozen viable embryos to the State Service in exchange for tax relief. She had been decanted in Brisbane and educated under the Colonial Necessities Act; her specialty had been agricultural genning and management, a skill lost to her now. She had met and married the young Gray McInnes at the orbital Emigre Academy.

And she had never been to Brussels.

Could there have been an unscheduled or unrecorded vacation? Well, perhaps so; but she doubted it. The State Service kept excellent records, especially in the case of a duty ward like Chaia Martine. If Chaia Martine had seen Brussels without registering the journey in her daily records, it represented a triumph of intrigue.

But Chaia Martine was nobody's rebel. She gave every evidence of being happy in her work. The prospect of traveling to Isis had apparently pleased her enormously. As had her marriage to Gray McInnes.

Then had come the Higgs translation, her first year on the planet, the terrible storm, her stupid heroism, lashing beacon pylons against the wind when the robots were disabled, and inevitably suffering for it—dying for it, essentially, when her skull was split and (according to the medical record) "large portions of the left and right parietal and occipital lobes were completely obliterated, with attendant massive blood loss and the penetration of untreated river water through the pontine and lumbar cisterns."

They could have let her body die, but enough of Chaia Martine remained intact that triage protocols dictated a cerebral rebuild. And thus the new Chaia Martine was born. With Gray McInnes, no doubt, weeping at her bedside.

Gray had avoided her assiduously for the first twelve years of her new life, because she had been, neurologically, a child—maturing in her adult body more rapidly than any normal child, but a child nevertheless. But he had remained loyal to her.

A loyalty born of guilt and grief, if Werner Eastman was to be believed.

But Gray loves me, Chaia thought. She had seen it a thousand times, in the way he looked at her, the way he held her. A love complete and forgiving and therefore terrible in its weight.

She scrolled deeper into the archives now, searching the name Zoe Fisher.

Zoe, the doomed colonist who had died in the digger warrens. Yes, here was Zoe, the records fragmentary, rescued from decaying atomic memory abandoned for years or pieced together from Terrestrial records equally incomplete. But enough to sense the shape of

Zoe Fisher, a clonal baby raised in the hothouse politics of twenty-second-century Earth, young, fragile, terribly naive. Zoe Fisher, born into a Devices and Personnel crèche in North America; lost for a time in the brothels of Tehran; educated in Paris, Madrid, Brussels—

Brussels.

Fat drops of rain pelted her face. Chaia hardly noticed them. The rain was bad, but the rain would inevitably get worse. A ridge of low pressure was flowing from the west, moisture from the equatorial oceans breaking against the Copper Mountains like a vast, slow wave.

She walked as if in a trance and found herself once more in the wildwood.

Had she been dreaming? Walking in her sleep? She was alone in the forest, well before dawn in the rainy dark. The darkness was nearly absolute; even with her corneal enhancements she could see only the scrim of foliage around her, and a glint that must have been the Copper River far down a slope of rock and slipgrass.

It was dangerous to be out at night in this weather. The rain and wind made it impossible for her insect-sized guardian remensors to follow her. She could not even say where she was or how she had come here, except that it looked like, now that she thought of it, the glade, her private glade where she came to be alone—the glade where she had seen the spiders take a human shape.

The spiders.

Chaia heard a rustly movement behind her.

She turned, knowing what she must expect to see.

She was not afraid this time; or if she was, the fear

was submerged in a thousand other incomprehensible feelings. She turned and saw the looming bulk of something as large as herself. It glistened in the rain that rushed from the forest canopy leaf-by-leaf, reflecting the firefly lamps she wore on her clothing. Its darkness was a deep amber darkness, and it smelled earthy and familiar.

She understood, now, that this was not something the spiders had done. The spiders were simply a vehicle. They were moved by something else, something vastly larger, something which had taken Zoe Fisher to its incomprehensible breast a hundred years ago and had recreated her now for some dire and essential purpose.

The creature spoke.

And Chaia Martine, at last, was ready to listen.

Gray McInnes found her in the glade a little before dawn, shivering and semiconscious; he carried her back through the wind-tossed forest to Humantown, to the infirmary, where she was dressed in warm hospital whites and put to bed with graduated doses of some gentle anxiolytic drug.

Chaia slept long and hard, oblivious to the wild wind beating at the shelters of Humantown.

She was aware, periodically, of the doctors at her bedside, of Gray (from time to time) or Werner Eastman, and once she thought she saw her therapy-mother Lizabeth Chopra, though nowadays Lizabeth worked in the orbital station a hundred miles above the Isian equator, so this must have been a dream.

She dreamed constantly and copiously. She dreamed about the ten million worlds of the Galactic Bios.

Zoe had explained all this to her in the glade above the Copper River.

Before the Earth was born, simple unicellular life had swept across the galaxy in a slow but inexorable panspermia. It was life doing what life always did, adapting to diverse environments, hot and frozen worlds, the icy rings of stars or their torrid inner planets. And all of this life carried within it something Zoe called a "resonance," a connection that linked every cell to every sibling cell in the way coherent subatomic particles linked Isis to Earth.

Life was pervasive, and life was a medium (immense, invisible) in which, in time, minds grew. Minds like flowers in a sunny meadow, static but ethereally beautiful.

Chaia was awake when the doctor (it was Dr. Plemyanikov, she saw, who wore a beard and sang tenor at the weekly Universalist services) told her he would be taking a sample of her cerebrospinal fluid for analysis.

She felt the needle in her neck just as the robotic anasthistat eased her back into dreamtime.

You have to warn them, Zoe Fisher insisted.

The walls of the clinic rattled with rain.

When she woke again, she found that the drugs, or something, had enhanced her sense of hearing. She could hear the rain battering the clinic with renewed intensity. She could hear the blood pulsing through her body. She could hear a cart rattling down the corridor outside her room. And she could hear Dr. Plemyanikov in the corridor with Werner Eastman, discussing her case.

—The contamination must have taken place during

her initial injuries, Plemyanikov said, *almost twenty years ago. . . .*

She opened her eyes sleepily and saw that Gray McInnes was with her, occupying a chair at her bedside. He smiled when he found her looking at him. "The doctors tell me you've been sick."

—*Some microorganism we didn't manage to flush out of her body after she was rescued from the river all those years ago, something almost unimaginably subtle and elusive. Lying dormant, or worse, riding on her neurological rebuild, feeding on it. A miracle it didn't kill her. . . .*

The minds that grew on and between the living worlds of the galaxy were sentient, but it was not a human sentience—it was nothing like a human sentience. Human sentience was a novelty, an accident. Once the minds of the Bios understood this, understood that mind could grow *inside the bodies of animals,* they regretted the deaths Isis had imposed on her first colonists and had attempted some small restitution by absorbing the mind of Zoe Fisher.

Gray McInnes took Chaia's hand and smiled. "You should have told me you were having problems."

—*Once we localized and identified the infectious agent, it was simple enough to engineer a cure. . . .*

Zoe Fisher had lived inside the Isian bios for more than a century, without body or location, preserved as a ghost, or a specimen, or an ambassador, or a pet— or some combination of all these things. She had even learned to control the local bios a little, in ways that never would have occurred to its native minds. The spiders, for instance, that had spoken to Chaia, or the delicately manipulated unicells that had invaded Chaia's broken skull and had made her meeting with Zoe possible.

"Chaia, there's nothing to be afraid of. Because the doctors say they can cure—"

—cure the dementia—

The meeting was important, because humanity needed to know that it was expanding into territory already occupied by minds hugely strange and not necessarily benign, minds diffuse and achingly beautiful but so different from human minds that their motives and desires could not always be predicted. The history of the future would be the history of the interaction between mankind and the Bios, between orphaned humanity and its ancient progenitors.

Gray said, "I couldn't sleep because of the storm. Too many bad memories, I guess. So I headed for the robotics bay to get a little work done. I saw the light in your shelter, but when I knocked and no one answered . . ."

—In fact, Plemyanikov said, *we've already administered a vaccine. . . .*

It was all alive with voices: the spaces between the stars, the spaces between any two living cells. The things that live there are the Lords of the Bios, Zoc had said, but they're invisible to human beings, and you have to tell people, Chaia, tell people about the Bios, *warn* people. . . .

"So I had the Humantown computer locate you, and I knew there was something wrong because you were out in the woods in a storm—God knows why—"

—She was rapidly approaching a crisis, and if Gray McInnes hadn't brought her out of the rain—

"But this time," Gray said, unable to conceal his pleasure, the gratification that welled out of him like fast white river water, "this time I wasn't too late."

—Fortunately the vaccine is already doing its work—

And something lurched inside Chaia, the voices fading now, even Zoe's strange and urgent voice, the voice of the forest, growing dim and oddly distant, and the word *cure* hung in her consciousness like a bright unpleasant light, and she struggled against the watery pressure of the sedatives and tried to tell Gray what was wrong, why they *mustn't* cure her, but all she could manage was "No, not like this, not this," before the tide of drugs took her and she slept again.

The storm broke during the night. By morning the winds had gentled. The air was cool, and the clouds were rag-ends and afterthoughts in the blue Isian sky.

It had been postponed a month while Chaia recovered, but in the end the wedding was a simple and pretty ceremony.

The vaccine had flushed the infection from her body. Her hallucinations were as distant now as bad dreams, fading memories, feverish delusions, and she knew who she was: she was Chaia Martine, nothing more, and she was marrying the man who loved her.

She walked up the aisle with Gray McInnes—good and loyal Gray, who had finally saved her from the river. Rector Gooding stood beneath the black circle that was the symbol of the Mysteries and said the binding words. Then Gray took the golden yubiwa from a filigreed box, and he placed one ring on her finger and she placed one on his, and they kissed.

She was fully recovered, the doctors had told her. She was sane now. The delusions were finished, and she recognized them as symptoms of her lingering illness, refractions of half-learned history, a peculiarly Isian madness that had ridden into her brain when she was opened to the planet like a broken egg.

She left the church with Gray at her side, flower

petals strewn at her feet, and she thought nothing of the spider that had nested at the side of the rectory, or the sound of the wind in the brella trees, or the white clouds that moved through the clearing sky like the letters of an unknown language.

THE SUSPENDED FOURTH
by Paul Levinson

Paul Levinson, Ph.D., is the author of the novel *The Silk Code,* and non-fiction books *Mind at Large, The Soft Edge* and *Digital McLuhan,* as well as more than 150 articles on the philosophy of technology. His science fiction has appeared in *Analog, Amazing,* and the anthology *Xanadu III.* He is also the president of The Science Fiction and Fantasy Writers of America, and visiting professor of communications at Fordham Univeristy.

The second planet around the G5 star in the Peacock was near Earth in more ways than one. Only nineteen light-years from Sol, it was little more than two months away by the faster-than-light star drives of the mid-twenty-second century. Its climate was a tad cooler than raw Earth's, but it sloshed with frothy seas and an atmosphere breathable to humans. It sported half a dozen land masses of varying size, all tied together in a biosphere conducive to all manner of creature from viruses to viverrines, butterflies to birds. Lots more of those, especially, than on Earth. But not so much as a primate, let alone anything with humanlike intelligence.

This was a planet, then, like Earth in many ways— but not like Earth in at least one way, the way that had become an obsession to the human species as it combed the stars for someone to talk to, someone other than humans. . . .

Twice the science teams had come, holding back the tourists and the settlers, pleading with governments and corporations back home to stay away a little longer, lest they trample some delicate intelligence hiding in the woods or seas—or destroy some fragile technology, a clue or a sign, that an intelligence might have managed to leave behind. But the science teams found nothing. Not in their extensive DNA sampling and genome mapping of organisms, not in their sifting and staring at the stuff of this planet until even the scanning equipment was bleary-eyed.

Nothing except a lot of fine feathers, a lot of fine birds who chirped in captivating triads, major and minor, and the occasional suspended fourth. . . .

The first settlement group arrived an Earth-year later.

"I love it," Yevgenia Prima said to her husband, Jack Swirl, as they took in the lush green foliage that worked its way down to the sea, at what would be the edge of their property. "It looks just like California, no?"

Jack smiled, put his arm around her. "More like Cape Cod than California," he said. "You've got California on the brain because of all that Mamas and Papas music you've been listening to."

"This place seems to be like that music," Yevgenia replied. "I heard something that sounded just like it in the trees, only yesterday—"

She was cut off in mid-sentence by a bolt of lightning that made Jack cry out in shock, and killed her on the spot.

A science team was back ten weeks later. Jack pleaded with the leader to let him stay. She was adamant that he could not.

"I'm sorry, Mr. Swirl. Death at this point—for any reason, even a lightning bolt from the sky—means the settlers must leave. Could be a symptom of some larger problem," Jenny Teng tried to explain.

"Could even be a sign of some intelligence acting to protect itself or this planet from our alien colonization," Ralph Giorgio, her second in command, added.

"You mean like on Orchard World?" Jack pressed. "Where the fruit trees were given a means of self-defense by their planters, whoever they were? I know all about that—Yevgenia's cousin was on the team that made that discovery. It was one of the things that inspired her . . ." His voice choked.

Jenny put an understanding hand on his shoulder. "It's hard to lose someone you love, I know."

"She was killed by a lightning bolt, for God's sake!" Jack pulled away. "You people think what? Some invisible intelligence that controls the weather on this planet hurled it down like Zeus?"

"That's what we're here to find out, Mr. Swirl," Jenny replied.

Jenny and Ralph were exoclimatologists—logical choices, since the proximate agent of death was a lightning bolt. The rest of the six-person team consisted of the standard exos—botanist, zoologist, archaeologist, technologist—found on every science team.

Jenny and Ralph spent six months hanging out near extinct volcanoes, mapping cloud formations, keeping careful track of every thunderstorm, every raindrop, every bit of bad or unusual weather they or their equipment could find. They found nothing out of the ordinary.

"Yevgenia's death was just bad luck—happenstance," Jenny said, as she finished her report. It would be relayed by tachyon spin to the proper authorities. Its conclusions would reopen the planet for settlement, once and for all.

Ralph shrugged. "Sometimes life is like that. Not everything has a reason."

"Jack Swirl's not going to like it."

"He was the one who said how ridiculous it was to suppose that his wife was killed by some alien intelligence," Ralph said. "Our conclusion should satisfy him on that score."

"He thought it was preposterous to think that his wife was murdered by a bolt from on high, yes," Jenny replied. "But he'll want to find some meaning, some larger purpose, in her death. He won't be satisfied in the least."

He was not.

Jack Swirl returned to the planet—now named Peacock Planet, even though it had no peacocks, just a lot of other pretty birds—to take up permanent, brooding residence.

He ran into Jenny two Earth-years later. By this time, more than fifteen hundred settlers had happily put down roots on four of the continents. None had died of old age—or anything else—as yet. Forty-three children had been born.

"What are you doing here?" Jack asked, grumpily.

"Same thing as you," Jenny replied. "Helping out on this construction project. This continent has my favorite views."

"I'm just passing through. You got tired of the science team?"

Jenny nodded. "I needed some time off. Eight years straight on science, with no result, was enough for me—at least for now. It's no fun coming up empty-handed."

"Who told you life's supposed to be fun?"

She ignored the jibe. "We may have to get resigned to the fact that there is no intelligence out here, other than us. Even on Orchard World—the intelligence of the planters is just hypothesis. No one's actually seen any alien intelligent being as yet."

Jack looked off into the distance. "So why did you come back here? Peacock has even fewer traces of possible intelligence than Orchard. As in, we apparently have none."

"I love the music," Jenny replied.

"The birds?"

"Yes," she said. "They're so soothing. It's like having a musical accompaniment just about everywhere you go. Hear that?"

A sweet madrigal emanated in the distance.

"Yevgenia taught rock 'n' roll in grad school back on Earth. She loved the music, too," Jack said.

"But not you?"

"I used to," Jack said. "Now . . ."

"I understand," Jenny said. "How about you help me with this porch?"

The porch work was actually a planting of a genetically tailored white birch sapling, which would grow in three months into a beautifully wide wooden porch.

Jack shook his head no. "Sorry. I've got my own work to do."

A terra-molding bull-droid crashed on the site three weeks later. Five people were crushed, one died. Jenny was about twenty feet away—she was unhurt, but very shaken.

Jack came back to see her, as soon as he heard.

"Do you remember what the birds were singing, the night before?" he asked.

"What? What do the birds have to do with this?"

"I'm not sure," Jack replied.

"They were chirping something that sounded deep-classic, I think—maybe Bachlike, I don't know. You know Bach?" Jenny asked.

"Of course I know Bach," Jack said. "That seems to be pretty common on this landmass. You heard nothing unusual—nothing discordant?"

"The unusual thing is that the damned bull-droid crashed!"

"Not really," Jack said. "You said so yourself: accidents happen. Circuits aren't perfect, you know that. Every once in a while, they malfunction. There's no particular astonishment in that. The deaths on this planet are still well below the acceptable statistical level." He winced, involuntarily.

Jenny softened. "So what are you hoping to find here?"

"Explanation, understanding," Jack said. "Not in the deaths themselves. But . . ."

"In the birds?" Jenny asked.

"Yeah. Maybe. It's just a feeling . . ."

"Tell you what—I know a splendid ornithologist—"

"Forget it," Jack said. "I've already interviewed six of them—Peacock's flapping with them, no surprise. They've been no help at all."

"You don't know Dinesh Rapadia," Jenny said. "He just got here last month. He's not only a birdman, but an accomplished digi-musician."

Dinesh's patio opened onto a field of wildflowers, velvet and violet. He offered his guests apple iced tea—pressed from a variety of apple that came with caffeine. "This comes from Mother Earth herself," he said, "and no one knows who created it. The old girl still has some surprises."

Jenny and Jack nodded, and sipped appreciatively.

"What was your profession, if you don't mind my asking, before you came here?" Dinesh asked Jack.

"Journalism," Jack replied. "An old family tradition. But I'd had enough of it. I met Yevgenia, we fell in love, we decided to come here and live like people used to . . ."

"Ah, yes," Dinesh replied. "So, you have no scientific experience in the study of birds?"

"Right, I have none," Jack began, defensively, "but that doesn't mean—"

"It's all right," Dinesh interrupted with a placating hand. "This means I take your point of view *more* seriously, not less. McLuhan said people inside a field are numb to its environment—they see everything too often. But people outside—they have the keener eye for something in the environment that may be significant, but was too obvious for the experts to notice. . . . You know McLuhan's work?"

"No," Jack said, and looked at Jenny.

She shook her head no.

"Not to worry," Dinesh said. "few people do these days. He was a philosopher who lived in the twentieth century—he said a fish is the last creature you should ask for the complete story of water, because the fish lives totally in the water, and thus knows nothing of the impact of the shore upon the water, you see. Anyway . . . you, Jack Swirl, are a man who might have fresh ideas about birds, precisely because you are not someone who has been totally immersed in that field. So . . . tell me what you know."

Jack told him about the last moments of Yevgenia's

life, and the conversation they had had about the
Mamas and the Papas and the birds—

"The Mamas and the Papas?" Dinesh asked.

"Yes," Jack replied. "They were a rock 'n' roll singing group in the twentieth century—"

"Oh, yes, I know who they are," Dinesh said. "They
were part of the 'flower generation' . . . about half a
century before the synthetic age in music, when everything became digital, even the generation of voices . . ."

Jack nodded. "That's why Yevgenia loved them so."

"I share her taste," Dinesh said. "There's something
authentic about those last analog recordings that have
come down to us, real voices singing out to us from
the past. But tell me, what was it in the birdsongs of
Peacock that you think reminded Yevgenia of the
Mamas and Papas?"

"I'm not sure . . ."

"Well, let's put it this way, then," Dinesh said.
"What is the most distinguishing feature of the Mamas
and Papas' singing—a characteristic that someone
could hear in the birdsong, and say: Ah! That recalls
the Mamas and Papas for me?"

"You asked me if I heard anything discordant,"
Jenny offered.

"Yes," Jack said. "It's a theory I have. I've listened
over and over again to every Mamas and Papas' song
I could find, and there's a chord that's prominent in
most of them. And . . . to me, that sound seems
fraught with danger. It's a kind of clashing sound, one
that makes you sit up and take notice. I think Yevgenia heard something like that from the birds here,
the day before she died."

"Let's see if we can specifically identify that sound
in the Mamas and Papas," Dinesh said, "so we can
know just what we're listening for in the birds. One

moment, please. Let me get my library." Dinesh stood up, then walked quickly into his dwelling.

"I told you he was good," Jenny said.

"We'll see," Jack replied.

Dinesh returned with a palm-sized device. "The speakers aren't the greatest on this, but they should serve our purposes. This has recordings going back to the beginning of the twentieth century."

Jack nodded.

"Mamas and Papas, mid-twentieth century, list of recordings, please," Dinesh instructed his device.

" 'California Dreamin' . . . 'Monday, Monday' . . ." the device began—

"Thank you," Dinesh replied. The listing stopped.

"Shall we listen to the first—'California Dreamin'?" he asked Jack.

"Yes. That was Yevgenia's favorite."

"And please identify for me the chord that you have in mind—the one that breathes impending peril," Dinesh said.

He instructed the device to play "California Dreamin' " . . .

"There!" Jack said. "That's it!"

Dinesh froze the recording. The word "day" hung in the air, at the end of the first verse. . . .

"Hmmm . . . yes," Dinesh said. "A suspended fourth. An unsettled chord—with the third moved out of its place to the fourth. It does give the feeling of waiting for the other shoe to drop—a transitional moment that hangs in the balance, a conduit to something else."

"So you think the birds on this planet sing a suspended fourth when they sense a lightning storm in the works?" Jenny asked.

"I think the birds here sing a suspended fourth when they sense a death in the works," Jack replied.

"But I didn't hear anything like it before the bull-droid crash," Jenny insisted.

"So maybe you're tone-deaf," Jack said.

"Funny," Jenny said. "But if I can recognize the suspended fourth in this recording, I can recognize it in the wild."

"Let's put this to the test," Dinesh said. "We can do it scientifically. We have two competing hypotheses. One—the far more plausible at this point, I must say—is that birds on this planet are attuned to emerging weather patterns. Birds are like that on Earth. Except here, they sing a suspended fourth—to warn their relatives about thunderstorms. Two—Jack's theory—is that the suspended fourth is somehow a warning about impending death."

"We have no way to test the second hypothesis," Jenny said, "other than waiting around for another fatality."

"So we test the first," Dinesh said. "If it proves out, we'll have our answer."

In the evenings and weekends of the next six months, Dinesh, Jenny, and Jack separately recorded 228 sets of birdsongs; 7 were succeeded within twenty-four hours by thunderstorms with lightning; not a single one of those 7 had a suspended fourth.

The three reconvened.

"Maybe we didn't get the right birds," Jenny suggested.

"Always a possibility," Dinesh said. "But at this point, we have to consider that thunderstorms per se have no connection to the suspended fourths."

"My point in the first place," Jack said, glumly.

"So what do we do now?" Jenny asked.

"We examine the second hypothesis," Dinesh said. "We wait for death."

Jack got the call, three months later, on the northernmost landmass, Feather.

"I'm down here on Beak," Jenny said, slightly out of breath. "A woman, about thirty, apparently died in her sleep last night."

"I'll be right down," Jack replied.

Dinesh joined them. "It still happens," he said. "Death by natural causes at those ages. From what I was able to learn, she apparently had a history of it in her family—aneurisms in the brain. She must have known someone in Records back on Earth—they never would have cleared her for settleship, otherwise."

"Are they going to investigate?" Jenny asked.

"Nah, no real reason to," Dinesh replied. "With four thousand settlers here now, and two hundred some-odd births, three deaths is still way under the alarm level."

"Good," Jenny said.

"But we'll conduct our own little investigation, of a different kind," Dinesh said. He pulled several little sound devices out of his pocket, and gave one each to Jenny and Jack. "Listen to this." Dinesh's fingertip touched a colored oval on his device. A sixty-second collage of suspended fourths—of various amplitudes, frequencies, and durations—ensued. "So," Dinesh said. "Now we conduct our interviews."

They each interviewed ten different people from the area, randomly chosen from the population.

Jack approached a blonde, about twenty, as she was about to take her lunch break.

"Excuse me, Nancy Keyes? I'm Jack Swirl—"

"Nice name." She smiled.

"Thank you. I wonder if you could spare a few minutes, and help me with a survey I'm conducting—"

"I have very normal preferences," Nancy said.

"Well, this is about the birds."

"Okay." She smiled again.

"I'd like you to listen to this, and tell me if you think you heard anything like it last night." Jack touched the oval, which called forth the sixty-second collage.

Nancy shook her head slowly. "You mean, did the birds sing like that last night?"

"Yes," Jack said.

"No," Nancy replied. "The birds I heard were much sweeter. With a kind of underlying refresho-beat."

"You sure?"

"Well, I guess sweetness is in the ears of the beholder. You want to come by my place tonight and listen?"

Jack had dinner instead with Jenny and Dinesh.

Their surveys produced the same results.

Two of the thirty subjects refused to answer any questions. Of the remaining twenty-eight, not a single one recalled hearing anything that sounded like a suspended fourth from the birds of Peacock—not the night before, not at any time.

Jack sighed. "It still doesn't mean I'm wrong—it just means we don't have the evidence."

"Jack, there comes a time when . . ." Jenny began, then thought the better of it.

"Surely the birds aren't prescient," Dinesh said, and put a local mushroom, thoroughly tested and sauteed, in his mouth. "A woman in apparently perfect health dies in her sleep of an aneurism, how on Earth—or on Peacock—could birds, anyone, possibly know that the night before?"

"The birds would have to be incredibly careful observers of the human condition," Jenny mused. "They would have to have recognized something in the woman's expression, demeanor, that alerted them that she was about to die that way. All but impossible, considering that our species arrived here such a short time ago."

"Right," Dinesh said. "Even if we start with the assumption that the birds are somehow observing events on this planet, and try to sound some kind of warning with that suspended fourth, for them, this death could not be much more than a random occurrence—unpredictable. So the absence of a suspended fourth in the instance of this woman dying disproves nothing . . ." He fiddled with his knife . . .

Then he suddenly lunged at Jack's face—

Jenny shrieked. "Dinesh!"

Jack's reflexes were quick. His hand was around Dinesh's wrist. The knife dropped to the cobblestone of the outdoor terrace.

"Okay, okay," Dinesh said, and pulled his hand free. "I've made my point. My apologies."

Jack glared.

"For God's sake, what point?" Jenny asked.

"No one could have predicted, last night, or even a few minutes ago, that I would jab at Jack like that," Dinesh said. "So, in that regard, this episode is just like the woman dying."

"So—?" Jenny began.

"But what I just did goes beyond someone dying unexpectedly in her sleep," Dinesh continued. "It shows much more convincingly that the birds are not connected to death."

"But you didn't kill me, didn't even hurt me, had no intention of doing either, so this has no relevance to the birds," Jack said.

"Yes, it does," Dinesh said. "Think about it: how could the birds have known the result of my action once it started? Look at how shocked both of you were. Why didn't the birds blare out a suspended fourth as soon as I made up my mind and tensed my muscles to come at you? Or even at the moment my arm went out? Listen . . ." Dinesh put a finger to his mouth. "Hear anything different?"

The same distant, soft variation on a serenade that they had been hearing all evening was all they heard now.

"I'm sorry," Dinesh said to Jack. "But I think the birds are no harbingers of death, or even danger—what just happened at our table proves it. And we've already proven that they have no connection to lightning."

"What about a connection to lightning that causes death?" Jenny asked, looking at Jack, desperate now to give him some thread to hold on to.

Dinesh shrugged in frustration. "How could we ever demonstrate that? It's such a rare occurrence. The first science teams made extensive recordings of the birdsongs on this planet. I had them scanned for suspended fourths—there were only three of them in more than five hundred hours of recordings. And none presaged lightning storms, or deaths—"

"Deaths as they recorded it," Jack objected. "Our science teams couldn't possibly have tracked the death of every organism in their vicinity, or even every potentially dangerous weather pattern."

"That may be so, but you can't support a hypothesis with unknown evidence," Dinesh said. "Our working theory would be, what? That the birds sound a warning when they see events—weather conditions, special kinds of storms in the making—that they know will cause death, have caused death in the past? Except we have no evidence that suspended fourths have anything to do with even bad weather on this planet, let alone death." He shook his head. "No. We would have to wait for another deadly thunderstorm, and who knows when that will happen."

"How about volcanoes, earthquakes, fires—there are other causes of death," Jenny said.

"You won't find them on Peacock in volcanoes and earthquakes," Dinesh said. "You know that. This planet is remarkably stable in those areas. As for fires—well, sure, that could happen. But my guess would be that, even with a deadly fire, we won't hear the suspended fourth. Jack, we may have to face the possibility that what Yevgenia heard was just coincidence. For all we know, it may be years or more before anyone hears a suspended fourth again from the birds here."

He was concerned enough about Jack's feelings not to say that it was also entirely possible that Yevgenia had not heard the suspended fourth in the first place.

But Jack knew that was what Dinesh was thinking.

Jack got up from the table, and took one look at Jenny.

"Thank you," he said softly, and left.

His phone rang almost fifteen months later, to the day.

"Jack—"

"Jenny—how are you?"

"I spoke to three people who heard it," she said.

He knew, instantly, what she was saying.

"When?" His mouth was dry.

"Late last night," Jenny replied.

"You're not just saying this to make me feel good?" But he knew Jenny would not do that.

"No. I just finished the interviews—the three folks I spoke to were sure. I've been quietly distributing Dinesh's sixty-second collage all year, figuring it couldn't hurt, and I got the call last night. Apparently lots of people here heard something a little after nine in the evening that sounded like a suspended fourth. I flew in first thing this morning with my own little player and confirmed it."

"Are you okay?" It suddenly came all over Jack that, if his wild theories were correct, she could be in trouble.

"I'm all right. The sky is clear, it's a beautiful day." Just like the day that Yevgenia died. "Where are you, exactly?" Jack asked.

Jenny told him.

"I'll be there in ninety minutes," Jack said. Travel between the landmasses was very fast.

Jenny was waiting to meet him at the shuttle-port. The weather on Wings was indeed lovely—not a cloud in the sky. Jenny looked good, too.

"Let's not be taken in by the blue skies," Jack said to her. "A bolt out of the blue may be just the sort of thing the birds try to warn about."

"I know," Jenny said. "I thought of that. But weather's my profession. I spoke to the people at the laboratory after we got off the phone—I've got the top man on this planet, and the best equipment, scrutinizing every vector on Wings and the nearest continents. The computers say there's less than a three percent chance of any rain activity, let alone thunderstorms, in this area. You can't get much more conclusive than that."

"Well, reality—what actually happens—always trumps a projection," Jack said.

"Of course," Jenny said. "I'm just saying—"

"I know," Jack said. "You were right to do the weather projections. I just don't want us to let our guard down. Can we go to the exact spot where they heard the suspended fourth?"

Jenny nodded, and flagged a ground transport.

Wings—the newest and last of the landmasses to have been opened up to settlement—was bustling with all kinds of activity.

"You know, it could be dangerous to go to the exact spot where the suspended fourth was heard," Jack said. "If I'm right about what that means, some kind of event leading to a fatality could occur there." He took his eyes off the pageantry of people and colors whirring by, and looked at Jenny.

"I realize that," Jenny said. "But what choice do we have if we want to investigate this?"

"You don't have to risk your life on this," Jack said. "You set the wheels in motion, you got me down here, that's more than enough. I'm the one with the personal mission."

"I'm doing what I want to," Jenny said. She pulled a sound device out of her pocket. "I interviewed seven more people who were in the area last night. Four said they recalled hearing something like the suspended fourth."

"Good work," Jack said. "One other question, though. How come you waited until morning to call me?"

"I was struggling with whether another wild goose chase would do you more harm than good."

*   *   *

They reached the site a few minutes later—an outdoor café that had sprung up on a hill on the side of the road, specializing in the local equivalent of clams and mussels, in zesty Italian sauces whose recipes had made the trip across the stars.

"Customers were having a late-night bite here yesterday when they heard the suspended fourth," Jenny said. "They say it was distant, but clear. The birds apparently repeated it several times, in the midst of what one man said was a neo-blues interlude. There were about twenty other people sitting around the tables then. This was the primary location."

"Looks like about twice that number now," Jack said. "Shall we join them? It looks like we can still get lunch."

Jenny nodded. A waiter seated them, and gestured to the menu-screens embedded on the table.

Jenny lit hers up. "The locals swear by the seafood," she said. "It's all been tested a dozen times to Sunday for human consumption, of course. You'll have no problem with it—unless you have uncorrected allergies."

"I love seafood," Jack said, and quickly lit up his menu and pressed the clams marinara. Then he looked at the sky.

"I still can't get over how much this sun looks like Sol," he said. "Maybe a little bigger, but the same color."

Jenny placed her order—for steamers—and stole a quick squint at the local sun. "Delta Pavonis is a bit bigger—and brighter—then Sol, but we're a bit farther away, which is why it's just a little more chilly here, on average, than it is back on Earth." She breathed in the fresh air. "But it suits me just fine."

"So you're becoming a permanent resident?" Jack said, his eyes still on the sky.

"Yeah," Jenny replied. "I'm working at the local climate lab on Beak now. I guess I've had enough starfaring for a while—"

"Jeez," Jack said. "What's that?"

Jenny followed his finger to the sky. A large nimbus cloud had suddenly appeared, and was drifting toward the sun.

"So much for your fine scientific projections—" Jack began.

Their waiter approached, dishes in hand.

Jack glowered at Jenny, the sky, the waiter, as a plate of clams marinara was laid in front of him.

"Is everything all right, sir? Can I get you something to drink? Chablis?"

"Water's fine," Jack grunted.

"Same for me," Jenny said.

The waiter nodded and retreated.

Jack pushed his chair away from the table.

Jenny whispered. "What do you propose we do? Tell everyone on this patio to take cover? One of the women I interviewed heard the suspended fourth across the street. A kid on a bicycle heard it down the road, maybe half a mile away. There's no telling where the lightning might strike, or even if there will be lightning at all. All we have so far is a dark cloud that I admit our projections missed."

"You're crazy," Jack said. He stalked off to find the café's proprietor.

Jenny followed a minute later. She found Jack gesturing to Leonardo, one of the owners.

Leonardo looked at her for guidance—she had impressed him with her intelligence earlier in the day.

"He may be right," Jenny said quickly, about Jack. "There could be some really nasty weather coming this way. Maybe you should urge everyone to go indoors until it blows over."

"We have no room inside," Leonardo protested.

"Well, then let them take their plates, and go someplace safe," Jenny said.

Now Leonardo looked at her like she was insane. He cursed in Italian, then made an announcement on the loudspeaker.

Jack and Jenny retrieved their food, and made their way to an indoor mall across the street. The place was soon packed with clanking plates and discontented patrons of the outdoor café.

Jack took a look outside. The gray cloud hung overhead.

"We should get some kind of public announcement out to the people around here," Jack said.

Jenny made the calls. Outdoor vendors took cover, cursing. Toddlers were scooped up from beaches and playgrounds by their parents. A recalcitrant couple ignored the announcement, and proceeded to make love behind a huge maplelike tree at the edge of the forest that trimmed the settlement. . . .

But the cloud was gone half an hour later, without incident.

Jack and Jenny took the slow way to the shuttleport—a long walk on a road that turned into a flat, grassy footpath. Jack took her hand, as they approached the gate. "Thank you," he said, quietly, "for at least believing in me enough to back me up back there."

"I do believe in you," Jenny said. "I admire people willing to move heaven and earth to pursue an idea—

that's what got our species out here in the first place. But . . ."

"I know," Jack said. "You don't need to say it."

"I have to say it," Jenny said. "I believe in *you,* but that doesn't mean I—or you—have to keep believing in this idea. You've given enough in pursuit of this suspended fourth—you've suspended your life for it. You don't have to do it anymore."

"I don't know if I can give it up," Jack said.

Jenny looked at him. Then she kissed him, and pulled away. "Well, you think about it," she said. "And if you think you might be able to give it up, you'll know where to find me. My shuttle leaves in the evening, then I'm back on Beak." And she turned and walked away.

Jack looked up at the sky, then through the gate of the shuttle-port, and then at Jenny's receding body. She was receding too fast. He liked what she looked like.

He thought about running after her.

He turned again to the shuttle-gate—his shuttle would be boarding in twenty minutes.

He looked again at Jenny—and something caught his eye, in the corner of the sky. . . .

He walked a few feet from the gate. He strained to get a better look, but couldn't quite make it out—

A call for shuttle-boarding boomed forth, but he could barely hear it.

He was concentrating on Jenny. He could barely see her now.

But the thing in the sky was clearer. It was gleaming . . .

"Jenny! Jenny!" He shouted, and ran after her, full speed.

He was in a race—he on the ground, the machine

in the sky. It seemed like they both were rushing in convergent lines that led straight to Jenny. The question was which one would get to her first . . .

"Jenny!" he shouted again, and again, but she was still too far away to hear him . . .

His blood pounded in his ears, his breath cut through his chest . . .

"Jenny, look at the sky . . ."

It was clear as day to him now. A goddamn bull-droid, way off course, hurtling in the sky where it had no place being, right toward Jenny . . .

"Jenny!"

Must have been some damn programming error that had made it crash two years ago, and now this one . . .

It was making so much noise—how could she not hear it—

"Jenny!"

Now she turned to look at him, then up at the thing in the sky.

It was whirling way out of control—

She tried to dodge it, but there was no telling where exactly this would crash—

It looked to Jack like it was making contact with her now, but she was still running, so that must be an illusion, and he was so close—

It hit the ground and burst into flames that engulfed Jenny, just as he reached her . . .

He grabbed her hand and pulled her away from the flames . . .

They ran and stumbled and both fell down. The bull-droid exploded, and the world went red and black—

*   *   *

His body was on top of hers. The air felt hot.

He held her face in his hands and kissed it all over. "Jenny, please be okay . . ."

Her arms went around him and her mouth against his . . .

"I'm sorry I didn't believe you," she murmured.

"It's okay, it's okay, you're all right." And they stayed that way for a long time. . . .

Dinesh flew in the next day, and joined them for lunch at the outdoor café.

The site of the bull-droid crash was a blackened scar, plainly visible down the road.

"You were right, I was wrong," Dinesh said. He gestured to the burned patch, and extended his hand to Jack.

Jack shook it, and motioned Dinesh to sit.

"Thank you," Jack said, "but I can't say I understand exactly how. What made the birds warn us about this bull-droid crash, and not the one two years ago?"

"They had no experience with our bull-droids," Dinesh said, and ordered the mussels in a light wine sauce. "How could they? No bull-droids were on this planet until we arrived."

"So they learned from the first experience—the first time the bull-droid crashed," Jenny said.

"Precisely," Dinesh replied. "Even on Earth, birds are extremely observant—they can make very fine discriminations about where food is, the best route to travel, based on the tiniest changes in the environment."

"So they observed the defective bull-droid the first time," Jack said.

"Right," Dinesh said. "They saw something in its behavior before it crashed that was unusual—however

slight a difference, but unusual. And they associated
the aftermath—the deadly crash—with this slight difference. Perhaps the bull-droid trembled when it flew,
perhaps it listed a few feet, who knows. But whatever
it was, it tipped off the birds. So, when they saw it
again, they knew what it could lead to. So they sang
out the suspended fourth."

"What the hell kind of intelligent birds are these?"
Jack asked.

"Not necessarily intelligent—but well-bred, or genetically engineered, to be able to sound alarums like
this," Dinesh replied.

"Maybe they evolved that way through natural se-
lection," Jenny said. "How can we know that these
guardian angels were deliberately bred to sound
warnings?"

"Think of who benefits from their suspended
fourths," Dinesh said. "The birds weren't hurt in the
bull-droid crashes—we were the victims. And birds
usually sit out thunder and lightning just fine. No—
they were bred to benefit someone else—their breeders. And our species is lucky enough to have been
the beneficiary."

"I knew it," Jack said. "I knew it about the lightning." And his eyes got teary, but he reached out for
Jenny's hand.

"Yes, you were right about that, too. We were close
to understanding that before. There must be some sort
of subtle, peculiar weather condition on this planet
that engenders sudden thunderstorms with lightning.
The birds were bred to alert everyone to that. But
even more impressive—"

"They were bred to learn—to learn about new dangers, and work those into their repertoires," Jenny
said.

"Yes," Dinesh said. His mussels arrived.

"There's nothing like those birds back on Earth," Jack said.

"Not that we know of, no," Dinesh replied.

"So who bred them here?" Jack asked.

"The science teams found no trace of any intelligent manipulation on this planet," Jenny said.

Dinesh smiled. "Well, it seems our California Dreamers proved them wrong."

The birds sang something in the distance. It wasn't "California Dreamin," but it came to rest in a wash of new horizons nonetheless. . . .

COMING OF AGE
by Edo van Belkom

Edo van Belkom is the author and editor of more than
a dozen books, and has published over one hundred
fifty short stories in a wide variety of magazines and
anthologies. He has won both the Bram Stoker and Au-
rora Awards for this short fiction with twenty of his best
tales collected in *Death Drives a Semi*. His fourth novel,
Teeth, will be published early in 2001. His website is
located at www.vanbelkom.com.

Jack Murray was awakened from a light sleep by the
sound of something heavy thumping onto the floor.
"William?" he called.

"Yeah, Dad, it's me."

Jack nodded slightly. Of course it was William. Who
else would it be?

"I just went over to Peckham Farm to see if I could
find any more solar panels."

"What do we need with more solar panels?" asked
Jack, shifting in his chair and feeling his bones ache
with stiffness. "We've already got six we're not using."

"I know, I know . . . I was going to try and get
them all hooked up and working."

"Why? We have more electricity than we can use now."

"But if we have to keep a light on through the
night, or run a machine during off hours, the batteries
won't last long."

Jack sighed, understanding the undercurrent of what

his son was saying all too well. At last Jack nodded. "So, did you find any panels?"

"No, but I did find a battery." He hefted the battery off the floor, barely able to lift it higher than his waist.

Watching his son struggle with the weight, Jack wondered how he'd managed to carry it all the way back from Peckham Farm. He'd been wondering about such things for some time now. Ever since his stroke he'd had no other choice but to sit and think, to take stock of his life and a long hard look at the future.

Well, the future hadn't looked very promising for years.

And now it was absolutely terrifying.

William dragged the battery through the house and out the back door. Jack could hear the thing clunk down the wooden steps, then only silence as it was pulled across the sandy ground to the shed where the rest of the generators, pumps, and batteries were housed.

The boy would work there for hours, jury-rigging the panels and batteries together so he could squeeze a few more watts of power out of the day. That would leave Jack alone in the house for a while with nothing else to do but sit and think.

His first thought was of *the boy*. Strange thing to call your twenty-five-year-old son, but that's what he was—a boy.

Always had been. Always would be.

They'd come to Effette IV forty years earlier, eighty-seven bright-eyed settlers eager to establish a new world better than the one they'd left behind.

All went well in the early years as the few dozen families carved out a life for themselves in the planet's rich and untamed wilderness. With a little planning and a lot of hard work, the land proved to be as bountiful as Earth's had once been. Life soon became peaceful and perfect, everything they dreamed it could be.

But it was all too good to last.

About fifteen years after their arrival, the settlers noticed that the development of their children's secondary sex characteristics seemed a bit slow. Those few children that had been born on the ship prior to the landing managed to squeak through puberty, but those born on Effette IV after the landing were not maturing into adulthood. They'd all ended up like William, grown to the size of a man, but without any of the characteristics that distinguished a man from a boy. His Adam's apple had never appeared; he was without facial hair; his body never gained muscle mass; and his voice had remained at a high pitch. Similar problems were experienced by the girls whose bodies failed to develop breasts or fill out in any other appreciable way.

The settlers soon realized that the children were also failing to develop primary sex characteristics, such as testes and ovaries, which were of course necessary for reproduction.

So what was the problem?

On Effette IV, it was a question for the ages.

Jack and the other settlers had spent nearly thirty years testing their food, water, sunlight, and air but had never found an answer. In time, two main theories were postulated. One suggested that Effette IV had some element or chemical unknown to human science that inhibited human sexual development. The other theory suggested that Effette IV lacked some element or chemical unknown to human science that fostered human sexual development.

Whatever the reason, the result was the same—a colony doomed to die out a generation after landing on their new world. The settlers had tried reassembling the generation ship they'd arrived in, but over the years it had been thoroughly cannibalized with many of the parts drastically modified to suit new applications. They also began broadcasting distress calls, but since Effette IV had been selected for colonization because it was so far removed from other colonized planets, there was little chance anyone would receive the message, let alone reach Effette IV, before the entire colony died out.

Jack took a deep breath and let out a long sigh. It wasn't the way he'd envisioned his final days. He was supposed to have many children and dozens of grandchildren, all of whom would share the burden of caring for his aged body and mind. Instead there was only . . .

For a few terrifying moments he forgot the boy's name. But then he closed his eyes and concentrated, traveling back through the years.

Billy.

The name seemed to come to him as if part of a song about youth and innocence. Yes, Billy was his name, but he didn't like to be called that anymore. It was *William* now. It sounded more mature, he felt, more grown up.

Well, if not the boy, then at least his name.

Jack retraced his thoughts. What had he been thinking about, before stumbling over the boy's name? Ah, yes, instead of a large close-knit family to support him in his waning years, there was only William to look after him, a man in the body of a boy barely able to look after himself.

But things could change, thought Jack, as he drifted off to sleep. Things would change. . . .

*   *   *

Jack awoke some time later, wondering if he'd slept the day away or just had a catnap. A glance at the clock told him it had only been twenty minutes, but it felt as if he'd been asleep for days. "William?" he called.

No answer.

Probably still in the shed. Jack rolled his body forward, grabbed his cane with his right hand, and slowly lifted himself to his feet. Standing was difficult. His hips and knees were always stiff and sore these days, and the stroke had made most of his left side useless. But despite the debilitation, Jack was determined to carry on as if nothing had changed.

At least for a little while longer.

He shuffled his way to the back door, stopping in front of the screen rather than opening it. William would be able to hear him through it easy enough. "How are you making out?"

There was a sound of metal striking metal, then silence. "Eh?" came William's reply.

Jack strained to speak louder. "How's it coming?"

"I've got all the panels relayed together," William said from within the shed. "And I think the battery's still got a charge."

Jack nodded. The boy was good with mechanical things. At least the farm wouldn't fall into disrepair. "What do you want for supper?" asked Jack.

The banging noises that had started again suddenly stopped and William appeared in the doorway to the shed. "I'll make supper."

"Never mind," said Jack, trying to wave his limp left hand. "I'll get it ready."

"No," said William. He picked up a rag and began wiping his hands on it as he started across the yard.

"I don't mind doing it." He opened the screen door and squeezed past Jack into the kitchen. "Besides, I was just about done out there. I can finish up in the morning, which will give me plenty of daylight to test it out."

Jack watched as William began moving about the kitchen, placing pots on the stove and gathering the rest of what he needed on the counter. It looked like it was going to be leftover stew again. Jack hated stew, but it was the only thing that made the meat of the dog-sized rodents native to Effette IV palatable. The settlers had brought their own livestock with them, but those animals had all died out within a couple of generations. What Jack wouldn't give to eat a steak with his potatoes, or bacon with his eggs. All they had was stew. It was nutritious enough, and it was all William seemed to have the time or the will to make for them since it could be left unattended for hours while it cooked on the stove. That, and the leftovers seemed to last forever.

"Here," said William, noticing Jack still standing by the door. "Let me help you back into the living room." He put a hand on Jack's shoulder and took firm hold of his right arm. "I'll call you when it's ready," he said.

Jack was perfectly capable of making it to the living room by himself, but he was glad for the help of his son. It made the steps easier to take, and getting seated in the chair wouldn't be so painful.

"There," said William. "I'll be back in about ten minutes to get you."

Jack nodded, tried to smile.

But inside, he wept.

*   *   *

Jack had often wondered what death might be like, trying to picture the peace and stillness of it in his mind. *Death.* It almost sounded nice, or at least better than what his life had become. Yet he still feared it, although the fear wasn't for himself as much as for William.

What would become of the boy after he was dead? What was William to do after he'd found the body? Certainly he wouldn't be able to lift it. He might be able to drag it out of the house and into the yard, but that didn't seem right to Jack.

And, truth be told, Jack didn't want William to find him dead. Although it was more than two years ago, Jack still vividly remembered the shock of finding his wife Margaret's body, bent, broken, and soiled as it lay splayed across the landing at the bottom of the stairs. Such an undignified end to such a courageous life. *No,* thought Jack, *I won't let that happen to me.*

Even worse, what if Jack didn't die? What if instead of a neat clean heart attack he suffered another stroke and lingered on for another dozen years? Would William dutifully feed, clean, and care for him, or would the boy be tormented by thoughts of putting a knife through his father's chest just to be done with it?

Jack preferred not to make that an option for the boy.

"Dad?" said William standing at the entrance to the kitchen. "Supper's ready."

"I'll be there in a minute."

"Do you want some help?"

"No." Jack couldn't keep the frustration from his voice.

"Okay, Dad."

William sat silently in the chair across the table from his father. While they'd dispensed with saying grace and giving thanks many years ago, William still waited for his father to begin the meal.

"Go ahead, you don't have to wait for me," Jack said. "I won't always be around to go first, you know."

"I know. You've told me enough times."

"Then get started, will you!" Jack said.

"Are you all right, Dad? Is something wrong?"

Jack was about to tell his son he was dying, but realized he would have to explain how he was dying mostly on the inside. He'd never be able to find the words. So instead, he took a deep breath and said, "I'm getting old, that's all."

"Not to me, you're not," said William, smiling bravely.

"You're a good boy, William. You don't deserve this." Jack didn't make any special gesture to let his son know that by "this" he meant coming to Effette IV and the whole sorry mess they'd made of their lives, but the boy knew.

"Nobody deserves this," said William.

They said nothing for several long moments.

"How's the food?" Jack asked. Anything to dispense with the silence.

"It's stew, you know."

"Yes," Jack nodded. "I know."

The shadows lengthened and vanished as the sun set on Effette IV and darkness nestled in for another long night. The house was secured and father and son sat quietly in the front room reading. In addition to the battery, William had found a few paperbacks at Peckham Farm and had busied himself with the new reading material shortly after sundown.

Jack had a collection of poetry on his lap, a book published on the ship some two generations back.

He'd read the book a dozen times before, but found that tonight the language that had so often intrigued him could barely hold his interest. He glanced from the pages to his watch every few minutes, silently cursing the minute-hand for moving so slowly.

"What do you think, William, almost time for bed?" he said after two hours had passed.

"I'm not that tired. I might stay up just a little while longer and see if I like this book as much the second time through."

"That good, uh?"

"Yeah."

"Well, I'm going to bed. I need to rest for tomorrow."

"Why, what's so big about tomorrow?"

Jack was surprised that he'd allowed himself to be so careless with his words. He wondered what was the right thing to say, the right way to tell his son of his plans, but he knew it would never come to him. He simply shrugged his shoulders. "Nothing, I guess. Just another day." He struggled to get out of his chair.

"Maybe I'll go to bed, too," said William, moving to his father's side and helping him to his feet.

They went upstairs together, then retired to their bedrooms alone.

Jack had finished his preparations and was ready to go, but somehow it didn't feel right. There was one more thing that he had to do.

He took his cane, went down the hall to William's room and cracked the door open slightly. William had already dozed off and was sleeping soundly on the bed. Jack hesitated in the doorway for several moments gathering his strength before entering. He tried to step lightly on the wooden floor, but the boards still moaned and creaked beneath his feet.

"Billy," Jack said, placing his bony hand on the bed to stop it from shaking. "William . . ." he corrected himself. "William."

William slowly opened his eyes.

"I just wanted to say good night to you," Jack said, his voice trembling.

"Good night, Dad," William said sleepily.

Jack's breath was rapid and shallow.

"Are you okay, Dad?"

"Of course I'm okay. Nothing wrong with a father saying good night to his son if he wants, is there?"

"No, I guess not," William answered. He was more awake now. Perhaps even aware of what was happening.

Jack reached out and held his son. William returned the hug with both arms.

"I want to tell you that I love you, Son. I haven't told you that in a while."

"I know that, Dad. And I love you, too."

Jack held his son as tightly as his feeble arms would allow.

William said nothing, pressing his lips together in a thin white line.

Jack rose up off the bed, shuffled out of the bedroom and closed the door gently behind him. Outside, he leaned against the wall and struggled to catch his breath. His heart was pounding out a painful, irregular beat, and there was a pain slicing through his arm again.

The morning sun cut through the thinly curtained windows of William's bedroom in dull beams of dusty sunlight. Noticing the light on his eyes, William quickly jumped from the bed and went down the hall to check his father's room.

The room was empty.

The bed was made.

From downstairs he heard the faint sound of the front door creaking shut. William's first inclination was to race down the stairs and out into the yard, but he decided against it. It would steal away what little of his father's dignity was left.

So instead, William walked slowly back to his bedroom, climbed up onto the bed and looked out the window at the road that led away from the house.

In the distance he could see the white-topped figure of his father hobbling down the road. There was a pack on his back and a cane in his right hand.

"Good-bye, Dad," William said.

There was a brave smile on his face.

But inside, he wept.

I AM A GRAVEYARD HATED BY
THE MOON

by Tom Piccirilli

Tom Piccirilli is the author of eight novels, including *Hexes, Shards, The Night Class, The Deceased,* and his "Felicity Grove" mysteries *The Dead Past* and *Sorrow's Crown.* He has sold over one hundred short stories to anthologies such as *Future Crimes* and *The Conspiracy Files,* and to magazines such as *Cemetery Dance* and *Hardboiled.* A collection of forty stories, *Deep into the Darkness Peering,* has just been released by Terminal Fright Press. Tom lives in Colorado, where's he's working on a horror novel, a mystery, and a western.

Jombu, now the monkey-god Hanuman, son of wind, born to aid Rama in his battle against Ravana, golden-bodied with a ruby muzzle and a devastating roar, turned to me on the living ice and said, "Bum a cigarette off you?"

I gave him one, and we stood there smoking and watching the frenzied lightning writhe inside the seething glacier cliffs. A pale crimson washed down the curtain of sky from Allfather Odin positioned in the eastern horizon. My black leather raincoat flapped in the vicious wind. Tides of ice reeled, rumbled, and pealed, roiling as they stabbed and spired into crystalline cathedrals, cities, a universe reshaping and collapsing and rebuilding. All its vastness thriving with the brilliant colors of an electrified madness gushing and sweeping across the wasteland.

"Menthol!" Jombu cried, coughing. "Christ, don't you have anything without a two-inch filter?" I checked another pocket and handed him an unfiltered Camel. He sucked the smoke into his lungs gratefully, making throaty noises of satisfaction.

A burning silver-blue glow threaded through the snow, sparking and striking at my feet. Black, emerald, and cobalt storms ignited a thousand feet deep, the lightning tumbling to the surface and exploding into the air. It was closing in on Absolute Zero as the planet Odin set, geo-glacial upheavals driving the rumbling mountains out of the frigid slag to crash against outcroppings of frozen stone. The mean maximum temperature remained a brisk -87° F.

We still didn't know what made this one farside continent convulse while the other four remained stable. Seven thousand square kilometers of alien arctic tundra that thrashed and flailed with an anguished, chaotic life. You could imagine God, or something, out there, abounding and determined to make itself known.

"Vishnu is angry tonight," Jombu said, the cigarette dangling from his lower lip *a la* James Dean.

"You're having identity problems again, Jombu."

"The hell you say." He shrugged and picked ice crystals out of his golden fur.

The light of all-seeing Odin began to fade. Crimson shadows rose around us, rippling against the crumbling spires of snow and ice, sending a billion shattered reflections streaking in all directions. Across the other ten moons we watched the eclipsing shade of this world, Frija, eleventh satellite of the superjovian planet called Odin, arch across their faces. Overlapping shadows ten moons deep created pockets of darkness that could drive a man insane if he fell into them.

"Morse." Elise's voice came down out of the stars, rushing at me from all around, loud as screams but as hushed as a whimper under the edge of my ear. She asked, "Have you spotted anything yet?"

"No," I said.

Lao Ti cut in. "You want to go out another eighty klicks into the hoary lands? The *Aerie* picked up a slight geothermal shift in meteorological readings. Might be worth a look."

Jombu chuckled and scratched his ass. "Hoary lands. You people have a real knack for names."

I grinned at him. "Says a dead test subject monkey who thinks he's a Hindu god called Hanuman."

"I am Hanuman!"

Elise shouted, "Morse!" This time the breath of her whisper, like her lips, barely brushed my sideburns.

"Yeah, I'm here."

"Your answer was garbled."

"Sure," I told her. "Into the hoary lands."

I had nothing better to do.

She'd already had the program set up to move me along the grid. In seconds I was spun across the na-noverse VR pattern another eighty klicks into the erupting wasteland, to witness more of the same destruction and birth and rebirth of a frozen hell devouring itself.

It was a lot easier exploring Frija this way than by using the crampons and spikes and nylon ropes and the plastisteel lines that had killed me three years ago and lost Lao Ti her legs. Jombu remained beside me, but he'd lost his cigarette. I gave him another, and he sat on the ice smoking happily.

It would have been much more beneficial to have settled on the superjovian itself, or any of the other ten moons, but Gunderson had made the big find on this one, so here the colonists stayed, shivering and wondering if their kids would ever be able to play outside in their lifetimes.

Elise said, "Is something wrong, Morse?"

I nearly burst out laughing. "No."

"I'm reeling you in."

"Okay."

It took her a few minutes to reinitiate the return program, and I waited with my eyes closed, smelling the odd burning snow stench and fried ice, feeling the white sparks snapping against my sneakers.

Jombu waved and said, "Later. Vishnu be praised."

I nodded to him and instantly the air around me folded into the four walls of the main lab of a habitat outpost station I'd named *Perdition* when I was alive.

Now that I was dead I realized just how accurate I'd been.

Elise's beauty still cut my breath away, as it had on Earth, as it had in life. I didn't have a heart, body, a soul, or even breath for that matter, but I could still lust. I ground my teeth together and tried to focus past my phantom pain-desires. It didn't work. Nothing ever did.

"You all right?"

"Yes."

Her hair rolled out in a heavy black bob, framing her face with those two feathery curls aimed toward the corners of her mouth. I'd always had to sweep those curls aside before I could kiss her, only to feel them flop back against my jaw as I pressed my lips to hers. Now an inch-thick trail of silver flowed back through her sable hair. Each line of her face had been etched in deeper, adding another level of character and resolve to her radiance. I could feel the nearness of her. The heat dropped over me like a bucket of burning sand, and I instinctively reached out—to touch, to hold onto anything—but could only stand there beyond her touch, just a shivering apparition.

It had been five years since I'd held her in my arms, and almost three since I'd last seen her with my own living eyes. The marriage had failed for reasons neither one of us completely understood. The love had still been there at the end as we touched down on Frija, the tenderness, the inner kindling. Perhaps there had simply been too much passion for us to take to another world; we'd never fallen into the comfortable standards of acceptance and domesticity that would have kept us together. The burn of our affections and wants had been too much even on this frozen planet.

Lao Ti scampered in front of me to a different monitor, checking the readouts of the telemetry sent down from the *Aerie*. She never appeared to be earthbound, not even on Earth. Her eyes retained her dreams and fantasies of journeying to other galaxies, and living those dreams hadn't stagnated them for her. She was as much a philosopher as a scientist, and she'd have made as fine a Buddhist priestess as an accomplished geophysicist. I invariably got the sense that she always knew more than she was telling.

The .5 g of the central lab allowed her to shove out of her seat and whirl across the room agilely by her arms when she needed to, hopping a little like Jombu does, swinging her torso up into the other seats before different instrumentation. She never wore her prosthetic legs—gams as long and lean as her own had been—and I thought that was as much a matter of comfort as acknowledgment.

She'd lost her legs in the same mission that had killed me.

The first time I'd awoken in the VR nanotechverse, three months ago, she'd been smiling at me while Gunderson sneered. Lao Ti took her time explaining how things would work from now on. I think she was actually having some fun explaining to me, until I started shrieking and they had to shut me down and reload. And reload. And reload.

"See anything at all?"

"This world is as empty as the 'narrow vale between the cold and barren peaks of two eternities.' "

"It's not a world, it's a moon," Lao Ti reminded me. "But you earn points for quoting Robert Green Ingersoll."

"It's four times the size of Earth, I'm calling it a world."

Gunderson, in typical fashion, continued to glower. "Let's run a diagnostic on the Morse program," he said.

Elise didn't like it when he simply called me a program, and I could see the hinges of her jaws begin to tighten. "Why?"

"I don't trust its readings."

I held a hand to my chest. "Take thy beak from my heart."

Gunderson did what he could to remind everyone on the station—most importantly me and himself—that I was no longer a man, and that in essence I was only a world-wide VR datum integration/impregnation program running fairly wild. He never caught the irony of his need to personalize this program, though: distrusting it, and personifying me back into existence. He liked arching his eyebrows and digging the crows' feet into trenches. He'd always mistaken fixation for dedication.

He blinked at me and licked his lips, slowly smoothing his blond beard. He liked to look thoughtful and dangerous, capable of great harm or mischief. Gunderson had discovered this galaxy through deep space probe satellite network telemetry, and saw it first on his little eight-by-five screen, while my back was turned, and so got to name the superjovian and its moons. Odd how a man can suddenly find pride in a heritage he'd long ago tried to break free from. Suddenly he embraced his Nordic heritage and started spouting off names of gods and fucking frost giants and fairies.

Actually, he didn't have the stomach for exploration and colonization, but his jealousy drove him into deep space following me and Elise to circle round Odin. Even now he glared at me with all the same hatred he'd felt when I was alive. He'd killed me once and undoubtedly had no reservation in fragging enough circuitry and throwing my head on the floor to destroy me again.

Lao Ti clambered to the other side of the room, half-floating and half-vaulting to different computers, checking the VR grid. "The integrity of his tracking signature is holding steady at ninety-eight percent."

"That's too great a variation." Gunderson continued smoothing his beard, in love with the feel of the thing. "See if you can lock it down to at least ninety-nine point two, which will clear our percentage of error variant. And the telemetric readings?"

"Within optimum operational parameters."

"Any memory slip?" Elise asked me. She sounded nearly hopeful.

"No."

She knew I was lying. She always knew but never said a word to the others. She imagined that I might be remembering the same beaches and bedrooms and

twisted sheets and promises in the dawn, seeping back
to our honeymoon in Rio and our first designate space
mission to the neutron sun of Daedalus, making love
in the light of the rings of Tantalus.

"Are you still seeing the monkey, Morse?" Gunderson asked.

"No."

"You were muttering to yourself again on the ice
plains."

"It's that damn Burma Shave jingle . . ."

"Are you still talking to the monkey?"

"No."

"You're lying."

I wandered over to the other side of the room and
stood before the containment vessel, following the
wires and tubes and machinery throbbing and clicking
and beeping. My face in the jar, with most of the nose
and ears gone from frostbite, forehead, cheeks, and
chin flayed in places where the ice chip daggers had
skinned me going down the fissure. They had dragged
me up from the chasm with my body no more than a
ruined red smear across the ice. Elise forced them to
put the VR chip in my brain and hook me into the
nanotech infrastructure. The amber synthetic amniotic
fluid that kept my head functioning pulsed with air
bubbles on occasion, twisting my face this way and
that like a sleeping, feverish child racked with
nightmares.

"You need me anymore right now?" I asked.

"No," Lao Ti said. "We'll keep working on your
tracking signature. You heading uptown to the
Aerie?"

"For an hour or so."

Elise couldn't get the sadness clear of her voice. I

was dragging her down into my own death. "Okay, we'll reel you in if we need you."

*   *   *

I stepped through the lab wall and out into Frija's welcoming frost. It was originally believed that enormous amounts of matter would need to cover *Perdition* station to protect colonists from radiation, cosmic rays, and solar flares, but the ice storms did an even better job than the atmosphere on Earth did to filter harmful EM. *Perdition,* built only slightly better than most of our Arctic research facilities, was an ice-strengthened research base habitat with extensive laboratory and computing capabilities.

The habitat station could house up to a thousand, but only half that number had settled here over the last three years since the big find: fossilized human DNA traces in the ice. Many of them were paleoenvironmentalists who studied glacial geology, ice dynamics, ice cores, numerical modeling, and remote sensing of ice sheets on all the five frozen continents. The glaciology of Frija followed no glacialogical paradigms as we understood them on Earth, and the hoary wastelands proved to be far too unstable to be explored by any of the research teams.

Colonist families each took separate sections, small communities living in different parts of the internal station, eager to confine themselves. Gunderson was no different, living among the corridors of shadow and loneliness.

From what I could discern, Gunderson and Elise no longer slept together. He roamed the halls in the green twilit mornings, snorting and lost in his own inner mayhem.

I got a real kick out of it.

Another three hundred and fifty colonists rotated

shifts aboard the space platform *Aerie* situated in geo-synchronous orbit above *Perdition.* The equator of the space platform was nearly a mile in circumference, with reflected light from Odin brought in through external titanium mirrors. The 1.9 RPM rotation produced a comparable Earthlike gravity, naturally diminishing to zero at the poles, where a corridor at the axis allowed 0-g flight from one end to the other.

I moved along the grid pattern until I stood in the low-g recreation areas of the *Aerie,* watching them dance and play sports. At the axis of rotation were huge circular swimming pools where they swam and relaxed on their off-duty hours. Some of them had been my friends once: Annette and Babbitt and Ridgeworth and Strothers. I sat among them in the dining halls, listening to their conversations, watching them primp their children and wipe the mouths of infants, nobody caring if I was built of bone or nano-technology. Friedman and Halliwell and Treamont. Judy Sanders and her kids, Mitch and Suzanne. Their names and faces registered but didn't mean much. Perhaps a lot of my feelings were in that last two percent of my signature. A few people even waved, and I smiled and waved back. The dull habits of life didn't leave you just because you were dead.

Lao Ti's voice came from everywhere, and if I'd had a real nervous system I would have been startled out of my seat. "Morse?"

"Yo."

"How about taking another run at Sector IV, Quad II, 3.2 on the hyperbolic graph?"

Even she thought calling them the "hoary lands" was pretty damn ridiculous. "Sure."

Children rushed by me laughing. I might not have much emotion anymore, but I did have my moods and

Lao Ti could read them. "Want to take a few minutes to get ready?"

"No need."

"Okay, if you say so."

I lit a cigarette and stood on the ice fields that stretched toward an eternal vanishing point, the single eye of Odin staring down at me, more bitter than usual. Frozen monolithic pillars toppled over one another, swallowing and vomiting greater gorges, cliffs, and caverns.

The blood-soaked shadows fell upon me one by one.

An ambulance siren drew me to my left, and Frija fell away like an awful dream and I was back in New York, on Twenty-third Street, visiting my parents. My mother stooped over the dining-room table, ladling stew into the bowl in front of me. The smell made my mouth water, heady and impossibly delicious. I tried not to groan but couldn't clamp it down.

My sister Sarah and her husband Paul talked about their new dog, a cocker spaniel named Pooh. My two nephews, Jimmy and Joey, sat on the living-room rug playing with the toy spaceships I'd bought them, the television blaring news reports on unfolding tragedies across the nation. I was twenty-one years old and had just received three degrees in molecular biology from the university. In two hours I'd be signing the papers necessary to join the initial phase of the Program. Separated, but still a part of me somehow, I could feel the old trepidation, hope, and yearning.

I'd just told the family my plans, a broad smile on my peach-fuzzed face, the old man blazing down at me as he'd done no matter what the reason, even when he was almost happy with two and a half bottles of wine in him.

The ladle hit the table with a thump that sent a

spatter of beef across my chest. "You can't," my mother said. Her numb hands hung in the air before my face like ghosts, floating and white, fluttering up and down. My father's face turned nearly the same purple as when he'd had his fatal coronary while screwing a teenage waitress in the back room of some bar off West Fourth. Despite his pressure for me to find a job, he hadn't expected this. He poured himself another glass of wine, soaking his bottom lip and sort of hissing. I enjoyed the way his eyes bulged, and his fury, like my own, was more palpable than usual.

"You going to go to Saturn?" Jimmy asked.

"Farther," I told him.

"Cool. How much farther?"

"About four light years."

"You going to fight space monsters?"

"Yes."

"What do they look like? They got tentacles? They got teeth that leak slime all over the place?"

I thought of Gunderson nearly slavering in the lab. "Some of them."

"Gross!" Joey said, grinning, holding out his rocket and swishing it along the coffee table. "No, they got claws and super-weapon laser guns and starships that let them teleport away."

"Space monsters are just people in space," I said. It sounded very profound.

My sister Sarah was crying. She was always crying.

"How do you know all this?" my father asked. "How do you know where they'll send you? What you'll be capable of?" He was dying in his seat, slowly turning to ash, still drunk and fuming. I couldn't think of him in any other way.

"Because, Dad," I said. "I've already done it all and now I'm dead but still living in world-wide virtual reality

datum integration/impregnation program through diamonoid mechanosynthesis molecular nanotechnology
that I created. I'm trapped with the evolving subcon-
scious pattern of a monkey named Jombu who was
the first test subject. He's also looped in the chip
they've got implanted in my most nonfunctional brain,
and the only relief he has in his insanity is to believe
himself the Hindu monkey-god Hanuman."

That about summed it up. They just silently stared
at me, and I started in on the stew. When I was finished, I said, "Pretty funny, huh?"

My sister sobbed even harder, trying to force out
the words. "And what relief do you have?"

"Memory funnels like this. See, they kccp me from
completely going over the edge."

A draft tossed Dad's ashes across the table. Sarah
twisted the border of the tablecloth until it shredded,
wet from her—*from my*—heartache. "Are you surc?"

"No, not really."

Joey wasn't all that impressed. He tossed the model
spaceship at my feet and it hit in slow-motion, shattering
into a dozen brilliant pieces of hideous mad shadow
as Jombu stared into my eyes, the snow covering his
ruby muzzle, and said, "And you tell me I have problems, eh?"

Gunderson enjoyed raging. It gave him something
to do. He could shake his head and get his hair flying
and take little jumps of anger that vaulted him across
the lab like a giant frog. "We need to take it off-line!
Despite what it says, it's still having memory slips."

Old habits don't die at all, especially four light years
outside the solar system where you were born. Elise
brought her hand up as if to stroke my face. She wrinkled her nose as if she could smell the cigarette smoke

she always hated. "Morse, is it true? These readings are incomprehensible."

"No, it's not true."

"It's lying!"

"You're cute when you get angry, Gunderson."

His jaws clenched so tightly that his teeth chattered. "You dare to insult me?" Three new staff assistants backed up against their consoles, and I could tell they were wondering just what in the hell they were doing here. I think everybody was feeling about the same way. They'd never seen him like this before. Petty and sarcastic and severe, sure, but never furious to the point of mania. He came hopping at me. "You dare?"

"Imagine that."

Lao Ti hung her head and said, "Oh, shit."

"You!" He wagged his finger in my nose the way he used to when I was only his assistant fresh in the Program, telling me how diamonoid mechanosynthesis could never work. "You're not even real! You're a three-month-old holographic virtual reality program that exists on a nanotech grid from micro-second to micro-second."

"A grid I created, by the way."

The fear in Elise came roaring up into her eyes. In lieu of grabbing me, calming me the way she had in the old days, she thrust herself against Gunderson's chest, patting him like she was trying to tamp down the beast. He reached past her shoulder, pointing, each of us egging the other on like we were about to get into a street brawl.

"You're not even a man!"

"More so than you."

I liked how the veins in his temples turned black and tried to crawl behind his ears. "You rotten son of a bitch!"

"How rude," I said, trying to sink my teeth into my lip. Biting, biting, with the blood of Odin dripping across the world. "Hey, Gunderson, I'm sick of your shit. Looky here." I brought a roundhouse up from my knees and smashed him backward over his computer terminal. The chairs flew and clattered, and he sat there bouncing on the floor, looking stunned. He held his hand up to his nose expecting to find it broken.

Actually, I hadn't even touched him, but he believed I was there, and reacted as if I had actually punched him, and he'd enacted the rest himself. It was a nice trick I could pull on them now and again.

My dead head in the jar looked moderately pleased.

Lao Ti followed Gunderson out of the lab, bounding on her arms and swinging her torso after him. She didn't do it to calm him or because she thought he might, but because—I felt sure—that she wanted to witness the strange sea-change of loathing that had been overpowering him since my rebirth. Maybe there was something to be learned by our conflict, but only Lao Ti would be able to find it.

I turned to the other three assistants, young as I'd been in the beginning, pale and hoping to someday touch the sunlight once more. "How about some privacy?"

They left without a word or gesture, treading single file out of the lab. Sometimes we were all just ghosts.

Elise sat in front of the nanotech VR grid board with her hands folded between her knees, watching my flayed face pressed against the glass. "I know you blame him for . . . for . . ."

"For my death, yes, but I'm still here, so I suppose it doesn't really matter very much."

She nodded. "You still hate him."

"I always hated him, no difference there either. The dumb shit doesn't know how to lead a research project, much less a colony of scientists and children. He couldn't even manage an expedition where he had to wear crampons and spikes and use plastisteel cords to climb snowbound peaks twice the size of Kilimanjaro."

"Morse, calm down . . ."

"I am calm. He wandered into a crevasse and got himself stuck in a fissure a thousand feet down, and I died going after him and Lao Ti lost her legs when a ledge collapsed under her. He sat on an outcropping like a side of beef for six hours, crying and praying while we croaked trying to reach him, and the fucker never even said thank you."

"He's afraid of you. More now than ever before."

"He's a dink who should have been left on Earth where his sourness wouldn't affect the mission. Everyone knows fear, but we all learn to contain it."

"And what do you fear?"

"Me?" There was only one thing. "Me? I'm afraid of waking up."

"What do you mean?"

I pointed at the glass jar. "I'm afraid of opening my eyes and finding myself staring out at this world from inside there."

She turned slowly and my lust caught me low in my guts, in the same place as always, each angle of her body coming into perfect view. She looked at my dead head, the hair floating in the amniotic fluid, half the skull exposed where the chip blinked and pulsed, and then spun back to me. "Oh, my God."

"Gunderson's big find is a wipeout. It doesn't matter that he found fossilized human DNA traces in that fissure, Elise. It means nothing."

"Oh, Christ, Morse, I know you're bitter because you died in that spot . . ."

"That's not it!"

"But how? How do you know?"

I wasn't sure how I knew, but I did. Jombu, now the monkey-god Hanuman, son of wind, let out a devastating roar capable of bringing down the pillars of the sky . . . but no, nah, it was only me screeching, deep in my head where all the rest of my screams squirmed.

I tried to concentrate past my mother's dithering. An autumn breeze hurled my raincoat across my shoulders, ten other moons circling wildly and All-father Odin rising as the spheres dropped upon my back like corpses. I was on seventy-eighth and Central Park West, being dragged along the sidewalk by the swarming tourists heading for the Museum of Natural History. My mother kept trying to hand me bags of fresh fruit and bottles of vitamin pills. My sister Sarah, lagging behind, walking her new dog Pooh, sobbed at my back.

"Mom, I'm sort of busy right now."

"Remember to dress warm."

"Of course I will."

"Take your vitamins."

"Okay, Mom."

Sarah wept, and even her dog seemed to be weeping, and the two of them sat on the curb with dried leaves kicking at their ankles, and they let me get the hell out of there without any more troubles.

The world turned white once more, and the hoary wastelands enfolded me in their frozen, thrashing embrace.

Lao Ti's voice reared and exploded across the sun

and under my skull. "Ready to tackle Quad III, 4.4 today, Morse?"

"Fourth continent. I've been on pins and needles just thinking about it."

"Figured you felt that way."

"Maybe we'll find a ski resort this time, huh?"

"Bring me back some hot chocolate if you do. Here you go. Sixty more klicks to the far side east."

"Make it one-fifty."

That stopped her, but I could hear her curiosity—the hopefulness of it. "Why? That breaks the hyperbolic graph pattern we've been following for weeks."

"Don't be so anal. Just do it. Call it a hunch."

"Okay. Confirmed. Initiating." Again the faith, and anticipation. "Holographic programs with hunches. "What the fuck is next?" The breath of her smile warmed the back of my neck.

Snowblind in the heart of the bellowing storm, rhapsody on the windiest evening, as slabs of stone and ice jutted wildly from the mountains.

Jombu smoked pack after pack and asked, "What the hell are we waiting here for?"

"Damned if I know."

"Soon I must join Rama and battle the evil Ravana. Let's move on."

"No point in doing that, but don't let me hold you up. I know you've got a busy schedule."

My own patience began to frustrate me. I should have been bored and strained, but instead I felt mildly anxious and didn't have a doubt that soon something would finally find me here.

The expectation grew in me as the horizon clouded with the motion of moons. Swirling banks drew me one way and then the other. I thought I could hear voices—not my mother's, not Elise's—but female, soft and melodic raining down in the spirals of snow. It took another hour.

"Oh, boy."

Three women came down from the peaks of the cliffs, twining slowly towards me. Jombu spit out his cigarette and started hopping up and down. "Hotchee Mama. Vishnu be praised."

"I might as well agree with that."

They stood nearly naked on the frozen plains, wearing banded wraps fastened at the shoulder, and saluted me with their fists held high above their heads in the gale.

"Okay, I might as well get this over with," I said. "Who are you?"

One woman stepped out of formation and came close. She smiled, kneeled, and began digging in the snow at my feet. She didn't have far to go before she pulled up a sword and shield. The other two came forward and continued digging in the same spot. After they'd collected their gear, one of them pointed into the hole. I could see that down there beneath the ice was a black outline at least two hundred meters across.

I nodded to them. They all looked vaguely familiar, and I couldn't shake the notion. The first reminded me of my sister Sarah. Another resembled Lao Ti, with similar sexy gams, and the third had the same features and frigid but burning eyes as Gunderson. She sneered at me, hefted her sword, and wheeled away. The other two women followed, and I watched them tramp and disappear into the storm.

"You probably won't want to mention this to base," Jombu said. "They already think you're pretty weird for a dead guy nanotech holographic molecular nano-technology program who talks to monkey gods."

"You might be right."

The sky thrummed like thunder, blaring with Elise's concern. "Morse, your readings are becoming irregular. Did you find something?"

"Yes, it's a ship."

Funny how you can spend years working up to a singular moment only to stall upon reaching it. She made a little hiccoughing noise. "What?"

"It's a buried starship. Looks similar to one of our own but much bigger. Swallowed by the currents of ice."

"I'm locking the *Aerie*'s scanners onto your position."

The shadow of the ship lay awkwardly within the freeze, twice the size of our largest space platform. Lightning swayed and whirled over it, slowly, caressing the damaged hull and engines. Emerald ice flared, then spit orange, yellow, and even gray. I could only make out the most basic specs: no insignia, no nearby bodies.

Gunderson let out a sharp braying. It took me a moment to realize he was laughing. He hadn't had much practice at it. "*Aerie* telemetry verifies the find, but they can't lock down the coordinates. There's too much interference from the storm."

Elise knew better. "How far down do you need to descend?" There was a mixture of fear and elation in her voice, just as when she repeated our wedding vows before our friends and families.

"Two hundred and twenty meters. Make it two twenty-eight."

"We've made contact!" Gunderson shouted. "Contact! This might prove that humanoid life began right in this galaxy, and that our extraterrestrial forefathers sowed their seeds in the primordial oceans of Earth."

"That's disgusting!" Jombu cried.

I swam down the grid until I was level with the
ship's battered gigantic hull. I stared inside the warped
metal and lit a match. I saw what I expected to see
and everything else dropped perfectly into place.

"Elise, send me along the grid back to the fissure
where we first had all the trouble."

"Where you died?" She didn't like saying it, and I
didn't particularly like hearing it.

"Yes, send me to the bottom. About four hundred
meters."

She did, but I still wasn't deep enough in the crevasse. I climbed down along the nanotech pattern, step
by step until I found the outcropping I was looking
for and spotted the frozen lump I expected to see.

"Reel me in."

I dissolved back into the white sterilized shine of
Perdition, and they immediately formed a ring around
me: Gunderson showing his back teeth in his delight,
still smoothing his Nordic blond beard; Lao Ti, always
so aware and accepting, with one eyebrow arched and
her mouth showing the barest hint of a dismal smirk,
waiting for the other shoe to drop; Elise knowing, in
her sad beautiful heart, that I could only bring darkness to the colony, understanding and forever expecting it.

"Get everybody uptown to the *Aerie*."

Without arguing, simply wanting to know the answer,
Elise asked, "But why?"

If possible, the bad feeling I had grew worse. I could
still care, in my fashion. "The ship is a fake."

"It's real!" Gunderson shouted, still parading his
molars. "We've finally locked our scans onto it. It's
right there!"

"It's there all right, but it's not real."

He did that braying thing again, no better at laughter. "Satellite telemetry is downloading data by the megabyte."

"The data stream will prove what I've said. You people need to get the hell out of here. Everybody on *Perdition* station. Now."

Elise, so lovely and near that my knees almost buckled, the warmth in my chest as bad as a heart attack, my fingers beginning to tingle. "Why? Tell us."

"Lao Ti," Gunderson said. "Take the Morse holographic nanotech program off-line. It's destabilized too much. We'll run a diagnostic on it later."

"Frija built the ship for us," I told them. "Drawing up the hard metals from its core, following your shape and wants, Gunderson. You couldn't conceive of a truly alien ship, you just don't have enough imagination. It's a phantom made real."

"No, not the ship!" Gunderson jutted his chin like a kid in a schoolyard about to jump another. "You! You—"

"Yeah, me, too."

"You—"

The correlated datum stream was being deciphered. Lao Ti merely stared at the numbers, the proof right there if you wanted it. She did something I'd never seen her do before. She touched her stumps. She was halfway to understanding.

"It's just an empty shell, Lao Ti. There's no intricate equipment or detailed machinery. It's a hoax. It's a trick."

"I see."

Elise wanted to trust me but couldn't do it yet, checking over the data and trying to make sense of it. I came up behind her and whispered in her ear, wanting to be the man I'd once been, whom she trusted with her life. "Just go, Elise. Move everyone off-planet, get to the *Aerie* and relaunch from there. Get the colonists out of this entire system. It wants us here too much."

"What about you?" she asked.

"Him!" Gunderson shrieked. "He's dead, and his programming has clearly had a schism. You're actually embracing the deranged notions of an unbalanced paranoid virtual reality pattern. Take it off-line now, we need to send an exploration party out there immediately." He turned on the comm-link ready to call in a team. At least he was no longer laughing. I wondered how much time there was left.

"You're dead, too, Gunderson," I told him. "You died in that same fissure before me."

My hands stopped tingling. I made a fist and put everything I had into it. This time I did strike him with a beautiful uppercut that in the .5 g of the room lifted and threw him nearly to the ceiling, because he was no more a man than I was. I felt his nose buckle beneath my human hate, and my knuckles burned with his hot spurting blood.

Elise said, "Oh, God. It's true."

I spun on her and said, "Do you think I'd ever lie to you, Elise?"

"But why be afraid?"

"It wants more now. It's tired of only dealing with me. Frija wants another team out there. It wants more flesh."

Gunderson wriggled on the floor at Elise's feet, his beard turning red. "You can't hit me, Morse," he said, denying everything in a strangely quiet, almost loving voice. "You're only a holographic image."

"No. I'm a *world-wide* VR datum integration/impregnation program. And on this world, that counts for a lot." Diamonoid mechanosynthesis molecular nanotechnology alive from micro-second to micro-second. Yes, I could touch a specter. "You're another wraith crated by this planet, Gunderson. The electrical activity in the crystalline structure of the ice of Frija is acting like a massive human brain. A mind with will and intent and desire. It ingested your frozen corpse in the fissure and you became a part of that will. It's taken what you wanted to find here and made it real."

"There's human life here," he said, reaching for Lao Ti's chair to prop himself up so he could stand. If she'd had legs, he would've been grabbing for her knee. She clambered over the console and started sending orders into the comm-link. Gunderson didn't seem to care as he dropped into the seat. "I discovered fossilized human DNA traces. I found them!"

"They were your patterns, you schmuck. You died in that crevasse and were reborn by Frija. We didn't make contact. It did. You came up carrying a sample from your own fossilized corpse. The world consumed you and spit you out again while Lao Ti froze her legs off and I broke my neck and back in that gorge trying to save you."

"But you—you say that because it's your petty existence."

"Even if the chip didn't work, I'd still be here, like you. Lao Ti feels it, too, her flesh a part of this planet."

Lao Ti said nothing, displayed nothing. "I've ordered an evacuation of the station. All hands will prepare for departure to the *Aerie* in minus fifteen minutes. What about you?"

"I'll be all right," I told her. "Just leave the head right there in its jar." It didn't matter. I was only walking thought. Frija had my DNA already, and could make as many samples of me as it wanted.

Gunderson sat in the chair shaking his head at his

monitors as the women in white-banded wraps fastened at the shoulders, carrying their shields and swords. The Valkyries born from our genetics, from Gunderson's heritage, darted across the snow with lightning in their hair, and giggled and snarled into the view screens.

The cold realization of seeing them shook him right out of his stubborn convictions. He crumbled like the living dust he was. "Get to the ship," he said. "Yes, we'll all get to the ship and figure this out on the platform. We'll be safe on the *Aerie*."

"It's too late," I whispered, and his bottom lip quivered.

Glaciers crawled forward burning crimson and throwing golden sparks, alive and drawing toward us. The electrical storms thrashed and formed shapes in the snow, blazing and screaming like an orgiastic feast of desire in a madhouse. Snow hurled down from the mountains, fissures opened and snapped shut with the thunder of a billion tons of cracking ice. The wasteland was upon us.

Jombu, now the monkey-god Hanuman, son of wind, turned his ruby muzzle to me and said, "I'm outta here. Vishnu protect you. Good luck!"

"You, too."

Lao Ti looked inexplicably pleased—perhaps because, like me, she'd left pieces of herself out there in the void and could accept the fact, and we could feel associated with the ice, if not altogether a part of it.

Gunderson just didn't want to be a corpse, and started weeping in the corner near the jar with my head in it—my eyes opening now, blinking at him, and smiling.

A man stepped forward across the monitor—grinning without real malice, but with a certain devilishness, just as a naughty child does. Just as Loki, god of mischief, would.

Elise, my wife and only love, took my hand, and I held it.

And this planet isn't Frija. Gunderson made a poor choice when naming these worlds.

This isn't Frija, with its tenfold bloody shadows.

This is Valhalla, land of the dead, blissfully pure and wonderfully cool against the burning of our confused souls.

THE EDGEWORLD

by Eric Kotani

Eric Kotani is a pen name used by an astrophysicist who has published seven science fiction novels with such authors as John Maddox Roberts and Roger Mac-Bride Allen. He also edited an anthology of stories in tribute to Robert A. Heinlein. For fifteen years he was the director of a satellite observatory at NASA, and, before that, headed the astrophysics laboratory at NASA's Johnson Space Center during the Apollo and Skylab missions. He has held professorships at several universities, including the University of Pennsylvania and the Catholic University of America. He has published more than two hundred scientific articles and edited eleven books on astrophysics. He has received several awards for his work in the science field, including the NASA Medal for Exceptional Scientific Achievement and the National Space Club Science Award.

One of his hobbies is martial arts. He holds a fifth degree black belt in judo and a sixth degree black belt in aikido, and has been teaching a class for the past few decades.

For the umpteenth time in the last few days, Steph MacNair wondered about the discovery on New Hope, another of the few dozen inhabited objects in the Edgeworth-Kuiper Belt, which the locals called the Edgeworld. *Is it a freak of nature, as has turned out to be the case before, or is it really an artifact?* She would very much like to be on the investigating team, but knew that there was little chance of anything like that happening, despite her professional training with a doctorate in exotic physics.

Steph looked longingly out the neo-glass window in the general direction of New Hope, without any expectation of actually seeing it from a distance of several billion kilometers. Myriads of unblinking stars, bright and faint against the blackness of space, appeared unhurriedly from one corner and disappeared from the other, thanks to Dyson's naturally slow rate of rotation. Even after a few months there, the view still fascinated her. Intellectually, she knew the starscape outside looked pretty much the same as the night sky at home in northern Arizona, but seeing it from these remote reaches of the solar system made a great difference in her perception.

She forced her gaze away from the glorious sky back to the plants in the huge greenhouse she had been tending. Closed ecosystem engineering was the professional qualification that got her this job in the pragmatic Edgeworld. The gene-adapted plants, especially designed for this environment, efficiently converted the carbon dioxide produced by humans and other animals into breathable oxygen, while consuming the locally available hydrocarbon compounds mixed with methane and ammonia as nutrition for their growth. The plants and the prawns grown in hydroponic tanks comprised the primary natural nourishment for the inhabitants. There was plenty of water, too, the single most essential ingredient for sustaining life, in the form of primeval ice. They were already exporting ice—compact cometlike objects—to space colonies closer to the Sun, using slow but economical orbits.

*   *   *

She was making a final adjustment on an instrument, when the communication unit lit up with a sharp beep, jerking her attention away from the routine task. The saccharine-sweet face of Rob Newman, her subsection chief, was peering out of the screen.

"We need you immediately, Steph! How soon can you get here?"

Her first reaction was to tell him to go fly a kite or something even less ladylike. She would have thought that his unsuccessful pass last week was sufficiently humiliating to his male ego, and, not coincidentally, painful to his wrist, to discourage his amorous advances for a while. Apparently not. The man definitely lacked *savoir faire.*

On the other hand, this emergency might be legitimate. She had heard that just before her arrival there had been an ecological emergency and the help had been a bit slow in coming; several people had had to be sent to the infirmary for a few days. She certainly wouldn't want that to happen on her watch. She took a glance at the three-dimensional display of Dyson next to the communication screen and located where he was calling from, then responded with a barely concealed disdain.

"What's the trouble, Rob? Under attack from a litter of puppies again?"

Rob reacted with his characteristic deviousness. "You'd better get out here *pronto* and find out for yourself."

Obviously, he was not going to give a straight answer; perhaps he was trying to pay her back for his earlier embarrassment or maybe he did not know the answer himself.

"I'll be finished here in fifteen minutes—should be

able to make it there in about thirty. Will that be
soon enough?"

His face on the screen exhibited a curious mixture
of expressions that were hard to read. "Yeah, that
oughtta do it, I guess. But hurry!"

After turning off the see-speak device, Steph read-
justed the nutrition supply control in the greenhouse
and restored proper sunlight to the plants; as the room
brightened, the magnificent starscape beyond the window faded away. Actually, the sunlight was quite feeble at the typical distance of the Edgeworld, it being
about a hundredth of a percent of what Earth received. The tenuous irradiation was gathered and fo-
cused by an array of huge collecting mirrors that
always faced the sun; the concentrated sunbeam, un-
thinkably stronger than the noontime sun in the Mo-
jave Desert, was directed to a receptor at the pole of
her world, where it was retransmitted or converted
into various useful forms of energy; the sunlight seen
by her growing plants was piped from the receptor.
The mirrors, each some tens of kilometers across, did
not have to be optically perfect for the purpose and
were economically manufactured using the locally
available material.

It took less than fifteen minutes to finish her remaining task. With a by now practiced, graceful gait
in her slightly magnetized boots, she stepped out of
the greenhouse into the hallway. When she pushed
the button on the wall for the shuttle, the door dilated
immediately, revealing a two-person capsule beyond.
Taking the nearest seat, she pushed a button for her
destination, Sector Seven. If it were not for the gentle
surge of the acceleration, she would not have sensed
the motion of her conveyance, so smoothly did the

superconducting magnet operate in the extreme low temperature environment of her miniworld.

Within a few minutes she emerged from the capsule into the hallway containing Sector Seven. It was a staging area for exploration and ongoing construction on the surface. Rob was waiting for her in the foyer and looked elated upon seeing her. Her strawberry-blonde hair was bound in a casual knot to avoid flying all over her pleasant oval face in this negligible gravity; she looked both neat and professional. It was a good thing that he did not try to hug her; she might have had to show her disapproval a bit forcefully—again.

Suppressing her personal predispositions, she spoke up first. "So, what's up now?"

Rob looked at her a moment as if to decide how to answer noncommittally. "Half an hour ago, Ali ran into an unusual object on his mining expedition on the surface."

Concealing her rising excitement, she attempted to extract more information. "That's interesting, but why did you want me here? I'm an ecosystem engineer."

He had a ready answer. "Director Conrad wanted you here, not me. As a matter of fact, he's on his way. Why don't you ask him?"

Even as he finished saying the last word, the door to the shuttle on the opposite side of the hallway dilated, and in walked a man of compact stature, light of hair and complexion, with merry, twinkling blue eyes. Before Steph had the chance to speak up, the director was already talking rapidly.

"You aren't suited up yet, I see. Let's climb into those monkey suits and go take a look at the *thing.*"

Although taken slightly aback by the swift turn of

events, she followed his example and quickly walked to the wall where the space suits hung. Thankfully, those suits operated under normal pressure and did not require prebreathing of pure oxygen lasting several hours like the suits used in an earlier century. With a practiced movement of many years he was almost finished donning his suit when she was still finding her way into hers. Just before he pulled down his helmet, she popped a question.

"What's this *thing* we are supposed to be inspecting, Mister Conrad?"

Casting an oblique glance at the subsection head, Conrad answered, "Oh, Rob hasn't told you yet? Ali found this strange object out there while on his routine job on the surface; we're now going out to see what it is. I told him not to do anything until we got there. It may be similar to the recent discovery on New Hope, though we still don't know much about what they found. We may have a chance to learn firsthand now. You are coming along because you are a trained exotic physicist. I understand you were involved in the analysis of that famous object from Titan a few years back?"

"Actually, that experience did not amount to much; as you probably know, the item turned out to be just a quirk of nature."

"Yes, I know, but you are the only expert here who has had any sort of experience in handling this kind of object." Peering into her green eyes, which had not yet been covered by the visor, he continued, "Aren't you interested?"

Steph's face lit up in excitement. "Of course, I am!" This was the kind of adventure she had come looking for.

*   *   *

In just a few minutes, they were stepping through the airlock into the forbidding world outside. The sun was above the horizon and provided adequate illumination once her eyes became dark-adjusted. Seen from a distance of some ten billion kilometers, old Sol shone as an extremely bright star, something like minus seventeenth apparent magnitude, still brighter than a full moon back on Earth; she avoided looking directly toward the sun to protect her dark vision. The craggy surface of Dyson looked eerie. It was bitterly cold beyond Pluto's orbit; the temperature was barely a few tens of degrees above absolute zero, where all gaseous motion would cease. Dyson was one of the countless such objects in the Edgeworld, ranging in size from mere pebbles to those measuring several hundred kilometers. The circumference of her mini-world was about sixty kilometers, and the farthest point from one of the dozen or so air locks could easily be several kilometers. Luckily for them, the site in question was a short distance from this particular gateway.

Walking on the surface was a bit tricky. The irregularly-shaped body of her home world had, at the surface, a gravitational field about one thousandth Earth normal, but the field varied considerably depending on where you were, thanks to its nonspherical shape. If she bounced around too energetically, she might accidentally catapult herself into a trajectory, landing a couple of hundred meters away. Following the examples shown by her boss, she took steps by pushing herself forward with as little up-and-down motion as possible, like some characters in classic Japanese *noh* plays. To help their progress on the surface, the space suit boots had rugged bottoms providing traction on the rocky surface, but spots with ice and carbohydrate were another matter altogether. She had to watch where she stepped. Such cautions tended to limit outdoor activities for the colonists, and consequently much of the surface of Dyson was still unexplored.

After several minutes of trekking, they were at their destination. Ali Al-Cadi, the resources specialist, was standing by the *object* when they arrived. He had been looking around for good icy-hydrocarbon compound deposits suitable for mechanized extraction. There was a dark object ensconced in the small pool of dirty ice in front of Ali. The *thing* looked like nothing she had seen before anywhere—certainly, not at all like the putative artifact from Titan. Illuminated by the portable light Ali had brought with him, the *object* looked grayish and had a dull surface appearance. It was about the size of an old-fashioned filing cabinet and had no particular shape to suggest its purpose, but something about it reminded her of an ultramodernist sculpture.

After receiving a go-ahead from the director, Ali crawled on all fours to the *object,* skillfully using gadgets that reminded her of rock-climbing gear on Earth, to avoid slipping off the icy surface.

Upon reaching the *object,* he put his right hand underneath to see if it was attached to the ice; it came up without any visible strain on him. That did not say much about the mass of the *object,* however; even if its mass had been a ton, it would have weighed only around a kilogram. To avoid ejecting it into orbit inadvertently, he had to raise the entire thing over the icy surface very slowly, and then push it to the rocky area where Steph and Conrad stood. Pushing it over the ice was actually trickier than it looked. Although the thing did not weigh much at all in the low gravity, it still had its inertial mass, which was nonnegligible. The Newtonian law of motion worked too perfectly there; Ali had to overcome the inertia of his burden by planting his ice-climbing gear firmly into ice, before pushing it ahead. Otherwise, his baggage would have pushed him right back with equal force, causing him to slide backward in the opposite direction.

When the *thing* reached the edge of the ice patch, Conrad barked a short order. "Leave it right there, Ali!"

Actually, Steph was about to issue a similar instruction. Neither of them wanted to risk lacerating the smooth-looking exterior of the *thing* by dragging it over the rocky surface even in this low gravity. Ali finished crawling the last couple of meters alone and stood up by their side.

Conrad pondered the situation momentarily and said, "Let's put it on the trolley and haul it back to the airlock so we could take a good look under better lighting and maybe run a few tests in the lab." His last words were clearly directed at Steph.

She dissented immediately. "Oh, no, Mister Conrad! We mustn't do that. The initial tests, at least, should be run outside in vacuum at low temperature. There is no telling what might happen if we put this *thing* in a lab. It could be dangerous."

"Hadn't they shipped that Titanian object back to one of those physics labs on Earth for analysis? All those experts must have thought it was safe enough." The voice of Newman, who had been monitoring outdoor communications from the base, cut in solicitously.

Here we go again, Steph thought to herself. She had no tolerance for professional incompetence even when the ineptitude had been exhibited by several distinguished members of the academy of science. Her impulsiveness had gotten her into trouble before, but she was feeling hot inside and, when she felt like this, did not care much about the consequences.

"It was pure luck that nothing happened in the process. Of course, in retrospect, nothing should have happened, seeing that it was just an unusual, humanoid-shaped rock formation. But they had no way of knowing that in advance. This *thing* here does not at all look like that object from Titan—nor like any other so-called alien artifacts before it. We should run our first tests outside. If the testing shows it to be safe enough, we will bring it into a laboratory that is kept in vacuum and at low temperature—directly through a door from outside. We can build one right next to the airlock for easy access."

Conrad was a little amazed at Steph's youthful vehemence. "Aren't we forgetting one important consideration here?"

Undaunted, Steph shot right back, "What have I forgotten? Whatever it is, it couldn't be more important than our safety."

"Ah, that's where you could be wrong. We stand the chance of becoming the first people to report the discovery of an authentic alien artifact. This could turn out to be the most significant discovery in the history of space exploration—short of an actual encounter with an ET, that is. We have no idea what they found on New Hope, but if the Edgeworld is indeed the place where we have a good chance of running into these objects, we may be in competition with a number of other colonies. Avoiding some minor risks, we may be conceding a defeat even before the contest is joined."

He added, as if as an afterthought, "Actually, I wouldn't be too unhappy if those guys on New Hope should become the first. They are pretty decent folks. But I'd kick myself if one of those scheming rascals elsewhere should beat us to it."

Steph mulled over his remarks. He had a valid point, but her keenly-honed instinct was horrified at the idea of exposing this strange object to a drastically different environment without some preliminary safety checks. She thought frantically, seeking a reasonable solution.

"Suppose we compromise, Mister Conrad? I'll bring my instruments here and start the testing immediately. That would be faster than taking this *thing* into a laboratory. I'll contact you right away if I find any convincing evidence that it is of alien origin. In the meantime, you can start building our new vacuum lab."

Conrad grinned thinly. "You are mighty free with our resources, aren't you, Steph? All right, go get the testing equipment, and I'll have the work gang start building a vacuum lab next to the airlock. We should be able to jury-rig one quickly enough. But don't fail to contact me as soon as you find anything important. Okay?"

"Yes, Mister Conrad."

When she started running preliminary tests to see what might be inside, the object turned out to be opaque to her apparatus. She took her time in conducting the experiment to avoid precipitating anything catastrophic, but further testing confirmed her initial results that the object was totally opaque to electromagnetic radiation in all frequencies from Gamma-ray to radio. This thing must have a surface layer whose atomic nuclei and electrons were packed together so tightly that no photons could get through.

Such tight bonding of atoms implied at least electron degenerate material as in white dwarf stars, or even nuclear degenerate matter as in neutron stars. In electron degeneracy, a cubic centimeter of the stuff masses around a ton; in nature, it is produced at the evolutionary end of a star when its nuclear fuel has been exhausted in the core. Nuclear degenerate matter of the same size weighs a few billion tons; it is created when electron degenerate matter becomes too massive to support its own weight, as happens at the core of a very massive star preceding a Type II supernova explosion.

The mass of the *object* was not much different from that of an ordinary rock; the degenerate matter must therefore be limited to the surface only—to an extremely thin layer, in fact. But, if so, how was the degenerate matter being kept in that state in the absence of the tremendous gravitational force of a collapsed star?

Steph was getting ready to start testing, with utmost care, the heat transmission property of the surface material when she was interrupted by a call from the director.

"Steph, leave that thing where it is and come inside right away."

"What's the emergency this time?"

"Something happened on New Hope. We don't know exactly what—as yet. We need to talk right away. I'll be in the little conference room next to the airlock."

"I'm on my way!"

She left everything, including her test equipment, on the ground and took off toward the airlock as quickly as possible, making sure that her hand slid along the newly installed safety line to avoid launching herself into a flight path by making too much haste.

As soon as she removed her space suit and hung it on the wall, she hurried into the adjacent meeting room; it contained a table, half a dozen chairs, some communication equipment and a computer terminal, and some sidearms on the wall. The chairs were not really necessary in the extremely low gravity environment, but they served as place markers at least.

Conrad was perched on a chair at one end of the oblong table, with his deputy, Tony Galvez, seated to his right. He indicated to Steph the vacant chair opposite Tony. Even as she was taking her place, the director was speaking.

"We sent a message about the discovery of our exotic object to New Hope. They had sent us a report of their find promptly and we wanted to reciprocate. New Hope is about four light-hours away from us, so it takes a third of a day to get a reply back."

When Conrad paused momentarily as if to consider what to say next, Steph posed a question that was foremost on her mind.

"Did they have anything to say about their test results?"

"Soon after acknowledging the receipt of our message, they started sending us a string of data in response to our request, but it stopped abruptly. All we got was an image of their object, which looked remarkably like ours."

"Was there a communication equipment failure?"

Tony Galvez jumped in at this point. "We checked our receiving system. It's working perfectly, receiving messages from other places in the Edgeworld and the inner solar system. If the breakdown had occurred at New Hope, they should have known it immediately, too, and would have switched to their backup set to complete the data transmission."

Reliable line of communication could literally be a matter of life or death to those living in the outposts of space. They took great care in setting up a fail-safe information exchange system with built-in redundancies.

"So, what do you think happened?" asked Steph.

The director answered. "We still don't know, but I can think of several possibilities. One, it is indeed a rare case of communication equipment breakdown at their end. Two, a natural catastrophe—possibly a collision with a big rock, but that's even less probable than an instrument failure. Three, they have been raided by one of the hostile Edgeworld colonies, who destroyed their communication equipment before getting away so the New Hope people could not contact one of the military garrison colonies quickly; there have been a few incidents of that sort lately."

Astonished at this revelation, Steph interjected. "Piracy in the Edgeworld?"

"Yes—although reports of such raids have not gotten into the news media much. But to complete the list of possibilities I was enumerating: Four, it had something to do with the object they had been testing in their lab."

"So, that's why you called me in so quickly!"

"Exactly! And, I am sure glad you persuaded me to let you test it outside first."

Steph was quite shaken—to think how close she might have been to a disaster. Galvez was now speaking. "Steph, you are still relatively new and haven't had the chance to find out how things really are out here. Much of what's going on has been prettied up for popular consumption back home for fear of creating crises among competing parent organizations and, most importantly, scaring off investors."

The competition to establish hegemony there had gotten fierce over the past few decades after transportation using continuous one-g acceleration became available; the new spaceships using antimatter-assisted nuclear propulsion system reduced the Earth-Edgeworld transit time from years to several weeks. Just counting objects larger than a few kilometers, the total surface area of the livable space in the Edgeworld was many times greater than that of the entire land area on Earth, an immense *Lebensraum* to the increasingly land-hungry population. The abundance of ice and hydrocarbon compounds, plus the ready availability of minerals, made the Edgeworld more attractive for permanent human settlement than asteroids and most other places in the solar system. In addition, those settlements would in time become excellent stepping stones for the much anticipated human migrations to the neighboring planetary systems.

Rivalry to outdo each other among the colonies, sponsored by various nations and megacorporations, had led to thefts of high-tech innovations and even to undermining of competitors in some instances; in these extremely hostile environments sabotage often caused destructions of lives. The stakes were high—domination of a vast virgin territory—and the basic aggressive nature of the human race had not changed much since time immemorial. Each nation or megacorporation wanted to be another Portugal or Spain in the new Age of Great Voyages.

Suddenly an idea popped into Steph's head.
"There is one other possibility for the communica-

tion breakdown, Mister Conrad—it's actually a combination of your third and fourth."

The boss looked intrigued. "Oh, really?"

Steph took it as an invitation to continue. "If there is such a fierce, clandestine competition among the various settlements, someone might have wanted to snatch the New Hope object, figuring that it could involve superhuman technology and offer a decisive advantage over others. After their piracy, they might have disabled New Hope's communication system or might have eliminated witnesses."

The director suddenly looked alert and thoughtful. "So far, the only people, outside of this place, who know about our discovery, are my counterpart on New Hope and his chief scientist. I know them both to be trustworthy people. I thought that by exchanging information we could help each other in reaching our common goal. At any rate, I wanted to wait for the results of your preliminary tests before announcing our discovery to the world at large. It occurs to me now it may be better not to announce it at all—for a while, at least. On the other hand, the raiders of New Hope, had there really been such, could have learned about our discovery already while paying an uninvited visit there."

Conrad must have been clearing up his own thinking as he spoke. Before he finished saying the last word, he was already punching the button of the communication apparatus.

"Security Alert! Watch out for any approaching ship. It may be using a stealth device against radar detection, so make full use of the optical surveillance, too. Do not, repeat, *do not* allow any ship to land on Dyson without my explicit authorization."

A voice responded almost immediately. "Security chief to the director. A full alert in effect now."

"Good! Issue a sidearm to everyone, Nick. And have a vacuum suit available within reach of all."

"Roger that, Chief!"

Turning back to Steph, Conrad said, "the risk of a raid is a long shot, but it never hurts to be prepared when our survival is at stake."

Steph did not anticipate that the security training she and her colleagues had undergone periodically would find such immediate application. As she started getting up to report to the security chief, Conrad waved her back down to her seat.

"You are in charge of testing and safekeeping of this object and are exempted from the general mobilization."

He stood up, took two weapons off the wall, gave one to Steph, and strapped the other on himself. His deputy was already helping himself to a third one.

"By the way, just before you walked in, I received a report that your vacuum lab is ready to receive the object. Haul it in there immediately, so nobody from outside can snatch it away easily. Be sure to avoid any testing that might precipitate a catastrophe. I'll try to find out what's really happened to New Hope and let you know."

Steph was not sure how she was to test the darned thing without any risk. Well, first things first. She had better drag it in right away and worry about what to do later.

"Yes, Mister Conrad. I'll get it inside instantly."

When she emerged from the airlock, she found that she was being followed by two assistants to help her with the chore.

*   *   *

Within a few hours of the meeting with Steph Mac-
Nair, Conrad started receiving reports, from a few colonies within several million kilometers of New Hope,
that the miniworld had exploded. The cause of the
blowup was still unknown, leaving several possibilities
open; since nobody was observing the colony when it
occurred, its exact timing was not in the news dispatch
either. A military garrison in the vicinity and a couple
of nearby colonies were sending out search and rescue
ships; they were not expecting to find any survivors,
but were looking to find out what had really
happened.

Since the warning about a possible buccaneer raid,
life on Dyson had become more like that of a military
outpost. Conrad seemed quite at home with the
change in lifestyle, as did his security chief, Nick
Hunter. Nick informed Steph that the boss had been
a military officer with the Team before becoming director of the Space Force laboratory on the Moon. He
then had been recruited to his current post by the
maverick multibillionaire CEO of Valhalla that ran
Dyson and several other pieces of choice real estate
in space. Nick seemed to assume she knew what the
term *Team* meant. Like others on Dyson, security specialists also had practical engineering or scientific
skills; everybody, including supervisors, had real work
to do on Dyson: producing useful things, performing
research or making equipment work, not just managing people.

One change since the latest development had been
a salubrious one for Steph. She was now directly reporting to Conrad—no more shillyshallying with that
slimeball, Rob Newman. She had carried out all the
safe, nondestructive tests she could think of and felt

that she should soon be able to make a comprehensive report but she had the feeling that she was still missing a key factor somewhere.

One early afternoon by the colony's clock, Steph was having a late lunch in the cafeteria. She was enjoying her meal when a fellow worker with a pleasant smile sat down next to her with his tray of lunch. The unpretentious young man had been hanging around her a lot lately, and she had not been discouraging his apparent interest in her. Derek Schuerman's graduate training had been in mathematical physics, but he now worked on Dyson as a computer engineer.

"Say, Steph, have you heard the big news?"

"What news, Derek? I've been out of touch in the vacuum lab for the last several hours."

After swallowing, he answered.

"Well, it appears we now have a well-confirmed detection of gravitational waves; the first report came from the new orbital array, but several other groups soon confirmed the detection with their own experiments. They all reported a magnitude ten detection! I'll bet someone is going to get a Nobel Prize for this; it's the first verified detection of the gravitational wave ever."

Steph became speechless, stopping her fork in midair, then she recovered enough to ask another question.

"When did you say the detection was made?"

"I didn't say, but I believe it was on the day you discovered the exotic object."

For the dozenth time in the past few days, Steph had to correct the error. "Derek, Ali discovered that object. Anyhow, was it before or after the discovery?"

"From the time given in the news, I think the event occurred several hours after the discovery."

Everything suddenly clicked together in her mind. Pushing away from the table and rising from her chair, Steph said, "Excuse me, Derek, but there's something I must do right away."

Leaving a dumbfounded Schuerman behind, she quick-marched out of the cafeteria to the hallway, where she pushed the button for the tube transportation. She did not even think to phone ahead, being so thoroughly preoccupied with the report she was now carrying. The shuttle arrived promptly, and it took only a few minutes to reach the director's office. When she knocked on the door, the familiar voice of Conrad boomed, "The door's open. Come on in."

As she stepped inside, Steph found Conrad seated at his worktable looking at a computer screen. The room looked spartan, as most rooms did in Dyson, but an array of latest model weapons and space suits on the wall reminded her of the martial law in effect. He waved her to a chair opposite him, and indicated a tray with a teapot and fresh cups.

"Help yourself, Steph. What's up?"

Unmindful of the invitation, she began speaking excitedly. "Mister Conrad, they detected gravitational waves!"

"Yes, I just heard the news," he responded, savoring his own steaming tea. "Does this detection have anything to do with your lab work?"

"Yes—well, maybe." Looking slightly uncomfortable, she added, "You see, I have been reporting test results only, excluding from my reports any hypothetical thinking on my part. I will offer my speculations now; you can then decide for yourself if the gravitational radiation detected had anything to do with the New Hope object."

Conrad appeared all ears, so she proceeded to tell

her tale. "What has confounded me most about the *object* has been how the degenerate matter on its surface is kept in that state without the benefit of the crushing gravitational field of a collapsed star. The report of strong gravitational wave detection shortly before or possibly at about the time of the explosion of New Hope provides the possible missing piece in the puzzle. I believe the extremely dense matter in the envelope is kept degenerate by a warped space inside."

The director looked genuinely intrigued. "Are you saying that the scientists on New Hope did something to the warped space, and the thing emitted gravitational waves?"

Steph was glad that she was reporting to a perceptive man. "Yes, something like that. I can think of several ways of that happening. Our colleagues on New Hope probably didn't suspect the existence of the warped space inside the *object*. In one of their tests, they might have placed it under extreme acceleration, disturbing the warp. That could have caused the gravitational radiation. Or they might have exposed the *object* to an intense local heating. It is even possible the hypothetical intruders might have accidentally grazed the *object* with their laser weapon."

"Was the explosion, then, caused by the gravitational radiation?"

"With what little I know, I can't tell if the emission of gravitational waves was connected with the explosion. We'll probably have to wait for the reports from the search and rescue ships that have been dispatched to the site."

Conrad was impressed by the way Steph was answering his questions—intelligently and honestly, without unnecessary equivocations. "Could such *objects* have been created naturally, or do you think they are ET artifacts?"

It was a tough question, but Steph gave a straight response. "They may indeed be alien artifacts, but we can't exclude the possibility that these *objects* have been created by nature. It is all but impossible to create two neutron stars in the proximity of each other, but a number of binary neutron stars are known to exist. Nature must have somehow provided for their existence."

Conrad's next question was a speculative one. "*If* they have been produced by an alien intelligence, have you got any idea why they are here?"

She looked pensive. "If that's the case, they could have been left here for any number of reasons. They might be something the ETs use in their spaceships— in propulsion system or scientific equipment, for example—and could have been just discarded where we found them. For all we know, those ETs could be cosmic litterbugs."

Steph smiled mischievously as if to make a naughty remark. "Or, maybe, they left it here deliberately as a trigger wire."

"What do you mean by that?"

"Well, I've got this idea from a classic flat movie I saw in college. Here is how it might work. By the time the indigenous race in this solar system—that's us— has advanced enough to reach the Edgeworld, we will be at the doorstep of interstellar exploration. We are then bound to find some of their souvenirs and fool around with them, causing one or more of them to emit strong gravitational waves. When the ETs receive the signal, they will know we have gotten this far."

Conrad was not finished with his questions. "What's

the chance of any other explanation for the gravitational waves?"

"The reported strength of the gravitational radiation was equivalent to a type II supernova—a most likely natural cause for such a strong emission—going off approximately one hundred parsecs away. No new supernova of any type has been reported within even a thousand parsecs of the solar system over the last few weeks; a supernova sighting like that would have been a big news item and we'd have heard it for sure. Considering the close coincidence in the timing, the radiation probably had something to do with the New Hope object."

He looked thoughtful. "That's a scary possibility. Do you agree, then, we ought to delay further testing, at least till we have a better handle on this 'space warp' effect?"

"Yes, it would be prudent to do so. I have already collected a lot of good experimental data; I'll shun all intrusive testing from now on and concentrate on data analysis to build a viable theoretical model. But there is no telling how long it will take before we understand the space warp. It may take years to figure out. At any rate, if I were to do the job properly, I would be needing a team of specialists supporting the analysis efforts."

Conrad looked undismayed at her request, as if he had been half expecting it. "Okay—have you got a list of names for your team?"

Steph had not thought things through that far and was caught unprepared, but one name occurred to her right on the spot. "I want Derek Schuerman. He's a first-rate mathematical physicist—just the kind of man I need for the theoretical model work. May I come back to you later with more names?"

"No problem. I'll tell Tony to reassign Derek to your project immediately. If you can't find all of the needed experts on Dyson, we'll talk about recruiting them from outside—even from Earth, if necessary."

What a pleasure it is to work for a man who gives such unstinting support to his people!, marveled Steph.

She used a momentary break to pick up the teapot and pour steaming tea into a fresh cup. The aroma was excellent and so was the taste. Conrad did likewise, then spoke again.

"Let's wait a while to find out what really happened on New Hope before we do anything, but it might be a good idea to move the object to an uninhabited world nearby; we'll of course set up tight security measures so it wouldn't be easy for anyone to steal it."

"That sounds like a logical approach. If and when the time comes, I'll volunteer for a detached assignment to the new laboratory—I imagine there will be experiments that could not be conducted remotely from a distance of millions of kilometers."

Seeing an expression of concern on her boss's face, she quickly added, "Don't worry. I'll take all reasonable precautions conducting my tests. I have no intention of turning it into a suicide mission. And, of course, if anyone comes with me, it will be strictly on a volunteer basis."

Conrad was touched to know that this bright young woman was willing to risk her life for a worthy purpose; he sensed the kindred spirit of a warrior. He was ready to treat her as a comrade. "In case ETs are coming back, we need to be ready for them, too, militarily or otherwise. There is no guarantee that they'll be friendly."

Steph looked simultaneously excited and apprehensive. "That is a possibility we need to take into account, however remote it might be." After a short pause, she observed thoughtfully, "I have little idea where all this will eventually take us, though."

The boss waxed philosophical. "Isn't that what we have come out to the Edgeworld for—to explore the unexplored and to go where we have not yet been?"

Her cheerful response mirrored his sentiment perfectly. "Yes, Mister Conrad, that's what I am here for—the challenge of the unknown and even the unknowable. The only thing I know for sure is I'll be working harder than I have ever imagined—and loving every living minute of it!"

She paused a moment for another sip of the flavorful tea before continuing. "But we have one important clue here that may help us in our quest. Space warp has been just an abstract concept up to this point; its physical reality has not been taken seriously by most working physicists. We now know we need to take it as a given; we have a working specimen! If—I should say—*when* we find the answers, we could even end up with something as fabulous as the much speculated warp drive."

Conrad reacted with a sunny smile. "That's the spirit, Steph. We may be holding the key to the universe right here in our hands!"

After securing the *object* in the vacuum laboratory under the new tight-security measures, Steph MacNair stepped outside. The sun was below the horizon and the ebony-black sky was studded with countless stars forming the familiar constellations, her old and trusted friends from childhood. It was a good place for reflection—to sort out her feelings about what had transpired. It seemed like only yesterday that Conrad had brought her out there to see the *thing* for the first time; the experience since had caused her perspectives to undergo major transformation. *Anything is possible in this universe.* She looked forward to working closely with Derek to start solving its mysteries. *Ad astra!*

Dedication

This story—"The Edgeworld"—was nearing completion when the tragic death of Astronaut Charles "Pete" Conrad on July 8, 1999 was reported to me by one of his long-time associates. I would like to dedicate this story to the memory of Pete Conrad, the Apollo 12 *captain, the* Gemini *and* Skylab *astronaut, the flight manager/pilot for the DC-X reusable launch vehicle, and the founder of Universal Spacelines—a real man of action, a true visionary, and a friend.*

FULL CIRCLE

by Mike Resnick and Kristine Kathryn Rusch

Mike Resnick is the multiple award-winning author of such novels as *Stalking the Unicorn, Ivory, Purgatory, Kirinyaga,* and *A Miracle of Rare Design.* His novella "Seven Views of Olduvai Gorge" won both the Hugo and Nebula Awards in 1995. He is also an accomplished editor, having edited such anthologies as *Alternate Presidents, Sherlock Holmes in Orbit,* and *Return of the Dinosaurs.* He lives in Cincinnati, Ohio.

Kristine Kathryn Rusch is an award-winning writer whose novels have also been on several best-seller lists. Her most recent novels are *The Fey: Victory* and *Hitler's Angel.* She has also coauthored *Star Wars: The New Rebellion* and several *Star Trek* novels with her husband, Dean Wesley Smith.

Sabrina's favorite landing site on Bupkis was eighteen klicks from the main city. A flat stretch of paved land—by the loose Bupkis definition of the term—was bracketed on one side by the ocean and on the other by a lush forest that smelled of roses, regardless of the season. She lied about her ship's configurations every time she hit Bupkis space traffic control (which was a nice polite way of referring to Jack Diamond, who had to be roused out of bed whenever a ship went into orbit) so that she could get to her favorite landing site. Finally Jack said to her, in tones that were both exasperated and sleepy: "Sabrina, we'll let you land at the goddamned ocean site. Just ask next time."

So this time she did. She really didn't want to bring her cargo into the city anyway.

She got out of the shuttle, reached her hands above her head, and stretched. The thin air smelled of roses, just as she had known it would, and the air was warm. The ocean was calmer than usual, its pale waters licking the black rocks that composed the shoreline.

Not for the first time, she thought she would retire here. Stop doing short cargo runs, stop solving middling emergencies, stop eating with spacers at terrible dives on horrible space stations. It was in one of those dives where she'd learned to call this planet Bupkis. It had some other, more official, designation, one she let her navigational computer worry about.

Bupkis it was and Bupkis it would remain as long as she flew here. An air cart pulled up beside the shuttle, and the colony's head, Elle Dorado, got out. She was a small woman possessed of a strong, wiry frame. She had single-handedly taught the two thousand colonists to clear the land and use that awful permaplastic to build what they called a city and what should more properly have been called a village.

They were still growing greenhouse food. Problems with a tiny insect, so small it was almost invisible, prevented actual farming.

The insect, the ghost fly, gnawed the leaves of growing plants, attached its egg sacs to the roots of new plants, and devoured any flowering plants.

Apparently the ghost fly lived on stimspice, a local plant, but seemed to prefer any other vegetation to it.

"You got 'em?" Elle asked. She never minced words, and usually Sabrina liked that. But this time Sabrina had traded the supplies that the colony had given her and thrown in a few favors of her own to bring what Elle wanted. The least Elle could do was give her a polite hello.

"Yes," Sabrina responded. "I wanted to wait until you got here. I've been assured that all we do is release them and wait."

"Wait?"

"They eat insects. We did the experiments you asked, and turns out they absolutely adore ghost fly. In fact, it's become their favorite food. The best estimate is that they will reduce the ghost fly population by a third within a month, and that before a year has passed ghost flies will be nothing but an unpleasant memory."

"And we don't have to breed them or nurture them or anything?"

"Nope," said Sabrina.

"Let's go, then," said Elle.

Sabrina put a hand on her arm. "Before I do, the xenobiologist I got these from told me to ask you a question."

Elle, never one to hide her impatience, began shifting from one foot to another like a child who had to go to the bathroom.

"You settled here because of the great soil, the wonderful climate, the access to water—" began Sabrina.

"I know, I know," Elle interrupted irritably.

"—and the absence, so far as we can tell, of indigenous life-forms. You didn't know about the insects, but obviously there are no pests. And now you want to introduce the chitmouse—"

"They're not really called chitmice, are they?" Elle asked.

"No," Sabrina said. This time she was the one who spoke rather impatiently.

"Their native name is *usianlubiancurscafilianxzynialetliacheenia.*" She had been practicing that for just this moment. "You really want to call them that? The spacer name for them is chitmouse. I'd stick with it."

"I hate spacer names," said Elle.

Sabrina turned away. She had been the one who had accidentally told Elle that the spacer name for this planet was Bupkis. The tirade that had followed that slipup hadn't been pretty.

"Fine," said Sabrina. "Call them what you want. I'm calling them chitmice."

"You're sure it's not chitmouses?" replied Elle sardonically.

Sabrina bit her tongue. "You want them or not?"

"Absolutely," answered Elle. "We have eight more pregnant colonists, and I don't have enough clear permaplastic for another greenhouse. Our food supply is stretched thin as it is. I don't know what it is about this planet, but it has our people breeding like rabbits, even when I've asked everyone to refrain from reproducing until the ghost fly situation is solved."

Elle had been asking everyone to refrain from reproducing for years now: first in the colony ship, then when they first landed on the planet, and now with the ghost fly problem. Sabrina had heard about that, too, from damn near every colonist, all of whom were beginning to conclude that Elle didn't want any of them to reproduce until she found a mate of her own.

Which would probably be never, knowing how difficult Elle was to be around.

"Well, we've solved it," said Sabrina. "Help me release these things." Elle frowned at her, but came to the side of the shuttle. The chitmice were stored in their own special box that had been built to help them withstand the pressures of the cargo hold in hyperspace. Sabrina opened the side of the shuttle, and then took two special pairs of gloves from on top of the box, handed one pair to Elle, and began working the door levers. Elle studied her for a moment, then began doing the same thing.

The sound of fingers scraping against the box's walls seemed to drive the chitmice crazy. They began to make noise, a high-pitched sound which was, appropriately, a chitter. It built and built and built as the women worked and then, just when Sabrina thought she couldn't stand it anymore, she got the door open.

Chitmice flowed out of the box like water. They were brown creatures the size of her fist, with snouts like a pug dog's and little legs with that terminated in hands. They had curly pigs' tails and they brought with them a stench that made Sabrina's eyes water.

"God!" she muttered, bringing the back of her hand to her nose. "If I'd known about that, I'd have asked for more insurance. If that box had broken open in space, I'd have died from the smell."

Elle's eyes were watering. She nodded, and watched the stream of chitmice flow into the woods. "I hope they get lots of ghost flies!" she said fervently.

"Let's hope the ghost flies don't have a sense of smell," Sabrina said.

Elle didn't smile.

After a moment, the chitmouse stream ended, leaving trampled underbrush, lots of droppings—and the stench. Sabrina closed the box and pulled it out of the shuttle, placing it on the landing site.

"Well," she said, "I guess that's yours."

"Lucky me," replied Elle dryly.

*   *   *

Six months later, Sabrina made another landing on Bupkis. Only this time, she wasn't that happy about it. Other spacers got to do the cushy runs, the simple runs, bringing supplies from one site to another—and it seemed like there'd been a lot of supply runs to Bupkis these days—but Sabrina got the tough ones.

She was tired and scraped and dirty, and her entire shuttle smelled of manure, but she had achieved her goal. Or rather, the colony's goal.

Muffkittens. Fifty breeding pair.

And this time she was doing no favors. She'd asked for payment up front, and now she was going to demand a bonus. She'd had no idea that muffkitten breeders lived in the ass-end of nowhere and expected buyers to catch the kittens themselves.

She deserved double—no, make that triple—her usual pay, and Elle was going to hear about it.

Only this time, as Sabrina opened the shuttle door, Elle wasn't there to greet her. And neither was the scent of roses. Maybe her sense of smell had temporarily deserted her after long, close quarters with the muffkittens, none of whom could be said to be housebroken, but it seemed to her that Bupkis now smelled like dirty socks.

The air didn't seem quite as clear either, and the ocean looked kind of droopy. But she was willing to write it off. She was tired, after all. Jack Diamond stood at the edge of the landing site, his hands clasped behind his back as he stared into the woods. He was a tall man with curly black hair and skin the color of good coffee. That, and the fact that even his muscles had muscles, always made Sabrina look twice.

"Muffkittens," Sabrina said without introduction, "may be cute when viewed holographically, but they have sharp little teeth, a nasty growl, and the ability

to fart whenever they're offended, which is pretty
damned often."

"Nice to see you, too, Sabrina," said Jack. Then he
wrinkled his nose. "Been out there a long time, huh?"

No man was going to tell her that she stank. He
wasn't even going to imply it.

"Those muffkittens were dear," she said. "You owe
me double. You should see the damage to my ship."

"Muffkittens?" he asked.

She put her hands on her hips. "It's spacer."

"I don't like spacer," he said and turned away.

"All right," she said, having practiced yet again.
"You can call them *neilthwaowaowasowasssohtlien* if
you want to. But I'm sticking with muffkitten."

A loud sound, rather like the chirping of a bird
crossed with the laugh of a hyena, echoed through
the woods. It grew louder, as more voices added to
the din.

Jack put his hands over his ears. After a moment,
Sabrina did too. Then, as abruptly as it started, it
stopped.

"What the hell was that?" she asked. Her ears actually ached.

"Your last lovely gift," he said. "Chitmice, remember? Guess where the chit came from."

"Hmm," she said. "They didn't do that on the
shuttle."

"They wouldn't." He shook his head. "Now, you're
sure that the muffkitten is the chitmouse's natural
predator?"

"I've watched one of these babies chomp chitmice.
It's not pretty, but it *is* thorough. And I've been assured that given the choice, muffkittens prefer chitmice to just about anything. Why? Didn't the chitmice
eat the ghost flies?"

"Oh, they did," he said. "And they burrowed under the greenhouses and have been having baby chitmice under the lettuce leaves. Chitmice eat green things until they mature and develop a taste for insects. Did you know that?"

Sabrina shook her head.

"And," he continued with barely a pause, "they have no natural predators here and their reproductive cycle is two weeks long and—"

That awful cry started again, joined by a thousand other voices. Sabrina plugged her ears and crouched, burying her head between her knees. It didn't block the sound, which continued for another minute.

When she finally raised her head, Jack was looking down at her. "I hope you brought enough muffkittens," he said.

"Fifty breeding pair," she said.

"They don't have any obnoxious habits, do they?"

"Besides the aggressive farting?"

He stared at her.

She held out her hands. "They're animals, Jack. Not native to here or to Earth. They've been in cages in the back of my shuttle. How the hell do *I* know if they have obnoxious habits?"

"You should have researched it," he said.

"Just a minute!" she retorted heatedly. "It's *your* goddamned colony, not mine! No one asked me to research it. You just asked me to bring something that ate chitmice." They stared at each other for a long moment. Finally she said, "Where's Elle, anyway?"

"In bed," he said. "Wearing earplugs and begging someone to soundproof her room."

"I thought nothing got to good old Elle."

"Nothing except loneliness and loud noises," Jack said.

"I think we have the cure for the loud noises," Sabrina said. "It's up to you guys to find the cure for the other."

"Not us," Jack said adamantly. "We know her too well."

Sabrina opened the hatch. The scent of manure floated out, so strong she could almost see it on the breeze. She peered inside the darkness, and then whistled.

"Hey, Jack?"

"What?"

"Remember that farting comment I made?"

"It's not the kind of thing you forget in less than an afternoon."

"Yeah? Well, try."

He came up beside her. "Why?"

"I think maybe something else was causing those Bronx cheers I was hearing." She pointed inside the shuttle, at the fifty individual cages.

"I thought you said there were fifty breeding pair," he said.

"There were."

He whistled softly. "Wow. These guys make rabbits look like slackers."

"Last chance to back out," she said.

He shook his head. "Hell, no. This is perfect. These creatures'll shut up those chitmice forever."

"Let's hope so," said Sabrina, wondering why she suddenly felt so uneasy.

The muffkittens *did* shut up the chitmice forever. But of course, that wasn't difficult, since they bred like . . . well . . . muffkittens, and by the time the last chitmouse was little more than a happily-remembered dessert there were well over three million muffkittens.

Well, said the powers-that-be, they'll all starve to death with no natural prey left on Bupkis, and that's certainly a pity, but it's hardly our fault, and besides, if any other world has a chitmouse problem, we'll sell them our muffkittens at a deep discount.

It was only after the muffkitten population reached four million that everyone realized that the little animals were *not* starving to death, but instead seemed to be thriving.

Then the reports started coming in from the outlying areas: two hundred thousand acres of corn gone. Three hundred thousand acres of wheat devastated. Five square miles of citrus orchards suddenly lay in waste.

Jack Diamond knew what had happened, but since it had never happened this fast before, he thought he'd better bring in a team of top exobiologists to confirm it. And confirm it they did: having run through their prey, the muffkittens, in overpopulated desperation, had mutated almost overnight into vegetarians. The original muffkittens were all dead—their life span was as short as their reproductive activity was vigorous—but every muffkitten born in the past six weeks was existing solely on fruit and vegetables.

And there were almost five million of them.

The newest order had been the toughest to fill, but with the proper financial incentives, Sabrina found herself returning to Bupkis once again, this time with five hundred catstalkers. The catstalkers—official name: *pellafeliniferousonitammelia*—looked like large terriers, perhaps ninety pounds apiece. They were gentle, loving, silent, lethargic, and serene—until they caught sight or scent of a muffkitten. Then they turned into growling, slobbering, rampaging engines of appetite and destruction.

"Yeah, they look pretty capable," said Jack, staring at the row upon row of caged catstalkers. "Where did you pick 'em up?"

"Terhune IV," answered Sabrina.

"Well, let's let 'em loose," he suggested. "Our problems are finally solved."

"Uh . . . I don't want to be a spoilsport or anything," said Sabrina, "but importing animals to kill the other animals didn't work with the chitmice or the muffkittens. Why do you think it'll work now?"

"Because you brought five hundred *males,*" said Jack with a smug smile. "If there's one thing I know, it's that we're not going to be overrun by catstalkers."

"Sounds good to me," said Sabrina, wondering why a little voice deep within her said it didn't sound so good to *her.*

Elle Dorado had worked out the math, and found it most disturbing. Juggle the figures as she might, she simply couldn't see how the catstalkers were ever going to eliminate the muffkittens.

"Look at the figures," she said to Jack Diamond, who was staring at her computer's holoscreen as it hovered between them on her patio. "The muffkittens are still reproducing at a rate of three thousand and seven hundred a day. And even allowing for exceptionally high metabolisms requiring twice the usual caloric and protein intake, five hundred catstalkers really cannot be expected to devour more than five muffkittens apiece, or a total of twenty-five hundred muffkittens per day." She grimaced and stared at Jack. "That's a net *gain* of twelve hundred muffkittens a day."

"I know, I know," he replied.

"Well, then, what do we propose to do about it?"

"Nothing."

"Nothing?" she demanded.

"Look, I don't know *why,* but the muffkitten population is plummeting. No one's seen one around here in more than a week, and I'm told that even the huge farms between the towns are almost free of them."

"They can't have migrated to another planet," said Elle. "What do you suppose is happening to them?"

"Beats the hell out of me," said Jack. "I suppose if they could mutate into herbivores, they could mutate into polar animals that live on icebergs and eat nothing but fish."

"That's just a bit far-fetched, isn't it?" replied Elle.

Jack shrugged. "Probably. But who cares *why* they're disappearing? The important thing is that there are a lot less of them than there used to be."

"Still, you have to wonder what's going on."

"Well, there's one thing we know: five hundred cats-talkers sure as hell couldn't decimate them to this extent. The answer must lie elsewhere."

But, of course, the answer didn't lie elsewhere.

What Jack hadn't known—and what the overwhelmed residents of Terhune IV had neglected to tell him—was that catstalkers were sex-changers. Every week half of the males became females.

Fertile females.

Romantically inclined females.

With an average gestation period of eleven days, and an average litter of fourteen.

And it didn't take long for a few million catstalkers to dispose of a few million muffkittens.

But unlike the muffkittens, they didn't mutate once

their prey was gone. They craved meat, and, more and more often, they turned their attentions to the cattle and sheep and goats that were being raised to feed the populations of a dozen hungry planets.

"You guys never learn," said Sabrina as Elle and Jack walked up to meet her at the cargo area.

"Bad luck, that's all it is," muttered Jack bitterly.

"Bad research, I'd say," replied Sabrina. "What's this current batch supposed to do? They don't look all that violent to me."

"Ah, that's because we've learned our lesson," replied Elle. "You brought us a thousand matched pairs of soothsingers."

"Soothsingers?" repeated Sabrina. "That's what they call them?"

"I can't give you the scientific name. It took up three pages when I tried to print it out. Basically, it translates as *'Cute little animals that sing a lot.'*"

"They look like a cross between bushbabies and koala bears," said Sabrina. "How are *they* going to stop these wolflike things from killing all your meat and dairy animals?"

Jack grinned triumphantly. "They're going to sing to them."

"I beg your pardon?" said Sabrina.

"Music hath charms to soothe the savage breast," quoted Jack. "Of course, your breast isn't so savage, so it probably doesn't apply to you."

"No matter what the subject, men always manage to bring it around to my breast," said Sabrina disgustedly.

"Right or left?" asked Jack.

"Cut it out, or I'm doubling my fee."

"My lips are sealed."

"Too bad the damned little soothsingers aren't sealed," responded Sabrina.

"What do you mean?" asked Elle.

"They're not the neatest animals in the galaxy. They like to press up against the edge of the cage and see how far they can shoot their urine and their stool. I'm going to be a month getting rid of the stench and the stains."

"They're not here to be neat, but to calm the catstalkers," said Jack.

"By singing to them," said Sabrina sardonically.

"When they're in love, their music is said to be positively mesmerizing," answered Elle. "It should have the same effect on the catstalkers as a tranquilizer. If they then behave themselves—the catstalkers, not the soothsingers—we'll permit a few of them to stay here, if only to keep down the spread of rats and other vermin."

"You have rats and vermin?"

"I have no idea. It's possible. We've been so busy arranging massive kill-offs that a few minor annoyances may have escaped our attention."

"And that's your sole weapon against millions of angry carnivores—a few matched pairs of creatures that sing pretty songs?"

"That sing pretty, *hypnotic* songs," Elle corrected her. "Don't forget the hypnotic."

"I flew them all the way here from Sondheim III, and *I'm* not hypnotized," said Sabrina.

"Did they sing *en route*?"

"No. I didn't know they *could* sing, remember?"

"Then that's your answer."

"No," said Sabrina. "That's your problem. Besides, even if they *can* sing the way you say, what makes you think they will?"

"Spring is in the air," said Jack. "It's all I can do to keep my hands off both of you women."

"I'm being serious."

"All right, then—seriously, there seems to be something about Bupkis that encourages every living thing to breed. I mean, that *is* the gist of all our problems, isn't it?"

"The gist of your problems is that you haven't thought out your solutions very well," said Sabrina. "It has nothing to do with your world's ability to encourage romance."

"Hah!" said Jack. "That just goes to show you don't know Bupkis."

Neither do you, thought Sabrina irritably. *And I have a terrible premonition that Time will prove it yet again.*

The soothsingers did their job. They took one look at each other, fell passionately in love, and spent all day and all night singing their spellbinding songs. The catstalkers were more than entranced upon hearing the haunting melodies; they were quite literally catatonic, and it took very little effort for human hunting parties—disposal parties, actually—to eliminate them.

This time the citizens of Bupkis were certain that they had solved the last of their problems . . . but the Higher Power—it doesn't really matter much if you call It God, Allah, Nature, the First Cause, or whatever—has a sly sense of humor, and It wasn't done with Bupkis yet. After all, It had not just created man, but also the ghost fly, the chitmouse, and all the other animals that man kept importing and then eradicating.

The soothsingers didn't mutate. They didn't eat meat. They didn't breed prolifically. All they did was sing.

And every man and woman of breeding age who heard them turned just as catatonic as the catstalkers.

Things didn't get much better during the following months as Sabrina kept transporting new "cures" to Bupkis.

The divebombers killed off all the soothsingers, but they also tended to fly off with small children to feed their own young.

So Bupkis imported dreadnuts (some people said the dreadnuts were so-named because they were all crazy; others said no, it was because of their huge testicles), and the dreadnuts killed the divebombers— but they also defoliated more than half the farms before Bupkis sent away for slydevils.

The slydevils were about the same size as lions (or tigers, if you prefer, and why shouldn't you, since the slydevils were magenta with glowing puce stripes). They decimated the dreadnuts, then started looking for tastier meals.

And easier ones.

And turned their multifaceted mauve eyes toward the colonists.

The only way to get rid of them was to bring in a few thousand bigtrains from Roundhouse VI. The bigtrains were huge lumbering beasts, herbivores all, with what seemed to be an inborn hatred of slydevils.

The battles were long and bloody, for the slydevils feared nothing, and they could be heard (and smelled) from miles away, but finally the last of the slydevils was dead, and the bigtrains, ten tons apiece, settled down for some serious grazing. Before anyone quite knew what had happened, they had turned half of Bupkis into a dust bowl and were busy defoliating the other half.

The colonists were grateful to the bigtrains, of course, but the situation was becoming intolerable. There was nothing for it but to spend the last of the planetary treasury on one hundred cock-o-the-walks— official name: *gudsluggeesichtenbechteinps*—which made Tyrannosaurs look small and spindly (and gentle) by comparison.

It was awful, seeing one gentle, unassuming bigtrain after another fall prey to these twenty-five-ton carnivores, but it had to be done, and in the end the planet began turning green once more.

Of course, the main reason Bupkis was becoming green was because the cock-o-the-walks ate only meat.

And by this point in the game, there was only one source of meat left on the planet.

"I can't help you," said Sabrina, having a drink with Jack Diamond and Elle Dorado while her ship was being refueled. "Even if there is something out there in the galaxy that can kill a cock-o-the-walk, I couldn't fit it into the ship. I think you're stuck with them."

"I don't think you comprehend the seriousness of our situation," replied Jack. "I've gone on safari after them. There isn't a weapon powerful enough to bring one down. Or if there is," he amended, "the radioactive fallout would kill every last man, woman, and child on Bupkis."

"Which the cock-o-the-walks will do anyway," added Elle morbidly.

"Of course, that'll be the end of them, too," said Jack. "When the last of us is gone, the last of them will starve to death . . . but of course there won't be any of us around to applaud."

"I wish I knew what to say . . ." began Sabrina.

"There's nothing *to* say," responded Elle. "Just stop

by in six or seven months and say a prayer over what's left of us."

"*Will* there be anything left of you?"

"Our shoes," said Jack.

"Your shoes?"

He nodded. "They hate shoes. They eat us whole, then spit out our shoes. So wherever you find a pair of shoes, plant a cross and say a brief prayer."

When her drink was done, Sabrina returned to her ship, feeling more like she had just been to a funeral than that she would be coming back to conduct one.

Sabrina returned seven months to the day after she had left, prepared for scenes of unimaginable carnage and devastation. Instead, she found a prospering colony without a single cock-o-the-walk in sight.

"What happened?" she asked as Jack came up to greet her. "I thought nothing could kill a cock-o-the-walk."

"It was the strangest thing," he told her. "Remember the ghost flies that started this whole mess?"

"Sure. The chitmice killed them all."

"Well, not quite all. It turns out that a few dozen survived in a swamp halfway around the planet."

"So what?"

"So it turns out that the one thing that can kill a cock-o-the-walk is a ghost fly's bite." He grinned. "It seems they're allergic."

"You're kidding!" exclaimed Sabrina.

"Look around," said Jack. "Do you see any cock-o-the-walks?"

"I'll be damned! So it really worked!"

"Right," Jack concurred. "This place is just about perfect again." He paused, frowning. "Except for one thing . . ."

"Oh?"

He sighed deeply. "How are we going to get rid of these goddamned ghost flies?"

Sabrina resisted the urge to laugh hysterically. It was *déjà vu* all over again.

All thoughts of retirement vanished from her mind. She could see where she was going to be employed for the next few years.

NO PLACE LIKE HOME

by Dana Stabenow

Dana Stabenow is best known for her gritty Alaskan mystery novels featuring Aleut detective Kate Shugak. During her rise in the mystery fiction genre, however, she also wrote three well-received science fiction novels, *Second Star, A Handful of Stars,* and *Red Planet Run.* She continues to write mysteries in and about Alaska, but from time to time revisits her science fiction roots.

We put down at the equator because it was the warmest latitude on the planet. Also the flattest.

"And the most boring," Grady said, hunched over the viewport.

"And the safest," I said, trying to peer over his shoulder.

"Well, it's no place like home."

"Not yet," I said. "Give us time."

There wasn't much of that going around, and we both knew it. "Look at that darker patch of ground over there. Do you remember if any of the scans showed iron ore deposits in this area?"

"There's nothing here, Grady," I said, relieved at the change of subject. "That's why we landed here, nothing to trip over. Don't worry, I'll have the rover up and running in a week and then you can prospect your little heart out. That ridge we scanned from our last orbit is less than fifty klicks away."

He didn't say anything, but then he didn't have to.
We came from the same place, a planet with too many
people and not enough room, where children went
hungry, and now some were starving because funds
and material had been funneled to this expedition. I
thought of my nieces, Joanna and Annie, and my
nephew, David. Odds were I'd never see them again,
but if I did my job and didn't screw up, I might help
give them a future.

The space station, the habitats at L-4 and L-5, the
colonies on the moons, they were self-supporting but
their capacity was limited. We needed somewhere to
go, a suburbial planet, a bedroom community for six
billion. Joanna was eighteen, David ten, Annie two.
This planet was theirs.

The plains stretched out in front of us, the far but
finite horizon jarring sensibilities accustomed to an infinite ebony expanse. The dirt was blood red, the sky
pastel pink. After twenty-five months in transit, sunshine diffused by an atmosphere hurt my eyes.

I felt a touch on my shoulder and turned to see
Esme Lauter. I stepped aside. Esme crowded in next
to Grady for his first, nontelescopic look at our brave
new world, and began a soft chant in Quarto, the language of the Universal Church of Being. The UCB
was the fastest growing organized religion back home;
at last count there were more Universalists than Cath-
ars. The Council, six of twenty-one senators UCB,
made it virtually impossible to assemble a crew for our
expedition without at least one pro-life, anti-capital
punishment vegan on board.

I understood; in a place of no hope, where daily
choices were made between who got to eat and who
didn't, a faith that preached the sanctity of all life was
some solace. It gave a spiritual underpinning to the idea

that everybody got to eat, although I never did understand the logic of a faith that forbade the eating of meat and allowed the eating of grains and vegetables. Life is life, isn't it? Either it's sacred or it isn't. Esme tried to explain it to me once—"We don't eat anything with eyes"—but I guess I'm just not the pious type.

I thought again of Joanna and David and Annie, not an ounce of spare flesh between them, as healthy as they were only because my brother-in-law was a commercial fisherman in Prince William Sound. They couldn't count the fish he caught until he got back to the dock, and there was a lot of open space between the dock and the fishing grounds. Everyone in our family was a card-carrying omnivore.

Esme finished his chant and explained that it was a prayer of thanksgiving offered up to the creator of all living things, sort of a verbal thank-you card to God for getting us safely to our destination. We murmured something appropriate, and he left.

We weren't on the ground more than two hours before Grady had us suiting up. It didn't take us long to get used to gravity again, and Hiroshi and Roberto had the drills out and in place before sunset. There was ice, all right, thirty-two centimeters below the surface. For once, the gnomes at home had interpreted the probe data correctly. Lucky for us, since our water tanks were running on empty.

"Cold," Hiroshi said, emerging from his goonsuit shivering and pinch-faced.

"Er than a witch's tit," Roberto agreed cheerfully. He'd been nauseous for two years; he didn't care how cold the planet was so long as it had enough gravity to keep his feet and his dinner down.

I'd been rearranging the furniture in the galley, unbolting tables and chairs from the bulkheads and placing them on what was now the floor. I'd reduced our dining room from three to two dimensions and our ten-man crew was shoulder to shoulder, but no one complained. Betty cooked, making a praiseworthy effort at extracting flavor from foil envelopes of alleged food packed two AUs away. Betty was a genius in the galley, but Betty Crocker herself would have been culinarily challenged by what we had left in the pantry. I'd have killed for a hot, meaty chili, smothered in onions and shredded cheese.

Grady made a little speech and raised a toast of eighteen—now twenty-year-old—single malt scotch, hoarded carefully for just this occasion. It didn't taste as smooth here as it did back home, but the flush started hot and low in my gut and spread up and out.

Esme followed the toast with a ceremonial chant. The UCB liturgy has a chant for everything, and encourages lay participation. Hiroshi, a Buddhist and very polite, bent his head. The rest of us waited with varying degrees of patience for it to be over, and went to bed.

It was Grady's night, and either the Glenmorangie or the gravity or both inspired him, because it was an inventive few hours before I got any sleep.

Engineers do it any way they can.

I was a mechanic. I'd spent the voyage out minding the drive, not that demanding a job given the passive nature of a nuclear propellant system: detonation, reaction, thrust, course adjustment, coast, detonation. After turnaround, about all I had to do was make sure the next charge was in the chute prior to launch, and that the thrust plate hadn't suffered a meltdown following detonation. Yawn. I was looking forward to handling tools again.

Landing+1 found me breaking out the components of the rover, essentially a perambulating platform with four enormous wheels. The engine was solar-powered, which made for a relaxed cruising speed and a guaranteed fuel supply. We weren't going anywhere in a hurry, but we would get there in the end. The cabin was a plated half-sphere. I christened it the Tortoise and the name stuck.

There wasn't enough oxygen or enough atmosphere to work unsuited, and working with gloves slowed me down. It took until lunch to get the platform assembled, and I'd just started to inflate the first segment of the first tire when Grady called us inside for a break and lunch. I unsuited in the airlock, indulged in a futile wish for a long, hot shower, and climbed through engineering and hydroponics to the galley.

Lunch was an herb omelet with a dusting of parmesan and fresh radishes. Grady complimented Betty, and Esme, our hydroponist, and inquired as to the menu for dinner. "Hot beef sandwiches," Betty said.

"Shit on a shingle," Hiroshi, the only ex-Marine in the group, said *sotto voce*.

"I'm going to need water," Betty said. "Soon."

"You'll have it," Hiroshi said, brightening. Half our crew complement was mining engineers; they were happy to be digging up anything. The sooner I got the Tortoise operational so they could go prospecting, the better.

That night was Esme's. He was very sweet, but he always had to be in love, and his brand of foreplay involved a lot of verbal reassurance that he was loved in return. If we hadn't been short one woman, and if I hadn't lost the toss between Aya, Betty, and myself with Kirsten already committed to Roberto, I would have been happy to forgo the pleasure. As it was, I murmured a lot of sweet nothings that seemed to satisfy him and fell asleep as soon as possible.

Farmers plant it deep.

By noon on Landing+2, we had water, about a liter, melted down from a core sample Hiroshi and Kirsten pulled out of the ground three meters off the starboard bow.

By thirteen hundred, Betty had run it through a filter, boiled it in the microwave, and we all had a ceremonial sip of reconstituted freeze-dried coffee.

By sixteen hundred, Hiroshi, Kirsten, and Aya had installed the drill, the liquifier, the pump, the filter, and the catch tank, and Boris had attached the flow line to the ship's potable water coupler.

By seventeen hundred we had running water.

By seventeen-thirty Betty was boiling more water for dinner.

By eighteen hundred, Betty was dead.

Grady had the crew assemble in the galley the next day at oh-nine.

"Let me get this straight," Grady said. "You slammed Betty's hand in the microwave door, and when she tried to fight you, you slugged her. Which blow, Aya reports, knocked her into the bulkhead, where she suffered a severe injury to the brain and died almost instantly."

Aya, our medic, nodded confirmation.

"Talk," Grady said. His face was set, and his skin was a dull red all the way up over his scalp.

"I didn't mean to kill her," Esme said. "But she wouldn't listen to me. I had to stop her."

"From doing what?"

"Committing mass murder."

There followed one of those silences that smells like a riot in waiting. "Okay," Grady said finally. "You mind explaining that to the rest of us?"

Esme was more than ready to. Like Betty, Esme needed water for his hydroponic system. He'd run a sample through the scope and detected what he unilaterally decided were bacteria, single-celled microorganisms, the lowest order of life, but life nonetheless.

And we hadn't brought it with us, it had been here.

"Wait a minute," Grady said sharply. "There isn't enough oh-two on this rock to sustain life. The imagers, the probes, our own scans from orbit proved that over and over."

"Bacteria don't need oxygen, or at least some of them don't. Facultative anaerobes prefer it, but they can live without it."

"It's as close to absolute zero out there as I ever care to get," Roberto said. "What lives in that?"

"Maybe nothing we know of—yet," Esme said. "But bacteria live in ice in the poles on home world. And one of the reasons bacteria survive so well is that they can go dormant for long periods of time."

It was about here that I pretty much zoned out of the discussion. Like I said, I was a mechanic. Mine was the care the gear engages. Mine was not the care and feeding of microbes.

For the next hour we sat as Esme showed us pictures of what looked to me like worms, displayed next to a red blood cell pictured in the same scale. It looked like a penny next to an eyelash. Roberto had to be restrained until Esme explained it was his own blood, not Betty's.

Esme juggled words like "heterotrophs," and gave

an impassioned disquisition on the subject of cyano-bacteria, which according to him had single-handedly created the atmosphere back home.

Esme looked Grady in the eye and said firmly, "I think we should shut down operations."

"And do what?" Grady said. "Esme, if we shut down operations, we stop acquiring water. Even with recycling every ounce of body fluid, we nearly ran out on the trip here. We won't survive."

"Then we don't," Esme said. "There is life indigenous to this planet, I have proved it, and I don't care if we die for it, we don't roll over the top of it just because we can. Life is sacred, Grady. Any life."

"They have eyes?" I said.

Esme's head snapped around. "What?"

"These bacteria. They have eyes?"

He flushed, almost as red as Grady. "They are," he said carefully, "the building blocks of life, of all life. Who knows how they will evolve, what forms they will take?" He drew himself up. "The point is, they are life-forms, indigenous to this planet, and we don't shove them out of the way just because we can. We have to stop operations. Now."

"What are you going to do?" I said that night.

"I don't know." Grady shifted next to me in the dark. "Why the hell did he have to look?"

I said nothing. I'd seen grief on Esme's face today, but no guilt, and no regret. He was convinced absolutely of the righteousness of his act, and he was no less certain of the course of our future action. We would cease operations, even if we died of it.

Evangelists do it with Him watching.

"How many of the crew do you think are with him?" Grady said.

"How many of the rest of them support Esme, do you mean? God, Grady, I don't know. None of them seem all that hot to become martyrs. Nobody except Esme talked much religion on the way out. Hiroshi's a Buddhist, and they have tremendous respect for life. Boris is his partner, but that doesn't mean anything. Aya, well, she's a healer. Franz says ve dee zuperior live vorms are, our need bevore dee bugs come. Roberto and Kirsten have gone into their cabin, and I don't think they're coming out until it's over, whatever 'it' is."

"Thanks."

"Always glad to be of service."

He rolled over on top of me. "Works for me."

Later, he repeated, "Works for me."

I understood.

The second ship put down next to us right on schedule. Every available cubic meter of space was crammed with supplies, including material for an expansion to the existing shelter that included a small water reclamation plant and a shower facility. The followers of the Universal Church of Being could have chanted a celebration to that with my right goodwill.

We invited the incoming crew to dinner. The news from home hadn't changed, although everyone had messages from family. Joanna had been accepted into the marine biology program at the University of Hawaii, David was driving his fourth-grade teacher insane, and Annie was talking in complete sentences.

In return, we caught up the second team on our progress to date—we'd already found deposits of iron ore and nickel. They asked about the two graves located nearby, and the next day in a small ceremony they added rocks to the cairns surmounting each one.

Their commiseration was sincere over Betty's freak accident—"Good cooks are hard to come by" their captain said with genuine sympathy—and they shook their heads over the faulty seal on Esme's goonsuit. It had resulted in the oxygen boiling out of his lungs while he was drilling a series of core samples on that promising ridge we had spotted from orbit. He'd had the Tortoise out that day, and he was only fifty-two kilometers away, but one of the tires had flattened before he had been able to make it back to base.

Mechanics do it with their tools.

THE VIETNAMIZATION OF CENTAURI V

by Peter Ullian

Peter Ullian is the author of numerous works of fiction and drama. He wrote the book for the musical, *Eliot Ness . . . in Cleveland,* which *Variety* called "a musical of great style and crisp wit . . . taut, absorbing . . . textured (and) rich in shading." Ullian's play *Hester Street Hideaway* was produced off-Broadway by En Garde Arts. His screenplays include *Justice* (Paramount) and *A Beginner's Guide to Armed Robbery* (Hollywood Pictures). His screenplay *Survivors* has been optioned by actor Alfred Molina and director Mark Rydell, with Sean Penn and Diane Lane committed to play starring roles. Ullian's previous fiction includes "Owen's Blood," published in *Cemetery Dance.* He is currently at work on a new project for director Harold Prince.

It was the day of what became known as the Sandy Hill Massacre on Centauri V that Corporal Richard Ryder lost all sense of certainty about everything he had been taught to believe.

Ryder's fellow soldier, Kay Willis, a Jesuit-trained Catholic, also suffered a crisis of confidence, and completely lost her previously solid religious faith that same day.

On the other hand, John Braddock, the third member of their team, who had never given theological matters much serious thought, quite unexpectedly found God.

The event that served as the catalyst for their re-spective spiritual journeys was the wholesale slaughter of the residents of a Centauri village by a platoon of Earth soldiers under the authority of the Inter-Planetary Treaty Organization.

Ryder, Braddock, and Willis didn't know the extent of the violence when they crested a hill overlooking a field of waving blue grass, their rifles at port-arms. But they heard the unmistakable burst of heat-seeking automatic rounds, and saw the IPTO soldier, no more than nineteen years old, firing at the Centauri female. Her age was hard to distinguish, but she appeared to be similarly in the bloom of late adolescence.

They did not see the Centauri girl right away, of course, because she was naked, and her blue skin blended in perfectly with the blue meadow plants around her. Not blue, Ryder thought. Azure. The Centauri grass, the sky, and oceans were not blue, they were azure. That was the word Ryder had come up with when he had been called upon to describe the planet to Terrans who only knew it from pictures.

The fact that the female was naked was no surprise, of course. The Centauri never wore clothes, except for the ones who had been compelled to do so after they moved to the Earth Colony settlements. The Centauri didn't even have a word for "naked" in their language. Such a word would suggest a choice between clothed and unclothed, and as the Centauri always went un-clothed, they had no word to suggest an alternative. The temperate climate they lived in did not require them to cover themselves, and their culture didn't either.

Red splotches dotted the Centauri girl's back when the rounds struck her. The impact knocked her off her feet, and she disappeared into the tall stalks.

A warm breeze wafted by, and the grass shimmered. The Centauri A sun was high in the afternoon sky, and the two other stars in the Centauri system were also visible. The sound of the shots echoed and faded, followed by an unsettling calm.

Braddock, a sergeant and the team leader, lead Willis and Ryder over the hill. Braddock and Willis went to the Centauri female, and Ryder cautiously approached the young Terran soldier.

Things have changed on this planet, Ryder thought, as he trudged through the grass toward the young infantryman. *Not like it used to be. Not like it must have been for the first Earth pioneers.* To them, arriving some fifty-odd years ago, the Centauri probably seemed to live in a paradise; a primitive, peaceful culture at one with their surroundings, living in close rapport with their natural environment. It must have been a heady experience for those first Terrans, to disembark into this tropical environment, having left behind an Earth where the ozone layer was so depleted that one couldn't venture outdoors without long sleeves, gloves, hat, dark glasses, and a complete coating of sunscreen, and where the natural vegetation was mostly withered and sun-blasted. The first Earth explorers must have thought they had stepped into a Garden of Eden, except that there was more than one Adam and one Eve, and their God, if he created them in his own image, had catlike pupils, long, limber arms and legs, and other biological singularities.

The Centauri were physically beautiful creatures, exotic, strange, but in some ways familiar. They were basically humanoid. The tallest stood about five feet, five inches. Their bodies were sleek, their skin smooth and almost hairless. Their hands and feet were wider than a human's, and slightly webbed. They could swim through water like sharks, and once ashore, the liquid would bead off their bodies like rain off a freshly waxed car. They stood erect, but they could scuttle on all fours with great agility if the situation called for it, gliding through tall grass without ever seeming to disturb a blade, and they could scamper up trees like lizards. They had little curved cups on their palms and hands, like the suckers on the tentacles of an octopus, and when the females were nursing, these cups filled in with a thin, mosslike substance, fuzzy little ciliary hairs which cushioned an infant's thin, membranelike skin. The Centauri's skin tone was chameleonlike, changing to match their environment, and sometimes to match their emotions.

The Centauri lived in communal social units, basically small tribes. They were nomadic, but they settled in one place for long periods of time, and built simple but effective shelters. Males and females shared most of the work equally, from hunting and farming to child rearing.

The Centauri reproduced sexually the same way humans did. The females chose their sexual partners. The Centauri did not mate for life, but each Centauri male remained responsible for the care of his own offspring. When sexually aroused, the Centauri, both male and female, emitted a strong, musky odor, and during intercourse, their glands secreted a lubricating substance that covered their entire bodies.

Not surprisingly, some of the human visitors found this repulsive. Also not surprisingly, other human visitors found this extremely enticing. As more and more Terrans came to Centauri V, some humans and Centauri engaged in sexual relations with one another. These humans usually reported extremely satisfactory results. Their less adventurous colleagues were satis-

fied to take their word for it, and leave it at that.
It was never determined how the Centauri felt about
coupling with humans, but as the years passed, human/
Centauri pairings continued to occur, not that frequently, but not that rarely either.

Looking back on it, Ryder could see the problem
was that the Earth colonizers had underestimated the
Centauri. Noble savages, they thought. Peaceful, pastoral creatures of nature. The mistake was to assume
that because they were a nontechnological people, the
Centauri were too unsophisticated to be dangerous.
They had welcomed the Earth visitors at first, but
when the settlements expanded and the Centauri felt
encroached upon, and when some of the colonists in
the outlying trading posts, unrestrained by the Colonial Authority, started to rape Centauri women, steal
Centauri land, and sell Centauri children into slavery,
the Centauri fought back.

And they proved to be just as vicious as any Terran
could be. On more than one occasion since the war
had begun, Ryder had seen fellow soldiers unfortunate
enough to have been captured who had been strung
upside down by their ankles, emasculated, with their
throats slit. Now, a year into the conflict, most IPTO
recruits would rather commit suicide than allow themselves to be captured by the Centauri.

"Son," Ryder said when he reached the soldier, although he himself was no more than a few years older
than the boy, "Hand me your firearm, son."

The soldier just looked at Ryder, his eyes blank,
and blinked a few times. His weapon was pointed directly at Ryder's chest. He didn't seem to know where
he was, or whom he was talking to.

Ryder decided not to try to get through to the kid,
who was probably so charged up with adrenaline, and

possibly Stim-Meds, that he didn't know what he was doing. Instead, Ryder shoved the soldier's weapon aside, and clubbed him on the temple with his own sidearm. The soldier's eyes lost focus, and he collapsed.

At the same time, Braddock and Willis had located the Centauri female, who was lying facedown. Her back was covered with blood, which was soaking the matted grass around her. They could see she was dead, but they rolled her over just to be sure. They also wanted to see if she was carrying a spear-stick. A spear-stick was about the shape and length of an arrow, and it was the Centauri's standard weapon. The IPTO soldiers had thought they would have no trouble putting down the Centauri rebellion, with their superior weaponry. But the Centauri had an annoying habit of jumping out of nowhere and driving a spear-stick through an IPTO soldier's heart and then disappearing again a split second later. They were spry creatures, and they could move fast and in peculiar positions, which would have been awkward for humans. It was at such times when the Centauri seemed somewhat less like exotic humans and somewhat more like creatures of another solar system.

The Centauri females fought alongside the Centauri males unless they were nursing their offspring, so it was not necessarily a breach of protocol for the soldier to have been shooting at this one, if she was carrying a weapon.

Braddock and Willis rolled the female over.

She was not carrying a weapon.

When Willis looked into the dead Centauri's girls eyes, she felt something snap inside of her, like a piano wire suddenly cut. Later that day, she decided it was her faith, broken in two with a deep, internal

shudder that she could only describe as a *twang*. She
was not immediately aware of it the moment it happened, but when she stopped to think about it, she
realized that for the first time in her life, she no longer
believed in God. She thought it was odd that one's
soul should be lost with a *twang*. She would have expected a more dignified noise, like the rumble of distant thunder, or at least the ominous tolling of a bell.

Braddock, on the other hand, looked into a different set of eyes. He looked into the eyes of the Centauri infant the dead girl had been carrying instead of
a spear-stick. The baby Centauri, unhurt, looked back
into his eyes and gurgled very much like a human
child.

Braddock, who was unmarried and had no children
of his own, was enveloped by an odd sensation, as if
his body was filled with a deep and cleansing warmth.
He thought the daylight itself grew somehow brighter.
He didn't know what it was at the time, but later,
when he stopped to think about it, he decided he had
found God.

Ryder's crisis was less spiritual, and less profound.
He just felt depressed. He didn't know what he was
fighting for anymore. He had been among the first
humans born on Centauri V, and although he had
been to Earth many times, and had been educated
there, Centauri V was his home, and he had joined
the IPTO to defend his home when the Centauri natives rebelled.

But, of course, it was the Centauri natives' home,
too. Indeed, the word the Centauri used for this planet
translated roughly into English as "Home." Centauri V
was the name the first explorers had given the planet,
simply because it was the fifth planet from the star
known as Centauri A.

Everything was wrong, Ryder thought, down to the names of things, even the way the Earth Colonists referred to the inhabitants of the planet. The Centauri did not call themselves the "Centauri." The word they used for themselves translated roughly as "the People."

So, Ryder thought, *I'm fighting for my home by fighting the People who are fighting for a place called Home.*

And now he was bashing his fellow soldiers on the head, because they were shooting Centauri females in the back. If that wasn't a ludicrous equation, he didn't know what was. Situation Normal, All Fucked Up. He had never understood those words in quite the same way before.

Ryder saw Willis and Braddock approaching him, with the Centauri infant in Braddock's hands. When they arrived, Braddock plopped the kid into Ryder's arms. The infant looked up and cooed at Ryder. Ryder gently touched its face, and the infant took his little finger in its mouth and sucked it.

"Congratulations," Braddock said. "It's a boy."

"Girl was unarmed," Willis said.

"Maybe our soldier-boy thought otherwise," Ryder suggested.

Then they heard the sounds of firepower unleashed at random from the other side of Sandy Hill.

By the time they reached the IPTO platoon, with the groggy soldier in tow, his head wrapped in a rudimentary bandage, they saw that the Centauri village in the glade below was engulfed in flames. Soldiers were running rampant, firing at fleeing Centauri, none of whom, as far as Ryder could see, were armed.

Closest to them, two soldiers were taking turns firing their rifles at another Centauri child, who was sitting in a clump of dirt, crying. The two men had disengaged the guidance system on their rifles, and were trying to shoot the child the old-fashioned way. The slugs were hitting the dirt about a meter short.

Ryder gripped the infant he held tighter in his arms.

"Gentlemen, you will discontinue this activity immediately, or I will place you both under arrest," Braddock said.

The two men looked at Braddock with an expression that strongly suggested contempt. They were both privates, so Braddock outranked them, but they did not seem particularly impressed with that fact.

"We're under orders, sir," the one who wore a small mustache said.

"Orders from whom?" Braddock asked, incredulous. In the distance, another soldier emptied his entire automatic rifle clip into a Centauri female, this one also carrying an infant. His clip was filled with explosive rounds, and both the adult and infant Centauri were blown to pieces.

"Jesus," Willis said under her breath, and then wondered who she was saying it to.

"Orders from our captain," the one with the mustache said.

"I'm countermanding those orders, soldier," Braddock said.

"He's a captain. You're a sergeant," the mustachioed soldier said, then aimed and took another shot at the child, missing by only inches this time.

Braddock drew his sidearm, and Willis did the same. Ryder shifted the infant to his left arm, and also drew his weapon. All three aimed at the two soldiers.

"You men are under arrest," Braddock said. "Violation of the code of military conduct, insubordination, and violations of the Geneva Convention, as amended by the IPTO Lunar Accord. Surrender your weapons, or so help me, I'll blow your brains out."

The two soldiers looked at Braddock, then at the infant, then at the three weapons only inches from their faces. Finally, they put up their hands.

"Willis, get that child sitting out there," Braddock said.

A moment later, Willis came back, the child limp in her arms. Ryder could see it was dead before Willis even came close.

"A stray slug hit him, I guess," Willis said, her voice calm, even, expressionless.

Braddock stared back at her for a moment, equally expressionless, then swung his sidearm across the mustachioed soldier's face. The soldier went down to the ground, conscious, but spitting out teeth and blood.

"Take me to your commanding officer," Braddock said. "Now."

From the top of Sandy Hill, Captain Justin A. Morray watched the battle below, and ignored Braddock's insistent tone as the sergeant pleaded with him to call off the attack.

"Have you seen what these creatures do to our boys?" Morray said. "The women too, not just the men."

"I know what they do, sir, you don't have to lecture me on that," Braddock said. "Those people down there are villagers, they are mostly females caring for infants, and the elderly; they are not soldiers. The soldiers don't live in the villages when the Centauri are at war, they hide out in the hills and the forests. You know why they do this, Captain? To prevent this very thing from happening. This very thing."

"Do you know what happened to my men just a few days ago, Sergeant?" The Captain said. "We stopped off at a Colonial outpost, about a hundred klicks from here. New Baltimore, you've heard of it? We thought we'd take a load off, a day or two of R& R, a drink or two, maybe some of the boys could dance with some of the outpost girls, if they'd a fancy to. Never expected trouble, 'cause New Baltimore's not in a hot spot, and the Colonials there have a pretty good relationship with the locals, lots of trade back and forth. The Colonials stay in their enclave, don't encroach on the Centauri territory, everything's jake. Well, guess what we find when we get there? All two hundred and forty some-odd Colonials, men, women, children, and babies, strung up by their ankles like fish by their gills, stripped naked like these savages, the men with their balls cut off, and all of them with their throats slit and the blood run out. They'd been there quite some time, and the birds and bugs had started in on them. We moved out ten klicks and sent in an incendiary, just torched the whole settlement to cinders. No point in trying to cut them down and bury them. None of my men had the stomach for it.''

But they have the stomach for this? Ryder thought, as he looked down on the continuing carnage below. The Centauri dwellings, mostly huts and lean-tos cut from the azure grass, were all in flames. Nearby, several soldiers were having their way with a Centauri female. Her skin color was changing rapidly, randomly, from green, to blue, to red, to brown, to tan, to black, to purple, as if desperately trying to lock on a hue which would allow her to disappear and escape. When one of the soldiers finished, he took out a knife and slit the female's throat. Another soldier, apparently angry at having been denied his turn, started a fist fight with him.

Ryder felt the bile rise in his throat. And then the feeling went away, and he felt nothing at all.

"I'm sorry about New Baltimore, sir," Braddock was saying. "This is the first I've heard of it. I had friends there, so I mean it when I say I'm sorry. But, sir, listen to me . . . the Centauri who did that are not the Centauri your men are slaughtering down there. I'll say it again . . . there are no Centauri soldiers in the villages during times of war. There are only females with infants, or pregnant females, or the elderly. It is inconceivable to the Centauri that anyone would want to harm these villagers, sir."

"Tell that to New Baltimore," Morray said. "The Centauri there didn't seem to show any mercy with our civilians."

"I realize that, sir," Braddock said. "That doesn't mean we have to do the same."

Morray, who had been studiously watching the attack on the village, now turned and, for the first time in the conversation, looked Braddock directly in the eye.

"Soldier," he said, "you have to get it out of your mind that these creatures are like us. They are not. They are not human beings. They are another species entirely. They are no more like us than a chimpanzee. Less, even, because a chimpanzee and you share ninty-nine percent of the same DNA. You cannot ascribe human worth to these creatures. Just because they have arms and legs and pretty blue eyes and tits and ass, does not make them like us. You think they are like us because their women let you screw them? I've got news for you . . . you could do the same with a chimpanzee, if you tried. The only reason you don't try is because humans don't like all that fur. If these creatures were furry instead of naked, you wouldn't raise any objection to what my men are doing down there."

The Centauri infant in Ryder's arms kicked and shrieked just then, catching Morray's attention.

"Hand me that creature," Morray said.

Ryder hesitated. He felt his heart sink. For a moment, he was torn; he did not know what to do. Then, in an instant, all his doubt disappeared, and he knew.

"No," Ryder said.

"Don't be difficult, Corporal," the captain said. "Hand it over."

"No, sir," Ryder said.

"I'll throw you in the brig, soldier."

"You don't have a brig out here," Ryder said. He had not intended to sass the captain, but somehow, it just slipped out.

The captain unsnapped the strap on his holster, and let his arm dangle by his sidearm. "I'll shoot you for insubordination, soldier," he said.

"You'll have to shoot me, sir, if you insist on taking this child from me."

"Damnit, soldier, it's not a child! That's what I've been telling you. It's a creature. An animal. A naked chimp."

"The Centauri are taller than chimps, sir," Ryder said, inadvertently sassing him again.

"Don't anthropomorphize the little beast," the captain said.

Then the captain pulled his sidearm and brought the barrel to the infant's head. He moved his thumb to click off the safety, but stopped when he felt cold steel against his neck and saw the knife in Ryder's hand.

"Begging the captain's pardon, sir," Ryder said. "But if you harm this child, I'll slit your throat."

"You're dead, son," the captain said. "You are finished."

"Begging the captain's pardon, sir, but if you don't move away now and reholster your sidearm, I'll slit the captain's throat, sir."

They stood there for several moments, which seemed to everyone nearby to last for several hours. Finally, the captain backed off.

"It's not a person, son, goddamnit," he said. "Don't you understand that? It's just another animal. A goddamn naked chimp."

Ryder clutched the infant tightly to his chest, and fingered the knife, which he did not return to its sheath.

"You don't believe that, Captain," Ryder said. "You think they are basically the same as us. Because you would never allow your men to do what they are doing to a bunch of chimps. You would never take a baby animal and shoot it out of caprice. People don't treat animals that way. They only treat other people like that, sir."

The captain stared at Ryder in contempt, and said nothing.

The captain did not have Ryder arrested, once Braddock used the phased-neutrino communicator strapped to his shoulder to call the United Nations Inter-Planetary Observers to the scene. But by the time the UNIPO had arrived, the massacre was finished, and not a single Centauri remained alive, other than the one Ryder held clutched to his chest. There was nothing for the blue helmets to do but record what they saw. Braddock wrote up a report on the incident, typing it into his hand-held log, took some digital pictures of the carnage and downloaded them, and beamed the whole thing to IPTO HQ.

He doubted that HQ would really give a shit.

"I'll tell you what," Morray said after the UNIPO representatives had left. He ignored Braddock and Willis as he spoke, looking only at Ryder holding the sole Centauri survivor of the village massacre. "You care so much about that little beast, you can take it to Fort Eisenhower. There's a Red Cross mission there. They'll take the creature off your hands."

"Eisenhower's in unpacified territory," Braddock protested. "It's supplied by air. There's no way to get to the fort on foot without walking through open field. We'd be sitting ducks, sir."

"I'm giving you a direct order, Sergeant," Morray said. "Or perhaps you'd like to defy me on this point, as well? I could have the three of you court-martialed as it is. Just push me a little farther and see what happens."

"You don't need to threaten us to get us to follow orders, sir," Braddock said. "We're soldiers."

"Then act like it," Morray said, and turned his attention to the smoldering village.

That night, Ryder, Braddock, and Willis camped under the stars and two moons of Centauri V. Ryder improvised a nipple from a rubber glove he fished out of the medkit, filled it with liquid Soya from the K rations, and fed the infant with it. The baby did not like the taste of the Soya at first, but soon it became hungry enough to take the nipple anyway.

They did not talk much about the massacre. They were tired, spent. For a long time they sat in silence.

Then Braddock and Ryder jumped when they heard

Captain Morray say, "Goddamnit, soldier, it's not a child! It's a creature! A goddamn naked chimp!" They turned and saw Willis, staring at the ground, trying to avoid eye contact with them as she desperately struggled to hold back her laughter. Her mimicry had been perfect: the timbre of Morray's voice, gruff and whiskey-coated, yet somehow affected at the same time. They all burst into laughter, and couldn't stop for several minutes. Every time the laughter threatened to diminish, someone would repeat the words "naked chimp" in Morray's pompous phrasing, as if Morray had believed he'd hit upon something very profound, and they would crack up all over again.

But eventually, the laughter felt sour in their chests, and they were silent again for a long time, until Willis said, "Anyone here believe in God?"

It was an odd and abrupt question, and yet, somehow, it did not feel totally inappropriate. Still, Braddock and Ryder were silent, not sure what the correct answer might be, afraid to reveal their own hearts.

Willis said, "I was raised Catholic, went to Catholic school, taught by nuns and Jesuits. I never doubted the existence of the Almighty for one second, not one second of my life. Until today. I looked that dead Centauri girl in the eye, and I felt God just fly right outta me."

Braddock thought about what Willis said for a moment. "I had the opposite experience," he said.

"What d'you mean?" Willis asked, not defensive, not accusing, just curious.

"I never gave religion much thought. Never went to church, except for weddings and funerals. Not exactly an atheist, just never gave the matter much consideration one way or the other. Until today. When I looked into that baby's eyes, I felt like my soul was all of a sudden filled up with something, and I knew there is a God. I could almost feel His hand on my shoulder."

Willis considered this. "Did you hear anything?" she asked.

"Hear anything?"

"When you felt God. What did it sound like?"

"I guess it didn't sound like anything. I felt a weird feeling. Like heat. Deep inside me. And the day kinda seemed to light up, like a cloud drifted away from in front of the sun. That was it."

"I heard something. The sound of something inside of me, like a cable snapping. It made me shudder, down to my marrow. It shook me. It made a kind of twang."

"A twang?" Ryder asked.

"Yeah," Willis said. "A twang. I think it's weird that a person would lose her soul with a twang. I would've expected something more, I don't know, Cecil B. DeMille. Instead, all I get is a twang. Funny thing."

"I guess it is." Braddock agreed.

"Also funny that you lose your soul with a twang, and you find it with silence," Willis said.

"That is a funny thing," Braddock agreed. "I would've expected something more . . . operatic, I guess."

Willis turned to Ryder. "How about you? What'd you feel today?"

Ryder thought for a second.

"I just felt like shit," he said.

Later, Ryder rocked the infant gently in his arms until the child fell asleep. *You don't look like a human being, it's true,* he thought, as he looked at the round, bald head of the azure creature. *But you're not that far off either. Or perhaps we're not that far off from you. You sleep, you eat, you cry, you shit. You feel love, at least I think you do. You feel loss, I'm almost positive. You must. And still, somehow, the Centauri heart will always remain inscrutable to the human, because our frames of reference are not the same.*

Was the human heart inscrutable to the Centauri? He doubted that it was. The human heart seemed too obvious to him, too full of violence, greed, venality, and lust. Too basic. Too primal. And they had thought the Centauri were the primitive ones. Humans do not learn from their mistakes. Do Centauri? He wondered if he would ever know the Centauri people well enough to find the answer.

The Centauri would lose the war, eventually. That, he knew. This planet was too rich in natural resources for running-on-empty Earth to let her go. The Colonists would win, inevitably. But winning would change them, and not for the better. Would losing change the Centauri? Probably. And not for the better.

The next day, as they cautiously made their way across a field of azure stalks that in some places came up to their chests, the Centauri child started to squirm. Ryder shouldered his rifle and held the baby in both his arms to keep it from wriggling its way out of his hands. That was why he was unarmed when the dozen or so Centauri rose from their hiding places in the tall grass. Until the Centauri moved, they had been completely invisible. The tone of their skin was a perfect match to that of the field around them.

Although Braddock and Willis held their weapons at port-arms, the appearance of the Centauri took them by surprise, and they had no time to react, or even to click the safeties off their rifles, before the two Centauri closest to them each drove a spear-stick through their hearts.

Ryder saw the surprise on his companions' faces. It was an expression he was getting used to, a familiar sight by now. Most Earth soldiers seemed to react to their own sudden deaths with complete surprise. The Centauri, in contrast, seemed to show no expression whatsoever when they met their ends. Ryder had seen that human look of surprise on the faces of a good number of his buddies by now. He wondered if Willis died knowing she would cease to exist, extinguished like a candle's flame, and if Braddock died knowing he would go to heaven, or at least get the chance to be judged one way or the other.

Ryder knew the enemy did not kill him only because he held the Centauri infant to his chest, and they could not do so without also killing the infant. He thought that he could drop the child and sling the rifle off his shoulder and make a stand. He could even switch the child to his left hand and unholster his side-arm with his right.

But he didn't do either of these things. He didn't move. He suspected that there was another Centauri at his back, and as soon as he reached for his sidearm, he'd be dead. Besides, if he was going to die, which he had every reason to believe he would, there was something he felt he had to do first, and it wasn't to take as many Centauri with him as possible. He didn't know if what he felt he had to do would make any difference in the scheme of things. He didn't really think it would. If the end meant anything more than permanent blackness, then whatever judgment he had coming had been pretty well established already, and what he did now was hardly likely to tip the scal's one way or the other.

He just hoped they would kill him quickly, and not take him captive and torture him.

Ryder stood as still as he could, and looked at the Centauri. He tried to keep his expression neutral, direct and unthreatening. The Centauri looked back at him, with their catlike, inscrutable eyes. Ryder thought they looked sad, but he knew he was just anthropomorphizing them.

No one budged. The baby squirmed.

Then, slowly, Ryder raised the child in his arms and held it out to the Centauri. The one closest to him, a female, looked at the child, and then at Ryder. Their eyes met. The Centauri female blinked twice. Then she took the child from Ryder, and held it close to her chest.

Then, in an instant, the Centauri were gone, diving back into the waves of grass, disappearing among the azure blades and scuttling away so quickly, silently and carefully that Ryder couldn't tell if it was the Centauri or the wind that made the grass shimmer and rustle.

Ryder stood still for several moments longer, waiting for the spear-stick to drive through his back and out his chest. When it didn't come, he cautiously turned around and saw that he was really alone. He felt alone, too, and lonely, in a way he hadn't since his first visit to Earth. He looked at his dead companions, lying in the grass, their red blood seeping into the soft dirt. He looked at his hands, and felt the ghost sensation of the weight of the baby who moments before he held in his arms.

Then he swung his rifle off his shoulder and gripped it tightly, and used his transmitter to call Medivac,

knowing that the next Centauri he saw he would probably have to kill before it killed him.

But as he stood in the silent field, his rifle felt heavy,
awkward in his hands. It felt alien to his touch, more
alien than the Centauri infant had.

He laid the rifle beside his fallen comrades, and
gently placed his sidearm there, too, like laying flowers
on a grave. He straightened and looked west, in the
direction of Fort Eisenhower, then behind him at the
trail the three soldiers had left, already being erased
by the waving grasses and gently blowing wind. Ryder
turned on his heel and started walking out into the
warm sunlit fields until he disappeared into the mead-
ows of tall azure grass.

DREAM OF VENUS

by Pamela Sargent

Pamela Sargent's recent work includes *Climb the Wind: A Novel of Another America.* Her other novels include *Ruler of the Sky,* an ambitious tale about Genghis Khan, told from the points of view of the women in his life, and the *Star Trek* novel, *A Fury Scorned,* coauthored with George Zebrowski. She edited the two ground-breaking science fiction anthologies, *Women of Wonder, The Classic Years* and *Women of Wonder, The Contemporary Years.* Her many novels include *The Shore of Women, Venus of Dreams,* and *Earthseed.* Winner of the Nebula and Locus Awards, she has been hailed by *The Washington Post Book World* as "one of the genre's best writers." "Dream of Venus" is set against the backdrop of her Venus trilogy, with the third book, *Child of Venus,* about to be published.

Hassan Petrovich Maksutov's grandfather was the first to point out Venus to him, when Hassan was five years old. His family and much of his clan had moved to the outskirts of Jeddah by then, and his grandfather had taken him outside to view the heavens.

The night sky was a black canopy of tiny flickering flames; Hassan had imagined suddenly growing as tall as a djinn and reaching out to touch a star. Venus did not flicker like other stars, but shone steadily on the horizon in the hour before dawn. Hassan had not known then that he would eventually travel to that planet, but he had delighted in looking up at the beacon that signified humankind's greatest endeavor.

Twenty years after that first sighting, Hassan was gazing down at Venus from one of the ten domed Islands that floated in the upper reaches of the planet's poisonous atmosphere. These Cytherian Islands, as they were known (after the island of Cythera where the goddess Aphrodite had been worshiped in the ancient world), were vast platforms that had been built on top of massive metal cells filled with helium and then covered with dirt and soil. After each Island had been enclosed by an impermeable dome, the surfaces were gardened, and by the time Hassan was standing on a raised platform at the edge of Island Two and peering into the veiled darkness below, the Islands had for decades been gardens of trees, flowers, grassy expanses, and dwellings that housed the people who had come to Venus to be a part of the Project, Earth's effort to terraform her sister planet.

The Venus Project, as Hassan had known ever since childhood, was the greatest feat of engineering humankind had ever attempted, an enterprise that had already taken the labor of millions. Simply constructing the Parasol, the umbrella that shielded Venus from the sun, was an endeavor that had dwarfed the building of the Pyramids (where his father and mother had taken him to view those majestic crumbling monuments) and China's Great Wall (which he had visited during a break from his studies at the University of Chimkent). The Parasol had grown into a vast metallic flower as wide in diameter as Venus herself, in order to allow that hot and deadly world to cool. Venus would remain cloaked in the Parasol's shadow for centuries to come.

Hassan's grandfather had explained to him, during

their sighting of Venus, that what he was seeing was, in fact, not the planet itself, but the reflected light of the Parasol. To the old man, this made the sight even more impressive, since the great shield was humankind's accomplishment, but Hassan felt a twinge of disappointment. Even now, as he stood on Island Two, the planet below was veiled in darkness, hidden from view.

The Venus of past millennia, with a surface hot enough to melt lead, an atmosphere thick with sulfur dioxide, and an atmospheric pressure that would have crushed a person standing on its barren surface, had already undergone changes. Hydrogen, siphoned off from Saturn, had been carried to Venus in a steady stream of tanks and then released into the atmosphere, where it was combining with the free oxygen produced by the changes in the Venusian environment to form water. The clouds had been seeded with a genetically engineered strain of algae that fed on the sulfuric acid and expelled it in the form of copper and iron sulfides. The Venus of the past now existed more in memory than in reality; the Venus of the future, that green and fertile planet that would become a second Earth and a new home for humankind, was still a dream.

As for the present, Hassan would now become one more person whose life would be enlarged by his own contribution, however small, to the great Venus Project. So Hassan's father Pyotr Andreievich Maksutor had hoped while meeting with friends and exerting his considerable influence on behalf of his son. Pyotr Andreievich Maksutov was a Linker, one of the privileged few who had implants linking their cortexes directly to Earth's cyberminds, a man who was often called upon to advise the Council of Mukhtars that governed all the Nomarchies of Earth and also watched over the Venus Project. Pyotr had convinced several Linkers connected with the Venus Project Council that Hassan, a specialist in geology, was worthy of being given a coveted place among the Cytherian Islanders.

Hassan, looking down at shadowed Venus through the transparent dome of Island Two, had been able to believe that he might have earned his position here until arriving on this Island. He had been here for two days now, and was beginning to feel as though his father's influence had always been a benign shadow over his life, one that had shielded him from certain realities. The passengers on the torchship that had carried him from Earth had been friendly, willing to share their enthusiasm for the work that lay ahead of them; the crew had been solicitous of his welfare, and he had taken their warmth and kindness as that of comrades reaching out to one who would soon be a colleague laboring for the Project. On the Island, he had been given a room in a building where most of the other residents were specialists who had lived on Island Two for several years, and had assumed that this was only because newcomers were usually assigned to any quarters that happened to be empty until more permanent quarters were found for them.

Now he suspected that the friendliness of the people aboard the torchship and his relatively comfortable quarters on Island Two had more to do with his family's connections than with luck or any merits of his own. The Venus Project needed people of all sorts—workers to maintain and repair homeostats and life support systems, and pilots for the airships that moved between the Islands and for the shuttles that carried passengers to and from Anwara, the space station in high orbit around Venus that was their link to Earth, where the torchships from the home world landed and docked. Counselors to tend to the psychological health of the Islanders, scientists, and people brave enough to work on the Bats, the two satellites above Venus' north and south poles, were all needed here, and not all of them were exceptionally gifted or among the most brilliant in their disciplines. Many Islanders, the workers in particular, came from the humblest of backgrounds; the Council of Mukhtars wanted all of Earth's people to share in the glory of terraforming, although the more cynical claimed that offering such hope to the masses also functioned as a social safety valve.

Hassan could tell himself that he measured up to any of the people here, and yet after only a short time on Island Two, he saw that many here had a quality he lacked—a determination, a hardness, a devotion to the Project that some might call irrational. Such obsessiveness was probably necessary for those who would never see the result of their efforts, who had to have faith that others would see what they had started through to the end. The Project needed such driven people, and would need them for centuries to come.

But Hassan was only a younger son of an ambitious and well-connected father, who was here mostly because Pyotr could not think of anything else to do with him. He was not brilliant enough to be trained for an academic position, not politically adept enough to maneuver his way into becoming an aide to the Council of Mukhtars, and he lacked the extraordinary discipline required of those chosen to be Linkers; his more flighty mind, it was feared, might be overwhelmed by the sea of data a Link would provide.

Hassan might, however, be burnished by a decade or two of work on the Project. With that accomplishment on his public record, he could return to Earth and perhaps land a position training hopeful young idealists who dreamed of joining the Project; that sort of post would give him some influence. He might even be brought in to consult with members of the Project Council, or made a member of one of the committees that advised the Council of Mukhtars on the terraforming of Venus. In any event, his father would see an ineffectual son transformed into a man with a reputation much enhanced by his small role in humankind's most ambitious enterprise.

Hassan knew that he should consider himself fortunate that his father had the power to help secure his son's position. He was even luckier to win a chance to be listed among all of those who would make a new Earth of Venus. His life had been filled with good fortune, yet he often wondered why his luck had not made him happier.

After the call to evening prayer had sounded, and the bright light of the dome high overhead had faded into silver, Hassan usually walked to the gardens near the ziggurat where Island Two's Administrators lived and ate his supper there. He might have taken the meal in his building's common room with the other residents, or alone in his room, but eating in solitude did not appeal to him. As for dining with the others, the people who lived in his building still treated him with a kind of amused and faintly contemptuous tolerance even after almost five months.

Hassan chafed at such treatment. Always before, at school and at university and among the guests his family invited to their compound, he had been sought out,

flattered, and admired. His opinions had been solic-
ited, his tentative comments on all sorts of matters
accepted as intriguing insights into the matters of the
day. His professors, even those who had expected
more of him, had praise for his potential if not for his
actual accomplishment. But many Islanders seemed to
regard him as someone on the level of a common
worker, no better or worse than anyone else. Indeed
the workers here, most of whom came from either
teeming slums or the more impoverished rural areas
and isolated regions of Earth's Nomarchies, were
often treated with more deference than he was.

And why not? Hassan had finally asked himself.
Why shouldn't an illiterate man or woman laboring
for the Project be given more respect than a Linker's
son? The workers, however humble their origins, had
to be the best at their trades, and extremely determined, in order to win a place here, and the main
reward they wanted for their efforts was a chance for
their descendants to have more opportunities than
they had been given and to be among the first to settle
a new world. Hassan's place was a gift from his father,
and he was not thinking of a better world for any
children he might have, only of hanging on to what
his family already possessed.

Hassan sat down at his usual table, which was near
a small pool of water. Other people, several with the
small diamondlike gems of Linkers on their foreheads,
sat at other tables around the pool and under slender
trees that resembled birches. As a servo rolled toward
him to take his order, he glimpsed his friend Muhammad Sheridan hurrying toward him from the stone
path that led to the Administrators' ziggurat.

"Salaam," Muhammad called out to him. "Thought
I'd be late—the Committee meeting went on longer

than we expected.'' The brown-skinned young man sat down across from Hassan. Muhammad's family were merchants and shopkeepers from the Atlantic Federation, wealthy enough to have a large estate near the southern New Jersey dikes and sea walls and well connected enough to have sent Muhammad to the University of Damascus for his degree in mathematics. Hassan felt at ease with Muhammad; the two often ate dinner together. Muhammad had a position as an aide to Administrator Pavel Gvishiani, a post that would have assured him a certain amount of status on Earth. But here, Muhammad often felt himself patronized, as he had admitted to Hassan.

''Let's face it,'' Muhammad had said only the other evening, ''the only way we're going to make a place for ourselves among these people is to do something truly spectacular for the Project, maybe something, God willing, on the order of what Dawud Hasseen accomplished.'' Dawud Hasseen had designed the Parasol almost three centuries earlier, and had been the chief engineer during its construction. ''Or else we'll have to put in our time here without complaining until we're as driven and obsessed as most of the workers and younger specialists, in which case we might finally become more acceptable.''

The second course was their only realistic alternative, Hassan thought. Their work here would not allow either of them much scope for grand achievements. Muhammad's position as an aide to Pavel Gvishiani required him to devote his time to such humble tasks as backing up written and oral records of meetings, retrieving summaries of them when needed, preparing and reviewing routine public statements, and occasionally entertaining Pavel with discussions of any mathematical treatises the Administrator had recently had transmitted to him from Earth. Lorna FredasMarkos, the head of Hassan's team of geologists, had given Hassan the mundane work of keeping the team's records in order and occasionally analyzing data on the increases in the levels of iron and copper sulfides on the basalt surface of Venus, work no one else was particularly interested in doing and that almost anyone else could have done.

"I don't know which Islanders are the worst," Muhammad had continued, "the peasants and street urchins who came here from Earth, or the workers who think of themselves as the Project's aristocrats just because their families have been living here for more than one generation." This was the kind of frank remark Hassan's friend would have kept to himself in other company.

Muhammad set his pocket screen on the tabletop in front of him. Hassan had brought his own pocket screen; although there was no work he had to do this evening, he had taken to toting his screen around, so that he could at least give the appearance of being busy and needed. The two young men ordered a pot of tea and simple meals of vegetables, beans, and rice. Hassan had come to the Islands with enough credit to afford a more lavish repast, even some imported foods from Earth, but he was doing his best to keep within the credit allotted to him by the Project, knowing that this would look better on his record.

"How goes it with you?" Muhammad asked.

"The way it usually does," Hassan replied, "although Lorna hinted that she might give me a new assignment. There's a new geologist joining our team, so perhaps Lorna wants me to be her mentor." He had looked up the public record of the geologist, who had arrived from Earth only two days ago. Her name

was Miriam Lucea-Noyes; she had grown up on a farm
in the Pacific Federation of North America, and had
been trained at the University of Vancouver. It was
easy for him to piece together most of her story from
her record. Miriam Lucea-Noyes had been one of
those bright but unschooled children who was occasionally discovered by a regional Counselor and ele-
vated beyond her family's status; she had been chosen
for a preparatory school and then admitted to the university for more specialized training. Her academic record was, Hassan ruefully admitted to himself,
superior to his own, and he could safely assume that
she had the doggedness and single-mindedness of most
of those who had come to the Cytherian Islands.
About the only surprising detail in her record was the
fact that she had spent two years earning extra credit
for her account as a technical assistant to a director
of mind-tours and virtual entertainments before com-
pleting her studies.

"Ah, yes, the new geologist." Muhammad smiled.
"Actually, I might be at least partly responsible for
your new assignment. Administrator Pavel thinks it's
time that we put together a new mind-tour of the
Venus Project. The Project Council could use the
extra credit the production would bring, and we
haven't done one for a while."

Hassan leaned back. "I would have thought that
there were already enough such entertainments."

"True, but most of them are a bit quaint. All of
them could use some updating. And Pavel thinks that
we have the capacity to provide a much more exciting
and detailed experience now."

The servo returned with a teapot and two cups. Hassan poured himself and his friend some tea. "I
wouldn't have thought," he said, "that an Administra-

tor would be concerning himself with something as
relatively unimportant as a mind-tour."

"Pavel Gvishiani is the kind of man who concerns
himself with everything." Muhammad sipped some
tea. "Anyway, Pavel was discussing this mind-tour
business with the rest of the Administrators, and they
all agreed that we could spare a couple of people to
map out a tour. This new geologist on your team,
Miriam Lucea-Noyes, is an obvious choice, given that
she has some experience with mind-tour production.
And when Pavel brought up her name, I suggested
that you might be someone who could work very well
with her on such a project."

"I see." Hassan did not know whether to feel flattered or embarrassed. Although cultivated people
were not above enjoying them, the visual and sensory
experiences of mind-tours were most popular with
children and with ignorant and uneducated adults.
They served the useful functions of providing vicarious
experiences to people who might otherwise grow
bored or discontented, and of imparting some knowledge of history and culture to the illiterate. With the
aid of a band that could link one temporarily to
Earth's cyberminds, a person could wander to unfamil-
iar places, travel back in time, or participate in an
adventure.

Hassan had spent many happy hours as a child with
a band around his head, scuba-diving in the sunken
city of Venice and climbing to the top of Mount Ever-
est with a party of explorers, among other virtual ad-
ventures. For a while, at university, he had toyed with
the notion of producing such entertainments himself.
He had managed to fit courses in virtual graphics, adventure fiction, music, and sensory effects production
into his schedule of required studies, and had been

part of a student team producing a mind-tour for the University of Chimkent to use in recruiting new students and faculty until his father had put a stop to such pursuits. He had given in, of course—Pyotr had threatened to cut him off from all credit except a citizen's basic allotment and to do nothing to help him in such a profession as mind-tour production—but he had remained bitter about the decision his father had forced on him. In an uncharacteristic emotional venting, Hassan had admitted his bitterness over his thwarted dream to Muhammad. Being chosen to work on the university's mind-tour remained the only privilege he had ever won for himself, without his father's intercession.

"It won't hurt to have such experiences on your record," Pyotr had told Hassan, "as long as it's clear that this mind-tour business is just a hobby. But it isn't the kind of profession that could make a Linker of you, or give you any chance in politics." His father had, for a while, made him feel ashamed of his earlier ambition.

"It's not that I'm doing you any special favors, Hassan," Muhammad said. "It's just that we don't have many people here who could put together even a preliminary visual sketch of a mind-tour, and Administrator Pavel thinks having people associated with the Project doing the work might impart a new perspective, something more original, something that isn't just the vast spectacle interspersed with inspiring dioramas that most mind-tours about the Venus Project are." He paused. "Anyway, it'll be something other than the routine work you've been doing."

Hassan found himself warming to the prospect. Constructing a mind-tour, putting together the kind of experience that would make anyone, however humble his position, proud to be even a small part of a society that could transform a planet—this was a challenge he was certain he could meet. There was also an ironic satisfaction in knowing that the pursuit his father had scorned might become his means of winning Administrator Pavel's favor.

Miriam Lucea-Noyes was a short, extremely pretty woman with thick dark brown hair, wide-set gray eyes, and a look of obstinacy. "Salaam," she murmured to Hassan after Lorna FredasMarkos had introduced them.

"How do you do," Hassan replied. Miriam gazed at him steadily until he averted his eyes.

"Hassan," Lorna said, "I feel as though we might have been wasting your talents." The gray-haired woman smiled. "You should have called your experience with mind-tour production to my attention earlier."

"It was noted in my record," he said.

"Well, of course, but one can so easily overlook such notations—" Lorna abruptly fell silent, as if realizing that she had just admitted that she had never bothered to study his record thoroughly, that she had given it no more than the cursory glance that was probably all the attention it deserved. "Anyway," the older woman continued, "Administrator Pavel is quite pleased that two members of my team are capable of putting together a new mind-tour. You will have access to all the records our sensors have made, and to everything in the official records of the project, but if there's anything else you need, be sure to let me know."

"How long do we have?" Miriam asked.

Lorna lifted her brows. "Excuse me?"

"What's the deadline?" Miriam said. "How long do we have to pull this thing together?"

"Administrator Pavel indicated that he would like to have it completed before the New Year's celebrations," the older woman replied.

"So we've got five months," Miriam said. "Then I think we'll see in the year 535 with one hell of a fine mind-tour."

Lorna pursed her thin lips, as if tasting something sour. "You may both have more time if you need it. The Administrator would prefer that you keep to his informal deadline, but he also made it clear that he would rather have a mind-tour that is both aesthetically pleasing and inspirational, even if that takes longer to complete."

Hassan bowed slightly in Lorna's direction. "We'll do our best to produce a mind-tour that is both pleasing and on time, God willing."

"And that isn't a sloppy rush job either," Miriam said.

"I may have to drag you away to our team meetings and your other standard tasks occasionally," Lorna said, "but I'll try to keep such distractions to a minimum." She turned toward the doorway. "Salaam aleikum."

"Aleikum salaam," Miriam said. Her Arabic sounded as flat and unmusical as her Anglaic.

"God go with you," Hassan added as the door slid shut behind their supervisor.

"Well, Hassan." Miriam sat down on one of the cushions at the low table. "I don't know if you've ever seen any of the mind-tours I worked on. Most of them were for small children, so you probably haven't. 'Hans Among the Redwoods'—that was one of our more popular ones, and 'Dinosaurs in the Gobi.' "

He tensed with surprise. "I saw that dinosaur mind-tour—marvelous work. Maybe you made it for children, but I have several adult friends who also enjoyed it."

"And 'The Adventure of Montrose Scarp.' "

Hassan was impressed in spite of himself. " 'Montrose Scarp?' " he asked as he seated himself. "My nephew Salim couldn't get enough of that one. He just about forced me to put on a band and view it. What I particularly admired was the way the excitement of the climb and the geological history of the scarp were so seamlessly combined."

"That was my doing, if I do say so myself." Miriam pointed her chin at him. "Joe Kinnear—he was the director I worked with—he wanted to put in more of the usual shit—you know, stuff like having the mind-tourist lose his grip and fall before being caught by the rope tied around him, or throwing in a big storm just as you reach the top of the escarpment. He thought doing what I wanted would just slow the thing down, but I convinced him otherwise, and I was right."

"Yes, you were," Hassan said.

"And every damned mind-tour of Venus has the obligatory scene of Karim al-Anwar speaking to the Council of Mukhtars, telling them that what they learn from the terraforming of Venus might eventually be needed to save Earth from the effects of global warming, or else a scene of New York or some other flooded coastal city at evening while Venus gleams on the horizon and a portentous voice quotes from that speech Mukhtar Karim supposedly made toward the end of his life."

Karim al-Anwar had been the first to propose a project to terraform Venus, back in the earliest days of Earth's Nomarchies, not long after the Resource Wars almost six centuries ago. " 'When I gaze upon

Venus'," Hassan quoted, " 'and view the images our probes have carried back to us from its hot and barren surface, I see Earth's future, and fear for our world.' "

"Followed by the sensation of heat and a hellish image of the Venusian surface," Miriam said. "And the three most recent ones all have scenes of explosions on the Bats, which I frankly think is misleading and maybe even too frightening."

The Bats, the two winged satellites in geosynchronous orbit at Venus' poles, serviced the automatic shuttles that carried compressed oxygen from the robot-controlled installations at the Venusian poles to the Bats. The process of terraforming was releasing too much of Venus' oxygen, and the excess had to be removed if the planet was ever to support life. The workers on the Bats, people who serviced the shuttles and maintained the docks, knew that the volatile oxygen could explode, and many lives had been lost in past explosions.

"There are real dangers on the Bats," Miriam continued, "but we don't have to dwell on them just for the sake of a few thrills. I'd rather avoid those kinds of clichés."

"So would I," Hassan said fervently.

"We should purge our minds of anything we've seen before and start over with an entirely fresh presentation."

"I think that's exactly what Pavel Gvishiani wants us to do."

"We're geologists," Miriam said, "and maybe that's the angle we ought to use. I don't think past mind-tours have really given people a feeling for the Project in the context of geological time. I'd like to emphasize that. Hundreds of years of human effort set against the eons it took to form Venus—and if we get into planetary evolution and the beginnings of the solar system . . ."

"I couldn't agree with you more," Hassan said.

"Most of the people who experience this mind-tour are likely to be ignorant and unschooled, but that doesn't mean we have to oversimplify things and lard the narrative with dramatic confrontations and action scenes."

"It sounds as though what we want is a mind-tour that would be both enlightening to the uneducated," Hassan said, "and entertaining and inspirational to the learned."

"That's exactly what I want," Miriam said.

It was also, Hassan thought, exactly what Pavel Gvishiani was likely to want. Judging by what Muhammad had told him about the Administrator, Pavel was not someone who cared to have his intelligence insulted. To have a mind-tour that would not just be an informative entertainment, but a masterpiece—

"We should talk about how we want to frame it," Hassan said, "before we start digging through all the records and sensor scans. Have a structure that encapsulates our vision, and then start collecting what we need to realize it."

"Exactly," Miriam said. "You'd be surprised at how many mind-tour directors do it the other way around, looking at everything that could possibly have anything to do with their theme while hoping that some coherent vision suddenly emerges out of all the clutter. That isn't the way I like to work."

"Nor I," Hassan said, gazing across the table at her expressive face and intense gaze, already enthralled.

Miriam, despite being a geologist and a specialist, lived in a building inhabited by workers, people who repaired homeostats and robots, maintained airships

and shuttles, tended hydroponic gardens, looked out
for small children in the Island's child care center, and
performed other necessary tasks. Hassan had assumed
that there was no room for her elsewhere, and that
her quarters would be temporary. Instead, Miriam had
admitted to him that she had requested space there,
and intended to stay.

"Look," she said, "I went to a university, but a lot
of students there didn't let me forget where I came
from. I feel more comfortable with workers than with
the children of merchants and engineers and Counselors and Linkers." She had glanced at him apologeti-
cally after saying that, obviously not wanting to hurt
his feelings, but he had understood. His family's position might have brought him to this place, but with
Miriam, he now had a chance to make his own small
mark on the Project, to inspire others with the dream
of Venus.

"The Dream of Venus"—that was how he and Miriam referred to the mind-tour they had been outlining
and roughing out for almost a month now. He thought
of what they had been sketching and planning as he
walked toward the star-shaped steel-blue building in
which Miriam lived. As they usually did at last light,
workers had gathered on the expanse of grass in front
of the building. Families sat on the grass, eating from
small bowls with chopsticks or fingers; other people
were talking with friends, mending worn garments, or
watching with pride and wonderment as their children
reviewed their lessons on pocket screens. All children
were schooled here, unlike Earth, where education
was rationed and carefully parceled out.

It came to him then how much he now looked forward to coming here, to meeting and working with
Miriam.

Hassan made his way to the entrance. Inside the windowless building, people had propped open the doors to their rooms to sit in the corridors and gossip; he passed one group of men gambling with sticks and dice. The place was as noisy and chaotic as a souk in Jeddah, but Hassan had grown more used to the cacophony. Since most of the workers could not read, the doors to their rooms were adorned with holo images or carvings of their faces, so that visitors could locate their quarters. Miriam's room was near the end of this wing; a holo image of her face stared out at him from the door.

He pressed his palm against the door; after a few seconds, it opened. Miriam, wearing a brown tunic and baggy brown pants, was sitting on the floor in front of her wall screen, a thin metal band around her head; even in such plain clothes, she looked beautiful to him.

"Salaam," she said without looking up.

"Salaam."

"We're making real progress," she said. "This mind-tour is really shaping up."

He sat down next to her. Unlike most of the people in this building, Miriam had a room to herself, but it was not much larger than a closet. Building more residences on the Islands would have meant cutting back on the gardens and parks that were deemed essential to maintaining the mental health of the Islanders.

"Before you show me any of your rough cut," he said, "would you care to have supper with me as my guest?" This was the first time he had offered such an invitation to her; he had enough credit to order imported delicacies from Earth for her if that was what she wanted. "We can go to the garden near the Administrators' building, unless of course you'd rather dine somewhere else."

"Maybe later," she said in the flat voice that was such a contrast to her lovely face and graceful movements. "I want you to look at this first."

They had decided to depart from tradition in their structure for "The Dream of Venus." Miriam also wanted to dispense with the usual chronological depictions, which she found stodgy, and Hassan had readily agreed.

The mind-tour would begin with Karim al-Anwar, as every other depiction of the Venus Project did, but instead of the usual dramatic confrontations with doubters and passionate speeches about Earth's sister planet becoming a new home for humankind, they would move directly to what Karim had envisioned— Venus as it would be in the far future. The viewer would see the blue-green gem of a transformed Venus from afar and then be swept toward the terraformed planet, falling until the surface was visible through Venus' veil of white clouds. Flying low over the shallow blue ocean, the mind-tourist would be swept past a small island chain toward the northern continent of Ishtar, with its high plateau and mountain massif that dwarfed even the Himalayas, to view a region of vast grasslands, evergreen forests, and rugged mountain peaks. Then the wail of the wind would rise as the viewer was carried south toward the equator and the colorful tropical landscape of the continent of Aphrodite.

Hassan was still tinkering with the sound effects for that section, but had found a piece of music that evoked the sound of a strong wind, and planned to use recordings of the powerful winds that continuously swept around Venus below the Islands as background and undertones. Near the end of the sequence, the viewer would fly toward a Venusian dawn, gazing at the sun before a dark shape, part of what remained of the Parasol, eclipsed its light. There were a few scientists who doubted that any part of the Parasol would be needed later on to insulate Venus from the heat and radiation that could again produce a runaway greenhouse effect, but most Cytherian specialists disagreed with them, and Hassan and Miriam had decided to go along with the majority's opinion in their depiction.

At this point, the viewer was to be swept back in time, so to speak, to one of the Cytherian Islands, in a manner that would suggest what was not shown in the mind-tour—namely that in the distant future, when Venus was green with life, the Islands would slowly drop toward the surface, where their inhabitants would at last leave their domed gardens to dwell on their new world. Hassan and Miriam had inserted a passage during the earlier flight sequence in which the viewer passed over an expanse of parklike land that strongly resembled Island Two's gardens and groves of trees. That scene, with some enhancement, would resonate in the viewer's mind with the subsequent Island sequences.

"What have you got to show me?" Hassan asked.

Miriam handed him a band. "This is some stuff for the earlier sequences," she said.

Hassan put the band around his head, was momentarily blind and deaf, and then was suddenly soaring over the vast canyon of the Diana Chasma toward the rift-ridden dome of Atla Regio in the east and the shield volcano of Maat Mons, the largest volcano on Venus, three hundred kilometers in diameter and rising to a Himalayan height. The scene abruptly shifted to the steep massif of Maxwell Montes rising swiftly from the hot dark surface of Ishtar Terra as millions

of years were compressed into seconds. He whirled
away from the impressively high mountain massif and
hovered over a vast basaltic plain, watching as part of
the surface formed a dome, spread out, grew flat, and
then sank, leaving one of the circular uniquely Venusian features called coronae. He moved over the
cracked and wrinkled plateaus called tesserae and was
surprised at the beauty he glimpsed in the deformed
rocky folds of the land.

His field of vision abruptly went dark.

"What do you think?" Miriam's voice asked.

He shifted his band slightly; Miriam's room reap-
peared. "I know it's rough," she continued, "and I've
got more to add to it, but I hope it gives you an idea.
As for sound effects and the sensory stuff, I think we
should keep that to a minimum—just a low undertone,
the bare suggestion of a low throbbing noise, and
maybe a feeling of extreme heat without actually making the viewer break out in a sweat. Well, what do
you think?"

Hassan said, "I think it's beautiful, Miriam." His
words were sincere. Somehow she had taken what
could have been no more than an impressive visual
panorama and had found the beauty in the strange,
alien terrain of Venus as it might have been six hundred million years ago. It was as if she had fallen in
love with that world, almost as if she regretted its loss.

"If you think that's something," she said, "wait until
you see what I've worked up for the resurfacing section, where we see volcanoes flooding the plains with
molten basalt. But I want your ideas on what to use
for sensory effects there, and you'll probably want to
add some visuals, too—it seems a little too abbrevi-
ated as it is."

"You almost make me sorry," Hassan said, "that

we're changing Venus, that what it was will forever be lost—already is lost."

Her gray eyes widened. "That's exactly the feeling I was trying for. Every mind-tour about Venus and the Project always tries for the same effect—the feeling of triumph in the end by bringing a dead world to life, the beauty of the new Earthlike world we're making, the belief that we're carrying out God's will by transforming Venus into what it might have become. I want the mind-tourist at least to glimpse what we're losing with all this planetary engineering, to feel some sorrow that it is being lost."

Hassan smiled. "A little of that goes a long way, don't you think? We're supposed to be glorifying the Project, not regretting it."

"Sometimes I do regret it just a little. Imagine what we might have learned if we had built the Islands and simply used them to observe this planet. There are questions we may never answer now because of what we've already changed. Did Venus once have oceans that boiled away? Seems likely, but we probably won't ever be sure. Was there ever a form of life here that was able to make use of ultraviolet light? We'll never know that either. We decided that terraforming this world and giving all of humankind that dream and learning what we could from the work of the Project outweighed all of that."

"Be careful, Miriam." Hassan lifted a hand. "We don't want to question the very basis of the Project."

"No, of course not." But she sounded unhappy about making that admission. Hassan would never have insulted her by saying this aloud, but she sounded almost like a Habber, one of those whose ancestors had abandoned Earth long ago in the wake of the Resource Wars to live in the hollowed-out as-

teroids and artificial worlds called Habitats. There
might be a few Habbers living here to observe the
Project, but they thought of space as their home, not
planetary surfaces. A Habber might have claimed that
Venus should have been left as it had been.

"You've done wonderfully with your roughs," Hassan murmured, suddenly wanting to cheer her. Miriam's face brightened as she glanced toward him.
"Really, if the final mind-tour maintains the quality
of this work, we'll have a triumph." He reached for
her hand and held it for a moment, surprised at how
small and delicate it felt in his grip. "Let me take you
to supper," he went on, and admitted to himself at
last that he was falling in love with her.

They would have a masterpiece, Hassan told himself. Three months of working with Miriam had freed
something inside him, had liberated a gift that he had
not known he possessed. He felt inspired whenever he
was with her. In his private moments, as he reviewed
sections of "The Dream of Venus," he grew even
more convinced that their mind-tour had the potential
for greatness.

There, in one of the segments devoted to the Venus
of millions of years ago, was a vast dark plain, an
ocean of basalt covered by slender sinuous channels
thousands of kilometers long. A viewer would soar
over shield volcanoes, some with ridges that looked
like thin spider legs, others with lava flows that blossomed along their slopes. The mind-tourist could roam
on the plateau of Ishtar and look up at the towering
peaks of the Maxwell Mountains, shining brightly with
a plating of tellurium and pyrite. What might have
been only a succession of fascinating but ultimately
meaningless geological panoramas had been shaped by

Miriam into a moving evocation of a planet's life, a depiction of a truly alien beauty.

Hassan had contributed his own stylings to the mind-tour; he had shaped and edited many of the scenes, and his sensory effects had added greatly to the moods of awe and wonder that the mind-tour would evoke. It had been his idea to frame the entire mind-tour as the vision of Karim al-Anwar, and to begin and end with what the great man might have dreamed, a device that also allowed them to leave out much of the tedious expository material that had cluttered up so many mind-tours depicting Venus and the Project. But Miriam was the spirit that had animated him, that had awakened him to the visions and sounds that had lain dormant inside him.

The fulfillment he felt in the work they were doing together was marred by only one nagging worry: that "The Dream of Venus" was in danger of becoming an ode to Venus past, a song of regret for the loss of the world that most saw as sterile and dead, but which had become so beautiful in Miriam's renderings. What the Administrators wanted was a glorification of the Project, a mind-tour that would end on a note of optimism and triumph. They were unlikely to accept "The Dream of Venus" as it was, without revisions, and might even see it as vaguely subversive.

But there was still time, Hassan told himself, to reshape the mind-tour when "The Dream of Venus" was nearly in final form. He did not want to cloud Miriam's vision in the meantime with doubts and warnings; he did not want to lose what he had discovered in himself.

He and Miriam were now eating nearly all of their meals together and conducting their courtship at night, in her bed or his own. He had admitted his love for

her, as she had confessed hers for him, and soon the
other members of their geological team and the residents of their buildings were asking them both when
they intended to make a pledge. Hassan's mother was
the cousin of a Mukhtar, and his father had always
hoped that Hassan would also take an influential
woman as a bondmate, but Pyotr could not justifiably
object to Miriam, who had won her place with intelligence and hard work. In any event, by the time he
finally told his father that he loved Miriam enough to
join his life to hers, their mind-tour would have secured their status here. Pyotr could take pride in
knowing that a grandchild of his would be born on
the Islands, that his descendants might one day be
among those who would live on Venus.

That was something else "The Dream of Venus"
had roused inside Hassan. He had come here thinking
only of doing his best not to disgrace his family. Now
the dream of Venus had begun to flower in him.

"We think that the Project has no true ethical di-
lemmas," Miriam was saying, "that it can't possibly
be wrong to terraform a dead world. We're not dis-
placing any life-forms, we're not destroying another
culture and replacing it with our own. But there is a
kind of arrogance involved, don't you think?"

Hassan and Miriam were sitting on a bench outside
a greenhouse near Island Two's primary school. They
often came here after last light, when the children had
left and the grounds adjoining the school were still
and silent.

"Arrogance?" Hassan asked. "I suppose there is, in
a way." He had engaged in such discussions before,
at university, and it had been natural for him and
Miriam to talk about the issues the Project raised

while working on "The Dream of Venus." Lately, their conversations had taken on more intensity.

"God gave us nature to use, as long as we use it wisely and with concern for other life-forms," Miriam said, repeating the conventional view promulgated by both the true faith of Islam and the Council of Mukhtars. "Terraforming Venus is therefore justified, since the measure of value is determined by the needs of human beings. And if you want to strengthen that argument, you can throw in the fact that we're bringing life to a world where no life existed, which has to be rated as a good. On top of that, there's the possibility that Venus was once much like Earth before a runaway greenhouse effect did it in, so to speak. Therefore, we're restoring the planet to what it might have been."

Hassan, still holding her hand, was silent; the assertions were much too familiar for him to feel any need to respond. He was looking for an opening in which to bring up a subject he could no longer avoid. "The Dream of Venus" was close to completion, and there was little time for them to do the editing and make the revisions that were necessary if their mind-tour was to be approved for distribution by the Administrators and the Project Council. He did not want to think of how much credit he and Miriam might already have cost the Project. All of that credit, and more—perhaps much more—would be recovered by the mind-tour; he was confident of that. But he had broached the need for editing to Miriam only indirectly so far.

"You could argue that all of life, not just human life and what furthers its ends, has intrinsic value," Miriam continued, "but that wouldn't count against the Project, only against forcing Venus to be a replica of Earth even if it later shows signs of developing its

own distinct ecology in ways that differ from Earth's
and which make it less habitable—or not habitable at
all—by human beings. You could say that we should
have abandoned our technology long ago and lived in
accordance with nature, therefore never having the
means to terraform a world, but that has always been
an extremist view."

"And unconstructive," Hassan said. At this point,
he thought, humankind would only do more damage
to Earth by abandoning advanced technology; solar
power satellites and orbiting industrial facilities had
done much to lessen the environmental damage done
to their home world.

"What I worry about now," she said, "isn't just
what terraforming might do to Venus that we can't
foresee, but what it might do to us. Remaking a planet
may only feed our arrogance. It could lead us to think
we could do almost anything. It could keep us from
asking questions we should be asking. We might begin
to believe that we could remake anything—the entire
solar system, even our sun, to serve our ends. We
might destroy what we should be preserving, and end
by destroying ourselves."

"Or transforming ourselves," Hassan interjected.
"You haven't made much of an argument, my love."

"I'm saying that we should be cautious. I'm saying
that, whatever we do, doubt should be part of the
equation, not an arrogance that could become a de-
structive illusion of certainty."

Those feelings, he knew, lay at the heart of their
mind-tour. Uncertainty and doubt were the instruments through which finite beings had to explore their
universe. The doubts, the knowledge that every gain
meant some sort of loss—all of that underlined "The
Dream of Venus" and lent their depiction its beauty.

And all of that would make their mind-tour unacceptable to the men and women who wanted a sensory experience that would glorify their Project and produce feelings of triumph and pride.

"Miriam," he said, trying to think of how to cajole her into considering the changes they would have to make, "I believe we should start thinking seriously about how we might revise—how we might make some necessary edits in our mind-tour."

"There's hardly any editing we have to do now."

"I meant when it's done."

"But it's almost done now. It's not going to be much different in final form."

"I mean—" Hassan was having a difficult time finding the right words to make his point. "You realize that we'll have to dwell less on the fascination of Venus past and put more emphasis on the glory that will be our transformed Venus of the future."

She stared at him with the blank gaze of someone who did not understand what he was saying, someone who might have been talking to a stranger. "You can't mean that," she said. "You can't be saying what it sounds like you're saying."

"I only meant—"

She jerked her hand from his. "I thought we shared this vision, Hassan. I thought we were both after the same effect, the same end, that you—"

"There you are." Muhammad Sheridan was coming toward them along the stone path that ran past the school. "I thought I would find you two here." He came to a halt in front of them. "I would have left you a message, but . . ." He paused. "Administrator Pavel is exceedingly anxious to view your mind-tour, so I hope it's close to completion."

Hassan was puzzled. "He wants to view it?"

"Immediately," Muhammad replied. "I mean to-morrow, two hours after first light. He has also invited you both to be present, in his private quarters, and I told him that I would be happy to tell you that in person."

Hassan could not read his friend's expression in the soft silvery light. Anticipation? Nervousness? Muhammad, who had recommended Hassan as a mind-tour creator, would be thinking that a mind-tour that won Pavel's approval might gain Muhammad more favor, while a failure would only make Pavel doubt his aide's judgment.

"It should be in final form within a month," Hassan said. "We're within the deadline still, but it needs more refining. Couldn't we—"

"Of course we'll be there," Miriam said. "I think he'll be pleased." There was no trace of doubt in her voice. Hassan glanced at her; she took his hand. "I want him to experience what we've done."

Hassan felt queasy, trying to imagine what Pavel Gvishiani would think of "The Dream of Venus," searching his mind for an excuse he might offer to delay the Administrator's viewing of the mind-tour. Pavel might have viewed it at any time; as an Administrator and a Linker, he could have accessed the work-in-progress any time he wished through the Island cyberminds. But Hassan had simply assumed that Pavel would be too preoccupied with his many other duties to bother.

"Well." Hassan let go of Miriam's hand and rested his hands on his thighs. "Presumably he understands that it's not in final form."

"Close to it," Miriam said in her hard, toneless voice. "Might need a little tweaking, but I don't see much room for improvement."

"And," Hassan went on, "I don't know why he wants us both there, in his room."

"It's a matter of courtesy," Muhammad said. "Pavel is most attentive to courtesies."

Hassan peered at Miriam from the sides of his eyes; she was smiling. "If you think about it," she said, "it's kind of an honor, being invited to his private quarters and all."

Hassan's queasiness left him, to be replaced with a feeling of dread.

The forty minutes of sitting with Pavel Gvishiani in his room, waiting as the Linker experienced the mind-tour, were passing too slowly and also too rapidly for Hassan; too slowly, so that he had ample time to consider the likely verdict the Administrator would render, and too rapidly, toward the moment of judgment and disgrace. While he waited, Hassan fidgeted on his cushion, glanced around the small room, and studied the few objects Pavel had placed on one shelf—a cloisonné plate, gold bands for securing a man's ceremonial headdress, a porcelain vase holding one blue glass flower.

Pavel, sitting on his cushion, was still. Occasionally, his eyelids fluttered over his half-open eyes. He wore no band; with his Link, he did not need a band to view the mind-tour.

I will think of the worst that can happen to me, Hassan thought as he stared at the tiny diamondlike gem on Pavel's forehead, and then whatever does happen won't seem so bad. Pavel and the Administrators would make him reimburse the credit the Project had allocated to him during his work on "The Dream of Venus." He could afford that, but his family would regard it as a mark against him. His public record

would note that he had failed at this particular task;
that humiliation would remain with him until he could
balance it with some successes. His father, after using
his influence to get Hassan a position with the Project,
would be tainted by his son's failure and was likely to
find a way to get back at him for that, perhaps even
by publicly severing all ties with him. Muhammad,
who had recommended him to Pavel, would no longer
be his friend. And Miriam—

He glanced at the woman he had come to believe
he loved. Her eyes shifted uneasily; she was frowning.
He felt suddenly angry with her for drawing him so
deeply into her vision, for that was what she had done;
she had seduced him with her inspiration. Maybe she
was finally coming to understand that their mind-tour
was not going to win Pavel's approval. If they were
lucky, he might settle for castigating them harshly and
demanding a host of revisions. If they were unlucky,
he might regard their failure to give him what he had
wanted as a personal affront.

Pavel opened his eyes fully and gazed directly at
them, then arched his thick brows. "Both of you,"
he said quietly, "have produced something I did not
expect." He paused, allowing Hassan a moment to
collect himself. "Your mind-tour is a masterpiece. I
would almost call it a work of art."

Miriam's chest heaved as she sighed. "Thank you,
Administrator Pavel," she whispered. Hassan, bewildered, could not find his own voice.

"But of course we cannot distribute 'The Dream of
Venus' in this form," Pavel continued, "and I am sure
you both understand why we can't. You still have a
month of your allotted time left. I expect to see an
edited mind-tour by the end of that time and, depending on what you've accomplished by then, I can

grant you more time if that's required. I won't insult your intelligence and artistry by telling you exactly what kind of changes you'll have to make, and I am no expert on designing mind-tours in any case. You know what you will have to do, and I am certain, God willing, that you'll find satisfactory ways to do it."

May the Prophet be forever blessed, Hassan thought, almost dizzy with this unexpected mercy. "Of course," he said. "I already have some ideas—"

"No," Miriam said.

Pavel's eyes widened. Hassan gazed at the woman who was so trapped in her delusions, wondering if she had gone mad.

"No," Miriam said again, "I won't do it. You said yourself that it was a masterpiece, but I knew that before we came here. You can do what you like with 'The Dream of Venus,' but I won't be a party to defacing my own work."

"Miriam," Hassan said weakly, then turned toward Pavel. "She doesn't know what she's saying."

"I know exactly what I'm saying. Edit our mind-tour however you please, but I'll have nothing to do with it."

"My dear child," Pavel said in an oddly gentle tone, "you know what this will mean. You know what the consequences may be."

Miriam stuck out her chin. "I know. I don't care. I'll still have the joy and satisfaction in knowing what we were able to realize in that mind-tour, and you can't take that away from us." She regarded Hassan with her hard gray eyes. Hassan realized then that she expected him to stand with her, to refuse to do the Administrator's bidding.

"Miriam," he said softly. You bitch, he thought, Pavel's given us a way out and you refuse to take it. "I'll begin work on the editing," Hassan continued, "even if my colleague won't. Maybe once she sees how that's going, realizes that we can accomplish what's needed without doing violence to our creation, she'll change her mind and decide to help me." He had to defend her somehow, give her the chance to reconsider and step back from the abyss. "I'm sure Miriam just needs some time to think it over." ¯

Miriam said, "I won't change my mind," and he heard the disillusionment and disgust in her voice. She got to her feet; Pavel lifted his head to look up at her. "Salaam aleikum, Administrator."

"If you leave now, there will be severe consequences," Pavel said, sounding regretful.

"I know," Miriam said, and left the room.

Hassan found himself able to complete the editing and revision of "The Dream of Venus" a few days before Pavel was to view the mind-tour again. This time, he went to the Administrator's quarters with more confidence and less fear. The mind-tour now evoked the pride in the terraforming of Venus and the sense of mastery and triumph that the Project Council desired, and Hassan was not surprised when Pavel praised his work and assured him that "The Dream of Venus" would become a memorable and treasured experience for a great many people.

Hassan had done his best to keep some of Miriam's most pleasing scenes and effects, although he had cut some of the more haunting landscapes of early Venus and the brooding, dark scenes that seemed to deny any true permanence to humankind's efforts. It was also necessary to add more of the required scenes of the Project's current state and recent progress. He had tried not to dwell on the fact that his editing and his additions were robbing the mind-tour of much of its beauty, were taking an experience suffused with the doubt and ambiguity that had made "The Dream of Venus" unique and turning it into a more superficial and trite experience.

In any case, Hassan knew, the merit of the mind-tour did not lie in what he thought of it, but in how Pavel Gvishiani and the other Administrators judged it, and they believed that he had made it into a work that would bring more credit to and support for the Venus Project, as well as the approval of the Mukhtars.

Miriam, with reprimands and black marks now a part of her record, and a debt to the Project that would drain her accounts of credit, had been advised by a Counselor to resign from the Project, advice that was the equivalent of a command. Within days after the Project Council had approved "The Dream of Venus" in its final form, which had required a bit more editing, Miriam Lucea-Noyes was ready to leave for Earth.

Hassan knew that it might be better not to say farewell to her in person. That would only evoke painful memories of their brief time together, and it could hardly help him to be seen with a woman who was in such disgrace. But he had dreamed of sharing his life with her once, and could not simply let her go with only a message from him to mark her departure. He owed her more than that.

On the day Miriam was scheduled to leave, Hassan met her in front of the entrance to her building. She looked surprised to see him, even though his last message to her had said that he would be waiting for her there and would walk with her to the airship bay.

"You didn't have to come," she said.

"I wanted to see you once more." He took her duffel from her and hoisted it to his shoulder.

They walked along the white-tiled path that led away from the workers' residence where they had passed so many hours together. There, at the side of one wing of the building, was the courtyard in which they had so often sat while talking of their work and their families and their hopes for a future together. They passed a small flower garden bordered by shrubs, the same garden where he had first tentatively hinted that he might seek a lasting commitment from her, and then they strolled by another courtyard, dotted with tables and chairs, where they had occasionally dined. Perhaps Miriam would suffer less by leaving the Island than he would by staying. Wherever she ended up, she would be able to go about her business without inevitably finding herself in a place that would evoke memories of him, while he would have constant reminders of her.

"Have you any idea of what you'll be doing?" he asked.

"I've got passage to Vancouver," she said. "The expense of sending me there will be added to what I owe the Project, and my new job won't amount to much, but at least I'll be near my family."

If her family were willing to welcome her back, they were showing more forbearance under the circumstances than his own clan would have done. As for her new work, he was not sure that he wanted to know much about it. Her training and education would not be allowed to go to waste, but a disgraced person with a large debt to pay off was not likely to be offered any truly desirable opportunities. If Miriam was lucky, she might have secured a post teaching geology at a second-rate college; if she was less fortunate, she might be going back to a position as a rock hound, one of those who trained apprentice miners bound for the few asteroids that had been brought into Earth orbit to be stripped of needed ores and minerals.

"Don't look so unhappy," Miriam said then. "I'll get by. I decided to accept a job with a team of assayers near Vancouver. It's tedious, boring work, but I might look up a few of my old associates in the mind-tour trade and see if I can get any side jobs going for myself there. At least a couple of them won't hold my black marks against me."

"Administrator Pavel was very pleased with the editing of 'The Dream of Venus,'" Hassan said, suddenly wanting to justify himself.

"So I heard."

"If you should ever care to view the new version—"

"Never." She halted and looked up at him. "I have to ask you this, Hassan. Did you preserve our original mind-tour in your personal records? Did you keep it for yourself?"

"Did I keep it?" He shifted her duffel from his left shoulder to his right. "Of course not."

"You might have done that much. I thought that maybe you would."

"But there's no point in keeping something like that. I mean, the revised version is the one that will be made available to viewers, so there's no reason for me to keep an earlier version. Besides, if others were to find out that I had such an unauthorized mind-tour in my personal files, they might wonder. It might look as though I secretly disagreed with Pavel's directive. That wouldn't do me any good."

"Yes, I suppose that's true," Miriam said. "You certainly don't want people thinking less of you now that you've won the Administrator's respect."

Her sardonic tone wounded him just a little. "I don't suppose that you kept a record of the original version," he said.

"I didn't even try. I guessed that my Counselor might go rooting around in my files to see if they held anything questionable, and would advise me to delete anything inappropriate, and I don't need any more trouble." She smiled, and the smile seemed to come from deep inside her, as though she had accepted her hard lot and was content. "Let's just say that the original may not have been completely lost. I have hopes that it will be safe, and appreciated. I don't think you want to know any more than that."

"Miriam," he said.

"You know, I never could stand long dragged-out farewells." She reached for her duffel and wrested it from his grip. "You can leave me here. You don't have to come to the airship bay with me. Good-bye, Hassan."

"Go with God, Miriam."

She walked away from him. He was about to follow her, then turned toward the path that would take him to his residence.

During the years that followed, Hassan did not try to discover what had become of Miriam. Better, he thought, not to trouble himself with thoughts of his former love. His success with the altered mind-tour had cemented his friendship with Muhammad, increased the esteem his fellow geologists had for him, and had brought him more respect from his family on Earth.

Within five years after the release of "The Dream of Venus," Hassan was the head of a team of geologists, was sometimes assigned to the pleasant task of

creating educational mind-tours for Island children,
and had taken a bondmate, Zulaika Jehan. Zulaika
came from a Mukhtar's family, had been trained as
an engineer, and had an exemplary record. If Hassan
sometimes found himself looking into Zulaika's brown
eyes and remembering Miriam's gray ones, he always
reminded himself that his bondmate was exactly the
sort of woman his family had wanted him to wed, that
his father had always claimed that marrying for love
was an outworn practice inherited from the decadent
and exhausted West and best discarded, and that taking Miriam as a bondmate would only have brought
him disaster.

Occasionally, Hassan heard rumors of various mind-
tours passed along through private channels from one
Linker on the Islands to another, experiences that
might be violent, frightening, pornographic, or simply
subversive. He had always strongly suspected, even
though no one would have admitted it openly, that his
father and other privileged people in his clan had enjoyed such forbidden entertainments, most of which
would find their way to the masses only in edited form.
It would be a simple matter for any Linker to preserve
such productions and to send them on to friends
through private channels inaccessible to those who
had no Links. Hassan did not dwell on such thoughts,
which might lead to disturbing reflections on the ways
in which the powerful maintained control of the net
of cyberminds so as to shape even the thoughts and
feelings of the powerless.

One rumor in particular had elicited his attention,
a rumor of a mind-tour about the Venus Project that
far surpassed any of the usual cliché-ridden productions, that was even superior to the much-admired
"The Dream of Venus." He had toyed with the notion

that someone might have come upon an unedited copy
of "The Dream of Venus," that the mind-tour he and
Miriam had created might still exist as she had hoped
it would, a ghost traveling through the channels of the
cyberminds, coming to life again and weaving its spell
before vanishing once more.

He did not glimpse the possible truth of the matter
until he was invited to a reception Pavel Gvishiani
was holding for a few specialists who had earned com-
mendations for their work. Simply putting the com-
mendations into the public record would have been
enough, but Pavel had decided that a celebration was
in order. Tea, cakes, small pastries, and meat dump-
lings were set out on tables in a courtyard near the
Administrators' ziggurat. Hassan, with his bondmate
Zulaika Jehan at his side, drew himself up proudly as
Administrator Pavel circulated among his guests in his
formal white robe, his trusted aide Muhammad Sheridan at his side.

At last Pavel approached Hassan and touched his
forehead in greeting. "Salaam, Linker Pavel," Hassan said.

"Greetings, Hassan." Pavel pressed his fingers
against his forehead again. "Salaam, Zulaika," he
murmured to Hassan's bondmate; Hassan wondered if
Pavel had actually recalled her name or had only been
prompted by his Link. "You must be quite proud of
your bondmate," Pavel went on. "I am certain, God
willing, that this will be only the first of several com-
mendations for his skill in managing his team."

"Thank you, Linker Pavel," Zulaika said in her soft
musical voice.

Pavel turned to Hassan. "And I suspect that it won't
be long before you win another commendation for the
credit you have brought to the Project."

"You are too kind," Hassan said. "One commendation is more than enough, Linker Pavel. I am unworthy of another."

"I must beg to contradict you, Hassan. 'The Dream of Venus' has been one of our most successful and popular entertainments." A strange look came into Pavel's dark eyes then; he stared at Hassan for a long time until his sharp gaze made Hassan uneasy. "You did what you had to do, of course, as did I," he said, so softly that Hassan could barely hear him, "yet that first vision I saw was indeed a work of art, and worthy of preservation." Then the Administrator was gone, moving away from Hassan to greet another of his guests.

Perhaps the Administrator's flattery had disoriented him, or possibly the wine Muhammad had surreptitiously slipped into his cup had unhinged him a little, but it was not until he was leaving the reception with Zulaika, walking along another path where he had so often walked with Miriam, that the truth finally came to him and he understood what Pavel had been telling him.

Their original mind-tour might be where it would be safe and appreciated; Miriam had admitted that much to him. Now he imagined her, with nothing to lose, going to Pavel and begging him to preserve their unedited creation; the Administrator might have taken pity on her and given in to her pleas. Or perhaps it had not been that way at all; Pavel might have gone to her and shown his esteem for her as an artist by promising to keep her original work alive. It did not matter how it had happened, and he knew that he would never have the temerity to go to Pavel and ask him exactly what he had done. Hassan might have the Linker's public praise, but Miriam, he knew now, had won the Linker's respect by refusing to betray her vision.

Shame filled him at the thought of what he had done to "The Dream of Venus," and then it passed; the authentic dream, after all, was still alive. Dreams had clashed, he knew, and only one would prevail. But how would it win out? It would be the victory of one idea, as expressed in the final outcome of the Project, overlaid upon opposed realities that could not be wished away. To his surprise, these thoughts filled him with a calm, deep pleasure he had rarely felt in his life, and "The Dream of Venus" was alive again inside him for one brief moment of joy before he let it go.

Science Fiction Anthologies

☐ **FIRST CONTACT**
Martin H. Greenberg and Larry Segriff, editors   UE2757—$5.99

In the tradition of the hit television show "The X-Files" comes a fascinating collection of original stories by some of the premier writers of the genre, such as Jody Lynn Nye, Kristine Kathryn Rusch, and Jack Haldeman.

☐ **RETURN OF THE DINOSAURS**
Mike Resnick and Martin H. Greenberg, editors   UE2753—$5.99

Dinosaurs walk the Earth once again in these all-new tales that dig deep into the past and blaze trails into the possible future. Join Gene Wolfe, Melanie Rawn, David Gerrold, Mike Resnick, and others as they breathe new life into ancient bones.

☐ **BLACK MIST:** and Other Japanese Futures
Orson Scott Card and Keith Ferrell, editors   UE2767—$5.99

Original novellas by Richard Lupoff, Patric Helmaan, Pat Cadigan, Paul Levinson, and Janeen Webb & Jack Dann envision how the wide-ranging influence of Japanese culture will change the world.

☐ **THE UFO FILES**
Martin H. Greenberg, editor   UE2772—$5.99

Explore close encounters of a thrilling kind in these stories by Gregory Benford, Ed Gorman, Peter Crowther, Alan Dean Foster, and Kristine Kathryn Rusch.

Prices slightly higher in Canada.   **DAW 104X**

THEY'RE COMING TO GET YOU. . . .
ANTHOLOGIES FOR NERVOUS TIMES

☐ **FIRST CONTACT**　　　　　　　　　　　　UE2757—$5.99
Martin H. Greenberg and Larry Segriff, editors

In the tradition of the hit television show "The X-Files" comes a fascinating collection of original stories by some of the premier writers of the genre, such as Jody Lynn Nye, Kristine Kathryn Rusch, and Jack Haldeman.

☐ **THE UFO FILES**　　　　　　　　　　　　UE2772—$5.99
Martin H. Greenberg, editor

Explore close encounters of a thrilling kind in these stories by Gregory Benford, Ed Gorman, Peter Crowther, Alan Dean Foster, and Kristine Kathryn Rusch.

☐ **THE CONSPIRACY FILES**　　　　　　　　UE2797—$5.99
Martin H. Greenberg and Scott Urban, editors

We all know that we never hear the whole truth behind the headlines—let Douglas Clegg, Tom Monteleone, Ed Gorman, Norman Partridge and Yvonne Navarro unmask the conspirators and their plots—if the government lets them. . . .

☐ **BLACK CATS AND BROKEN MIRRORS**　　UE2788—$5.99
Martin H. Greenberg and John Helfers, editors

From the consequences of dark felines crossing your path to the results of carlessly smashed mirrors, authors such as Jane Yolen, Michelle West, Charles de Lint, Nancy Springer and Esther Friesner dare to answer the question, "What happens if some of those long-treasured superstitions are actually true?"

Prices slightly higher in Canada.　　　　　　　　　　**DAW 215X**

JULIE E. CZERNEDA

"One of the fastest-rising stars of the new millennium"—Robert J. Sawyer

The Trade Pact Universe
☐ **A THOUSAND WORDS FOR STRANGER (Book #1)**
                            0-88677-769-0—$5.99

☐ **TIES OF POWER (Book #2)**   0-88677-850-6—$6.99
Sira, the most powerful member of the alien Clan, has dared to challenge the will of her people—by allying herself with a human. But they are determined to reclaim her genetic heritage . . . at any cost!

Alos available:
☐ **BEHOLDER'S EYE**   0-88677-818-2—$5.99
They are the last survivors of their shapeshifting race, in mortal danger of extinction, for the Enemy who has long searched for them may finally discover their location. . . .